Before she could stand, a flash of light shot through the snow, through the room. The building shook and a tremendous boom shattered the morning.

"Oh, Faulkner," Helma said, already hurrying to the window where Glory stood, gazing into white. As was her habit during any unusual or calamitous event, she glanced at the time. The clock above the circulation desk read 11:08.

"Is this the Big One?" George asked behind her. "The monster quake?"

"It was an explosion," Glory whispered. "It came from up there, where they're building the new library."

They all peered vainly through the windows for the source of the light flash. The falling snow blocked their view.

"I'm going to find out what happened," Helma told them. "I'll ski toward the northwest and if I don't come upon something extraordinary in ten minutes, I'll come back."

"This is a bad idea, Helma," George told her, frowning. "It's dangerous out there. Deadly even."

"I love Miss Zukas mysteries!"
—Carolyn Hart

Books by
Jo Dereske

CATALOGUE OF DEATH
BOOKMARKED TO DIE
FINAL NOTICE
MISS ZUKAS AND THE STROKE OF DEATH
MISS ZUKAS AND THE ISLAND MURDERS
MISS ZUKAS AND THE LIBRARY MURDERS

CATALOGUE OF DEATH

Jo Dereske

AVON BOOKS
An Imprint of HarperCollinsPublishers

AVON BOOKS
An Imprint of HarperCollins*Publishers*
10 East 53rd Street
New York, New York 10022-5299

Copyright © 2007 by Jo Dereske
Excerpts copyright © 1994, 1995, 1995, 1998, 2006 by Jo Dereske
ISBN: 978-0-06-079084-4
ISBN-10: 0-06-079084-9
www.avonmystery.com

First Avon Books paperback printing: April 2007

Avon Trademark Reg. U.S. Pat. Off. and in Other Countries,
Marca Registrada, Hecho en U.S.A.
HarperCollins® is a registered trademark of HarperCollins Publishers.

Printed in the U.S.A.

10 9 8 7 6 5 4 3 2 1

For Chuck and Dee Robinson

Contents

CATALOGUE
OF DEATH

Chapter 1

Snow Business

On Wednesday morning, in the dead center of February, Miss Helma Zukas awoke, not to the music of her clock radio, but to a drowsy awareness of unusual light. She snuggled against her 100 percent goose-down pillow, filled with contentment in the warmth of her queen-sized bed, wondering for a single delusional moment if her father had already stoked the furnace.

Helma didn't move but her eyes flew open. Her father had been dead for seventeen years, and she'd lived on the waters of the Pacific Ocean for longer than she'd ever lived in Michigan. In the temperate climate of Bellehaven, Washington, it either rained or it didn't rain. Little else.

But she recognized that soft cushiony light, that diffused, coming-from-nowhere-and-everywhere blue creaminess that muffled sound and movement: snow.

Lots of snow.

Helma flung back her covers, forgetting her strategically placed slippers, leaving her robe draped across the foot of her bed with its sleeves open and folded back. Some people would have been shocked by the sight of Miss Helma Zukas running barefoot to her living room and throwing open the drapes that shrouded the sliding glass doors to her balcony.

Her apartment was flooded by signature whiteness, and for the briefest instant she squinted her eyes against it. Outside, snow fell in feathery flakes, too thick to glimpse the water of Washington Bay or even Boardwalk Park nestled below the Bayside Arms. Only the movement of white, the air itself seeming to shift and drift and circle downward, was visible.

Four inches, at least, humped along the railings, softened the floor and turned the chairs and small table on her balcony into pillowy shapes.

In fact one of the mounded shapes on the balcony floor moved. Eyes blinked and Boy Cat Zukas rose, snow sliding from his black body. He gazed coolly at her. Helma didn't ascribe human emotions to animals but there did appear to be a hint of accusation in his gaze.

She unlocked her door and slid it open to create an eight-inch gap. Boy Cat Zukas didn't move, only stared unblinking at the entrance toward warmth and comfort, as if waiting for a better offer. Icy air spilled into Helma's apartment, bringing the sting of snowflakes with it.

Only when she began to pull the door closed did Boy Cat Zukas slink through the narrowing gap and take up residence in the wicker basket beside the door—as far as he was allowed into her apartment.

Helma Zukas did not converse with nonhuman species, so she said nothing to the cat as she blotted his wet tracks from her carpet and briefly considered, then rejected, toweling Boy Cat Zukas dry. She'd never touched a cat and she supposed he'd been wet multiple times in his previous life roaming the streets of Bellehaven.

Rarely had Helma seen *snow* actually moving ashore across the waters of Washington Bay. The air was too temperate, the climate too mild. In the mountains to the east behind Bellehaven, yes, but seldom at sea level. She stood beside her glass doors and watched the downy flakes descend. Beneath that very snow, moss roses already bloomed, daffodils poked up fat green spears, and yesterday she'd remarked on a yellow forsythia blooming against the south wall of the courthouse.

As photo-perfect beautiful as the snow was, even at only a few inches, Helma knew what this meant: Bellehaven was about to be brought to its knees.

"The mayor requests that citizens postpone all nonemergency travel," announced Gillian Hovel, the TV reporter who always pronounced her last name with the accent on the second syllable, as if she'd been challenged too many times in her life, her face brightened by the excitement of bad weather and the possibility of disaster. "All county schools are closed. No city buses will operate until further notice."

The city of Bellehaven didn't own a single snow-plow. Its citizenry barely owned winter coats. And unless they played at winter sports, any boots residing in closets were intended for rain or high fashion, not snow.

"Only essential city offices will be open today," the reporter continued, "offering limited services."

The Bellehaven Public Library was certainly an essential city service. Of course, its doors would open to serve the public. And most definitely, Helma's skills were essential to its operation.

Her phone rang.

"Have you looked outside?" Ruth screeched, and Helma pulled the receiver farther from her ear. "It's a *blizzard* out there."

"It *is* snowing," Helma agreed. "You're up early."

"Haven't been to bed yet. I've only got two weeks to finish this stuff. And don't say it."

She didn't. There was no point in reminding Ruth that the opening date for her art show had been on the calendar for six months. She'd avoided her paintbrushes until two weeks ago and now lived in a frenzy of belated creativity.

"It's a good day to work inside," Helma said judiciously. A slab of snow slid from the apartment building roof, scattering in front of the window like confetti.

"*Inside*? On a rare day like this? Want to go for a walk?"

"No thank you. I have to work."

"Work? Where? Nobody's going to the library in this stuff."

"They may," Helma told her. "And I intend to be present to assist them."

"You are *so* misguided," Ruth said, adding a barrage of tut-tut sounds. "How are you getting there?"

"I have means."

"'Means' means you don't want to tell me, right? Okay, then, I'll talk to you later. Sit in a stuffy library all by yourself when you could be out ... " And here Ruth broke into song, "'walking in a winter wonderland.'"

After she hung up and was properly attired in clothing from a twenty-year-old box marked WINTER OUTERWEAR, Helma pulled open the front door of her apartment and stood taking in the morning. There was the curious magnification yet minimization of sounds. The spinning whine of tires, a child's shout of pleasure, a chime like sailboat rigging, the murmurs of men's voices. If anything, snowflakes now fell more thickly.

From beneath the guest bed in her back bedroom, she had pulled a pair of cross-country skis, poles, and boots. And now she carried them down the three flights of stairs of the Bayside Arms and began her preparations.

"Hey, Helma, isn't this something?"

It was Walter David, the manager of the Bayside Arms, face tipped up to the sky. He wore a woolly cap advertising beer, and in his arms, wrapped in a red, white, and blue afghan, rested Moggy, his white Persian cat.

"It's a surprise," she agreed.

"I haven't seen skis like that in years," Walter said, tucking an afghan corner more securely around Moggy's head, until only the cat's oddly flat eyes were visible. "You aren't going out in this, are you?"

"They'll be expecting me at the library."

"Might be tough to find your way. Everything's white." He shivered and squinted at the definitely white landscape.

"I'll recognize landmarks," Helma assured him. "Moggy looks cold."

"Yeah, I'm going in. Want to take my cell phone? You know, just in case?"

"No thank you."

Walter shook his head doubtfully as Helma buckled on her skis and prepared to leave. "Well, be careful, then."

She was hesitant at first, naturally, since she hadn't skied—except accidentally during a past desperate situation—since she was a junior in college and had reluctantly enrolled in a cross-country skiing class to secure a much needed single credit. By the time the class had ended, she'd wished it had been a five-credit course, since she earned the only A the instructor had bestowed in the past six years.

But within fifteen minutes Helma found her snow legs, and if there'd been traffic, drivers would have let up on the gas to watch her striking figure swoosh through the picturesque winter scene.

A tasteful blue coat and pants with black piping, a blue and black stocking cap, tall argyle wool stockings with a matching scarf, and overlong skis. No step-slide, step-slide movements forward; she sailed along, the tracks behind her evenly spaced herringbones. Her pack—also a remnant from twenty years ago—containing library-appropriate clothing, swayed against her back. Unhampered by traffic, poles cadenced with skis, as swift and precise as if she were destined to ski on forever. The elastic on her old snow goggles had rotted and her face was bare to the weather. Flakes brushed against her eyelashes. The air pleasantly stung the insides of her nostrils. She smiled.

By the time Helma reached the untracked snows of the Bellehaven Public Library's parking lot, her cheeks glowed pink and a sheen of perspiration warmed her body. Snow topped her stocking cap and epauletted her shoulders. As she bent to unbuckle her skis, she spotted yellow flashing lights through the dense snow.

The library stood in the midst of Bellehaven's civic buildings—the courthouse, city hall, and the hospital—so flashing lights were a common enough occurrence. Helma brushed the snow from her skis and propped them against the wall of the loading dock, unlocked the rear door and entered the library workroom.

She was eight minutes late but the workroom was silent, the lights off, the crowded room bathed in snowy blue light. When she flicked on the lights, it was apparent that she was the first of the staff to arrive. Ms. Moon's office was dark, the computer screens black. No coffee odors drifted from the staff room.

In the public area of the library, lights shone down on the circulation desk, where she was relieved to see

Dutch, the circulation manager, checking in books from the drop box. An electronic beep sounded as he passed each bar-coded book beneath the scanner to check it in.

"Are you the only staff member here?" Helma asked him.

"So far, ma'am," he said briskly.

Dutch was a retired military man who'd worked part-time at the circulation desk before taking full command. He didn't know Poe from Pope, or *Where the Wild Things Are* from *Where's Waldo*, and Helma had had her doubts when Ms. Moon hired him. But Dutch didn't gossip, kept the youthful circulation staff on task, reshelved books in a timely fashion, and disarmed unruly patrons with a single glance. He was also a man so private that his only address was a post office box

"I'll help prepare for the public," she told him.

He inclined his thumb-shaped head toward the windows. "It may be a quiet day."

Helma Zukas was not only a degreed and experienced librarian; she had made it her business to learn every job responsibility in the library, from reshelving books to assigning Dewey decimal numbers.

She also knew where Jack the janitor hid his "best" supplies, how to "jimmy" the heating and air-conditioning systems, and who to call when vandals stuffed the public toilets with rolls of toilet paper.

The library's main phone rang. Helma let Dutch answer it as she walked through the building, flipping on lights, starting the photocopiers and computers. After reading the directions on the back of a package of "fair-trade, handpicked, gently roasted" grounds, she even made coffee. Although she didn't drink the brew, the fragrant roasty odor seemed appropriate for a snowy morning.

The phone rang again, and when Helma saw that Dutch was wheeling a cart of books toward the fiction section, she picked it up at the reference desk.

"Bellehaven Public Library," she answered.

"Oh good, you're there," a woman's breathless voice responded. Panicky, Helma judged.

"The library is here to serve the public," she assured the caller. "We'll be open at ten o'clock as usual."

"Great. We're sending them over right now."

"Sending what over?" Helma asked. But the caller had hung up.

Helma hung up, too, and looked out the library's wide windows at the white, white world, puzzled. The flashing lights still gyrated through the falling snow, and from this vantage point they seemed close, very close. Forty minutes until the library officially opened, and at a time when the building was usually buzzing with staff members preparing for a day of dispensing information, only she and Dutch were on duty.

She had only been gazing out the window a few moments when a sound made her turn. An indistinct figure bumped against the front doors and a mittened hand pounded against the glass. Had someone become lost and disoriented right in downtown Bellehaven and by happenstance stumbled onto the library's front door? Frozen and desperate for rescue?

Helma rushed to their aid, jerking open the door and admitting a blast of snow and cold air. The figure nodded to her and turned back, calling behind him, "Inside. Inside, ladies."

He held open the door by leaning against it and counted aloud, as one by one through the front door of the library struggled a line of smallish muffled figures. "Seventeen," he ended, closing the door and adding in a sigh of relief, "That's everybody, the whole kit and kaboodle. I was afraid I'd lose somebody in this mess."

He removed a billed blue cap and pushed back a sweatshirt hood, revealing a young man about thirty, slightly taller than she was, with straight black hair and a dark complexion. Helma recognized him as likely a member of the Nettle tribe. The Nettles lived north of Bellehaven on ancestral land, a politically savvy Indian tribe who, as her friend Ruth said, "the government couldn't push any farther west without drowning them in the ocean."

"I'm Jimmy Dodd." Despite the cold and peril, his eyes twinkled. "They told me you were expecting us."

"Who did?" Helma asked, not really hearing his answer, if he did answer, as she watched the group of small figures in the library foyer begin to unwind their scarves and coats and sweaters. Their voices rose and fell in melodic excitement as they emerged from their wraps, already combing hair and briskly rubbing cold flesh: seventeen elderly Asian women.

Chapter 2

Stranded Players

"*Who* sent you?" Helma asked. "Who *are* you?"

The young man named Jimmy Dodd grinned at her and swatted his cap against his leg. Snow shimmered and dropped to the floor. "City hall swore you'd take us in and save us from a snowy death. Our bus got caught in the storm, and here we are, at your mercy." He was enjoying the situation far too much.

"A city bus?" Helma asked, confused, watching as the snow from the women's outerwear fell to the library floor, puddling and melting. One of the women had taken charge and was gathering the group in a circle, giving directions and motioning for the other women to sit around two of the long library tables. She was the tiniest of the seventeen, by far the oldest, dressed beneath her coat as if it were summer: in a sleeveless shirt and light green pants, and even sandals over white—and wet—ankle socks.

"Today is Ladies' Day at the casino," Jimmy Dodd explained. "We were coming down from Canada. This is my Chinatown run."

"Where's your bus?" Helma asked, peering out the library's front doors. The wind had risen and now the snow that fell from the sky was being mixed with snow billowing upward from the ground.

"Out there," he said, waving his hand toward the windows at the back of the library. "I left the emergency lights on so nobody'd hit it."

That explained the yellow lights flashing through the snow. The new Nettle casino, built on the edge of the reservation, had proven to be popular beyond everyone's expectations except the Nettles. Since the Canadian border was only twenty miles from Belle-haven, the cross-border Nettle-owned casino buses—"Win Big!"—had been an innovative, and profitable, move.

"We're understaffed today," Helma told him. "But you're welcome to stay here until the weather lets up. I don't expect we'll have many library patrons."

"You never know: somebody might need an emergency book on frostbite," he said. Either Jimmy Dodd had a tic in his eye or he'd just winked at her.

The tiny elderly woman suddenly stepped between them. "You are . . . ?" she asked Helma, tipping her head back to look up at Helma, who wasn't tall.

"Miss Helma Zukas," Helma told her.

"Miss Zukas," the woman said, nodding slightly. "I am Bonita Wu." She nodded slightly again. Her hair was short and white, crisply cut into a pixie, her face a mass of deep wrinkles, and her bare arms ... well, any sort of covering would have been advisable, Helma thought. And immediately chastised herself, thinking that perhaps Bonita Wu was so old she was beyond caring about the state of her arms. Helma's eighty-eight-year-old Aunt Em claimed, "At my age, if it still works, I flaunt it."

Bonita Wu removed a pair of tinted glasses from her pants pocket and balanced them on her nose, where the nose piece disappeared into a crevasselike wrinkle and the lenses immediately steamed over. She pulled the glasses from her face and returned them to her pocket. "I would like for my women, hot water for tea, a ... towel, and where are your facilities, please?"

Helma rarely pointed inside buildings, and never toward private facilities. "The facilities are behind me to the left. I have coffee prepared and we can heat water, plus I believe there is a selection of tea. As for a towel ... perhaps paper towels from our facilities?"

Bonita Wu nodded with a single deep incline of her head. "You are kind," she said, and turned back to the two tables she'd commandeered where the sixteen women waited, all eyes on Bonita.

"That one's the dragon lady," Jimmy murmured when Bonita was out of hearing. "I put her in the seat behind me because she's so old I thought she'd die before we got here. Instead, she spent the whole trip hissing into my ear in a *Bridge on the River Kwai* voice. Giving me driving tips," he finished with an upward roll of his eyes.

"I believe the *Bridge on the River Kwai* portrayed a

somewhat fictionalized account of a Japanese incident," Helma pointed out. "These women are Chinese."

"Yeah, well you get the idea," he said. There went the roll of the eyes again. "Think cross-cultural. I mean, did you ever hear of a Chinese woman named *Bonita*? Or hey, that I'm named Jimmy Dodd, instead of something more culturally authentic like White Feather or Dancing Snake? Or what about those flashy casinos on honest-to-God ancient tribal Nettle land?" His voice rose. "I'm talking about, what do you call it, anomalies?"

"Or snow in Bellehaven," Helma contributed, distracting Jimmy Dodd from further explorations of the world of melting pots. "I'll show you where you can heat water and find cups. Today we can stretch the library's rules about food and drink."

"I'm just the bus driver," he said, grunting and pulling his sweatshirt hood back up over his head as if he were about to disappear inside it.

Suddenly, Dutch stepped up beside Jimmy Dodd, shoulders back, buzz-cut head erect. "*Just* the bus driver?" he repeated in a tone that would have dropped a platoon to their knees for a hundred push-ups. "That makes *you* responsible for the well-being of your passengers."

The words were pulled from Jimmy's mouth as if he had no will. "Yes, sir," he said, his back straightening, sweatshirt hood pushed back with a swipe of his hand that could have doubled as a salute.

Duty completed, Dutch spun on his heels and returned to the circulation desk.

Jimmy frowned and looked over at Bonita Wu, who stood between the two tables, apparently issuing assignments. "She doesn't look like much of a tipper," he commented to Helma, too low for Dutch to hear.

When Helma only gazed at him, he held up his hands in surrender. "Okay, okay. Lead the way to the tea and crumpets."

She led Jimmy Dodd behind the public area into the library workroom and the staff lounge. Through the windows, there was no green, only curtains and walls and mounds of white.

"Crowded back here, isn't it?" he asked, gazing around at the crammed work spaces, the stacked boxes, the narrow aisles. "Cold, too. You need a bigger library."

Helma nodded. "If all goes as planned, we'll be moved into a new building by this time next year."

So far, the new library existed as an excavation two blocks away, begun two weeks ago, since in normal Bellehaven, Washington, weather, construction took place year-round. After years of make-do and months of controversy, when bonds were floated, fought over, and rejected, a local citizen had stepped forward with an offer city officials could not refuse. The new Bellehaven Public Library would soon be fact, and Miss Helma Zukas had played a modest but vital role in the blossoming reality. Ms. May Apple Moon, the director, was in a constant frenzy of excitement.

Helma left Jimmy gathering up cups and coffee and condiments with an efficiency that belied his earlier reluctance. In the public area, tapping sounded from the front door. It was 10:05, five minutes past opening.

A solitary muffled figure tapped at the plate glass with a key. Insistent. Dutch unlocked the doors and pulled them open. Fully twenty feet away, Helma felt the shiver of icy wind. Snow swirled inside with the figure.

"Can't let a little snow and ice put a stop to reading, can you?" a man asked from inside a heavy coat, scarf, and cap. His cap was red plaid, like the old-time hunting caps from Helma's Michigan childhood, before neon orange became the rule. Flaps covered his ears and silver hair. "Bet you don't recognize me in all this insulation, do you?"

He unwound his scarf. Steamed glasses blocked his eyes. Helma might not have recognized him in all his layers, but immediately recognized the red childish backpack hanging off his shoulder, which he jokingly said left his hands free to hug a pretty woman, but in actuality left his hands free to steady his balance. A yellow hard hat was attached to a strap. "Hello, Mr. Harrington. I'm surprised you're out in this weather."

Franklin Harrington was routinely the first person to enter the library and had been for years. It wasn't just that he was a favorite patron and enthusiastic library supporter that set him apart; it was Franklin Harrington who'd donated the land for the new library.

"It's just weather," he said now. "I've been through worse. Once I got caught in a blizzard that lasted for weeks. *Weeks*. At my age, I don't have time to slow down for a little snow."

"The newspapers haven't been delivered," Helma warned him. "So your *Wall Street Journal* isn't here."

"I'm here to do a little last minute research," he told her, and carrying his coat to the vestibule, he hung it above the plastic mat that had been placed there to catch rainwater dripping from coats and umbrellas. "Weather doesn't affect history, at least not the past."

Franklin was also a history buff who'd self-published two slim volumes on Bellehaven history and was now completing what he called his "opus," the story of "the Harrington empire." The Harringtons were one of the city's founding families, a force to be reckoned with from Bellehaven's toughest and rawest beginnings forward.

"You holding a tea party?" he asked, seeing Jimmy Dodd pushing a book cart laden with tea supplies, coffee, cups, and what appeared to be every single leftover snack that had been abandoned in the staff lounge.

"A busload of passengers is stranded until the weather clears," Helma explained. "That's their driver."

Franklin frowned at Jimmy, his eyes narrowing. Then he looked at the tables containing the seventeen women

"They were on their way to the Nettle casino," Helma explained. "From Canada."

"I see. Canada," he said, his eyes still on the women. He smiled at Helma. "I need to look at some old newspapers on microfilm."

"Of course. I'm the only—"

He waved his hand at her. "I know my way around

the public space, her small arms outstretched as if she were running headlong into an embrace.

"Isn't this glorious?" she cried eponymously. "Snow! I love, love, love it! I simply *love* it!" It was herself she embraced, her pink-cheeked face rosy in rapture.

Glory, who was as petite as an eleven-year-old, wore a baby blue parka. White faux fur trimmed its hood, hem, and cuffs. The hood hung down her back because a pink fuzzy hat with tiny fake cat ears crowned by a yellow pom-pom contained her abundant overly red hair. Her calf-high boots were trimmed in fur, and her gloves, which she was pulling off, were white with roses embroidered on the backs.

Jimmy Dodd stood transfixed as Glory began to wiggle out of her clothing in the center of the public area.

Off came the gloves, one finger at a time, the hat, the parka, all landing on the floor. She shook out her red hair. Light blue spandex pants clung so tight Helma made out the brief outline of a thong. And all the time, Glory chortled in excitement, her voice as high-pitched as a seven-year-old's. "Oh, what a fabulous day. And a wonderful walk through the snow. But oh," she breathed as she pulled her Irish sweater over her head to reveal more spandex, "I'm so hot." With thumb and forefinger she stretched the neckline of her top and blew downward. Dutch had glanced up briefly at the squeal then returned to sorting books. So far, Helma and the seventeen women hadn't penetrated into Glory's line of vision.

The library telephone rang and Glory leapt for it, leaving her shucked clothing in a pile behind her.

"Bellehaven Public Library," she cooed, "this is Glory," then paused, her head tipped as she listened. "Of course I'm here, May Apple, I mean, Ms. Moon. I wouldn't let the library down by not coming to work, although it *was* a long walk." Glory finally saw Helma and waggled her fingers at her.

"Oh no," Glory continued, speaking to the director. "There are a few patrons here." She turned her back to Helma but Helma still heard her say, "No, I didn't see any other staff members in the workroom. But don't worry. I can handle it until the others arrive."

She hung up and turned her beaming eyes to Helma. "That was Ms. Moon. She's going to be late, but she *is* coming in. I told her we could handle it."

"You walked?" Helma asked judiciously.

Glory giggled. "Kind of. My neighbor works at the post office and you know how they are about rain and hail and gloom of night, so I rode on the back of his … oh, I don't know what they're called. People ride all over the mountains on them, like four-wheel motorcycles."

"All terrain vehicles?" Helma offered, although she herself had never ridden on one. "ATVs."

Glory put her small hands together in fierce little claps that made no sound. "That's right! I knew you'd know the answer. You're such a wonderful librarian. Isn't this snow beautiful?" Glory finally saw the seventeen Chinese women and stopped. "Who's that?" she whispered to Helma.

At the same time, Helma noticed Bonita Wu say something in a low voice to the women surrounding her, and as one, all the faces went blank, all except Bonita's; she continued to coolly watch Glory.

"A busload of Canadian women on their way to the Nettle casino. They're stranded here until the weather lets up. The lights blinking in the snow belong to their bus."

"Ooh," Glory breathed. "Stranded here in the library. I'll see if I can help them."

Franklin stood by the microfilm reader, frowning toward Glory and the Chinese women. Then he turned and gazed out the window at the falling snow, his expression vague.

"Are you all right, Mr. Harrington?" Helma asked, already counting off in her head the ABCs of emergency heart attack care: Airways, Breathing, Circulation. Maybe he'd tried to shovel snow before coming to the library, or the walk through the cold and snow had been too much for him.

Franklin turned to her, blinking his eyes. "I'm fine. Just woolgathering. This snow takes me back. Way back." He laughed. "But that's fitting, isn't it? Me and history?"

"A lot of local history would be lost without all the work you're doing," Helma told him. "When will your new book be available?"

"My Harrington history?" He patted his red backpack, which bulged with his notes and books. "I have to clear up a couple of last minute details but it's actually finished: a surprisingly big book. The Harrington family had their nose everywhere: mining, logging, fishing." He shook his head, with a gleam in his eyes that Helma had seen in teachers obsessed by their subject. "Quite the empire, beginning in the 1800s with our great-grandfather." He winked. "An old scoundrel by today's standards. Now look at us: three tottering old brothers and only two offspring to carry on the family legacy."

Without their wealth and influence, the "three tottering old brothers" would have been well known simply because of their existence: triplets nearly eighty years old. Triplets had been a rarity when they were born in 1931. And even more than that, the "Harrington boys" had been identical, although the years had muted and altered Franklin, Rosy, and Del.

"The library will certainly purchase copies," Helma told Franklin.

He shook his head. "I'll be proud to *give* the library copies. Someone might stumble across it and read it here. None of my lot gives a rip."

"Someday they will," she reassured him.

Wasn't everything appreciated once the instigators, the main characters, were gone? she thought. Even the most troubling, outsized personalities turned into lovable eccentrics once death rendered them powerless to influence the present and future, once those they'd driven to distraction no longer bore the responsibility of dealing with them. Look at her father and uncles.

"May I help you with any of your research?"

He shook his head. "Not today. I know exactly what I'm looking for and where to find it." He nodded toward the Chinese women. "That's a coincidence, isn't it?"

Helma looked, uncertain what he meant. Glory Shandy was waxing, gesticulating at the snow, the rhythm of her voice rising and falling across the room in the way of people who raised their voices when they believed their language wasn't being understood.

Jimmy Dodd sat in the magazine section, flipping pages of a *People* magazine, every little while glancing up at Glory, who, although she didn't acknowledge Jimmy, had placed herself so no shelves or tables blocked his view of her.

A man wearing a bundle of clothes of the drab color achieved when too many shades of children's clay were mixed together entered the building and shook snow off like a dog. On unsteady feet he looked at Helma and said, "This is a public building, is it not?"

"Yes it is," Helma told him.

"I'm the Homeless Citizen," he announced, as if it were his name. "But I'm here. And I'm cold." He spoke in a staccato fashion, rocking precariously. "Can I read?"

"Yes, you may. Magazines are always a good choice."

"Yeah, something short." He shambled to the magazine section and immediately dozed off over an unopened magazine on his lap.

Jimmy Dodd, sitting across from the man, raised his eyebrows and fanned the air, then moved to a table on the other side of the Chinese women.

The library phone rang again, and this time Helma answered.

"Oh God," a man groaned. "We're open today."

"Good morning, George," Helma said, recognizing the voice of the library cataloger, George Melville. "The library *is* a vital city service."

"The power's still on; why can't they all stay warm at home and play on the Internet. Who's there?"

"Glory and Dutch and I are the only staff here at the moment."

"Is the Moonbeam coming in?"

"Ms. Moon is planning to come in, yes."

"Just my luck. I'll see if I can dig out my boots and mittens. There's probably a nest of mice living in them by now." He hung up, and as the phone descended, Helma heard him grumbling about snowplows and frozen personal body parts.

Another snowy figure entered the library, bringing a draft of cold air. The large figure stopped inside the door and brushed snow from his shoulders. He removed his hat, and his graying hair fell forward to cover his widow's peak. It was the chief of police, Wayne Gallant.

Glory abandoned the seventeen women midsentence and beelined toward the chief. She fairly danced across the floor.

"Wayne! Isn't this snow just amazing? I was just discussing it with these women. Their bus was stranded and I was assuring them I'd do everything I could to keep them safe here in the library."

Wayne Gallant's face reddened even more than it had from the cold. He smiled vaguely, glanced at the women, flashed his cool policeman's gaze around the library, and didn't meet Glory's eyes.

Helma would never, ever delight in anyone else's discomfort, but there had been an incident the preceding autumn concerning the chief of police and a shocking lapse in judgment on his part.

And now, as Wayne Gallant smiled at her over Glory's head, she smiled, too, nodding slightly, but busying herself at the reference desk.

She and the chief were working their way back to where they'd been before the unfortunate incident, tentatively, carefully. Helma Zukas did not hold grudges; she *did* believe that those who erred had a certain responsibility to, not *prove*, but at least *assure*, that the error was a onetime event.

"Good job," Wayne said to Glory. "Excuse me."

Glory faltered and chewed her lip, then spun and trilled to Jimmy Dodd, "It must have been so spooky scary driving in this."

Wayne Gallant approached Helma, hat in hand. "I heard the bus passengers were diverted over here. Can the library handle it?"

"The library, *and* the staff," Helma told him.

The homeless man abandoned his magazine and approached Wayne. "You're the police, right?"

"That's right," Wayne told him.

"I knew it." He nervously buttoned and unbuttoned the bottom button of his coat. "I can tell. I'm not doing anything illegal. I fix anything I do wrong."

"Good for you," Wayne said, and the man walked away, nodding to himself.

Wayne stamped his feet as if he'd just trudged through fields of snowdrifts instead of across the street from the police station. "When this lets up," he told Helma, "we'll get the bus passengers to a hotel. Until then ... "

He looked harried, distracted. His city was in the capricious grip of dangerous weather.

"It's warm here, we have plenty of snacks, and I'm sure it'll be a slow day. At least for us," she added, nodding graciously toward him, "but for you ... "

"Yeah, the calls are backed up." He gestured toward the homeless man who was pulling volumes of the *Encyclopaedia Britannica* from the shelves, shaking them close to his ear as if listening, and neatly reshelving them. "Want me to take him to the mission?"

"He'll be fine here," Helma assured him.

"Thanks. I'll talk to you later." And he returned his hat to his head, lightly touching Helma's shoulder as he raised it.

"Bye-bye, Wayne," Glory called after him.

"We would like to hang our coats, please," Bonita told Helma.

Helma motioned toward the vestibule. "There may not be enough hangers," she warned her.

"We will manage," Bonita said. She had divided the women into groups. One headed for the facilities, another arranged the drinks and food that Jimmy had delivered. And another group, their arms laden with all the women's coats, marched behind Bonita to the vestibule.

Franklin Harrington sat at a microfilm reader, looking up occasionally at Bonita and the Chinese women, or out the window at the falling snow, then back to the reader, bending his head close to the screen of the aged machine. The microfilm was destined to be digitized, and in the new library the floor space taken by the clunky old microfilm machines would be freed to satisfy the public's hunger for more Internet computers.

From somewhere in the ceiling, metal rattled ominously, once, then again. Jimmy and Glory looked at each other, then at Helma as if she could explain its origin. Behind Helma, Dutch said, "That was either the furnace or the wind."

"The wind would be preferable," Helma said.

The front doors flew open and George Melville, the cataloger, banged inside, dressed in layers of sweaters and scarves, a stocking cap pulled over his ears and sunglasses over his eyes. With his beard speckled with snow, not a square inch of flesh was visible.

"I hope there's hazard pay for this," he grumbled as he pulled off hat and gloves. "There's a drift blocking the back door, a friggin' *snowdrift*," George continued. "I didn't pass a single open store. The weather's sideways and everybody's shut tight but us."

"The police are also on duty," Helma pointed out.

"Oh goody. The library and the police taking care of business. Keeping the lifelines open. 'Stuck in the snow? Here, warm up with a few pages of *War and Peace*.'"

Despite his apparent disgruntlement, Helma noted an unusual level of intensity, even excitement, in George's voice. He saluted Dutch in exaggerated military fashion and Dutch briefly nodded back.

"Who's that?" George asked, nodding toward Bonita.

"A busload of passengers on the way to the Nettle casino."

"Oh yeah, it's Ladies' Day, isn't it?"

"I wouldn't know," Helma told him, "but that's what their driver claimed."

"And that?" George asked, looking at the homeless man who was now gathering pencils from tables and stacking them into miniature log cabins on tabletops and low bookshelves.

"He said he's a homeless citizen," Helma told him. "Come in to get warm. Aside from being restless, he's not causing any trouble."

"Yet," George said.

George spotted Franklin Harrington at the microfilm reader. "Ah, our benefactor. Can't believe he's out in this stuff. I guess when you're that old, you've seen worse."

"That's exactly what he said," Helma told him.

"Well, he's a tough old bird. Probably beat me all hollow in a foot race." George straightened his collar, smoothed his beard and hair. "I'll unload this stuff and be back in a minute to keep the women under control."

"Excuse me, Miss Zukas," Franklin Harrington said, approaching the desk. "Might I use your telephone?"

"Of course," Helma said. She pushed the telephone toward Franklin, then gave him privacy while she retrieved a mop from Jack the janitor's closet and left it near the front door to mop up melting snow. At least it was clean water.

The metallic rattle sounded from the ceiling again and George looked up. "That's the furnace. One more good reason for a new library." He saluted Franklin, who was just hanging up the telephone. "Thanks to you, sir."

Franklin Harrington actually blushed. "My pleasure," he said. "I hope this weather doesn't slow down construction."

The library would be Bellehaven's first building with an underground parking garage that descended three levels beneath the street. The evolving hole drew scores of citizens every day to watch, and a few to protest this new assault on the landscape. Only big cities built underground parking, some people claimed, and Bellehaven had no right to put on big city airs.

Franklin himself stopped by the excavation site so often that the construction crew had presented him with a yellow hard hat of his own. F. HARRINGTON was printed across the brim. He carried it with him everywhere, attached to his backpack. "Never know when I might want to check up on the boys," he liked to say when anyone asked, then would pause to judge if they had the patience to hear an expanded tale of the hard hat's origin.

Glory had abandoned the Chinese women to their own devices and now asked Helma, "Do you go out much?"

"I beg your pardon?" Helma asked. She tucked an old advertisement that had been left on the desk back into its envelope and dropped it in the trash.

"Like on dates. Do you go out with any city employees?"

Helma did not participate in abstruse conversations. "Are you referring to employees of the police department?"

Glory's cheeks pinked. "Maybe. Do you?"

"My private life is not a component of my professional life," Helma assured her.

"I mean ... "

But a noise by the vestibule caught Helma's attention and she turned to see Franklin buttoning his coat, donning black leather gloves. His hard hat sat on the table beside him.

"Mr. Harrington," she said, leaving Glory to her musings. "You're not leaving, are you?"

"I'm finished here for now, so I think I'll walk past the construction site and make sure everything's all right."

"In the snow?"

"How about if I walk over with you?" George asked.

Franklin shook his head. "It's only two blocks. I can walk two blocks—in any weather. And then I'll be back to warm up."

There was no changing his mind. Franklin tugged down his earflaps, smiled and waved, and was out the door, saying, "I'll see you in fifteen minutes."

George looked after him. "Do you think I should follow him?" he asked Helma, gazing toward the front doors where Franklin had already disappeared into the white landscape.

"I think he'd be insulted," she said.

"Yeah, you're right." He shrugged. "Besides, I'd probably get turned around and he'd have to rescue *me*." George checked his watch. "Eighteen minutes," he said. "I won't worry for eighteen minutes, how's that? Can't let a benefactor flounder around in the snow." He gave Helma a thumbs-up. "Our benefactor, thanks to *you*, that is."

"I did nothing except provide Franklin with our usual high standard of library service," Helma demurred.

"That, too." George grinned. "With maybe a few judicious comments about this creaky, crappy, snake pit of a building."

Helma *may* have pointed out the overburdened electric circuits to Franklin Harrington, or even mentioned that the historic volume he needed was stored off site due to lack of space. And there *was* that time she'd grabbed his arm to keep him from tripping over a stack of overflow magazines.

"I need a cigarette."

It was the homeless man, standing at Helma's elbow. He was younger than she first believed, with the look of the lost in his eyes. "I don't have cigarettes," she told him.

"No." His face scrunched like a child's frustrated by adult backwardness. "No. *I* have cigs. I need to smoke one."

"Not in here," Helma informed him. "This is a public building."

"Then I'll go outside."

"You may do that."

"Aren't you afraid I'll freeze to death?"

"No."

He appeared hurt.

"But," Helma continued, "please stay within sight of the library, even if you must smoke within the twenty-five-foot banned area."

"Okay then," he said, giving her an exaggerated nod. "That I can do. Yes, I will. Uh huh, you bet."

A few times more Helma felt blasts of icy air, as if the front doors had opened. Each time she checked, no one was there, and she glanced apprehensively at the heating vents.

"Look. It's getting worse," Glory said. "The flakes are bigger."

"Actually," Helma said, drawing on her Michigan background, "that's an indication the air is warming up."

"Oh." Glory's face fell. "It's not stopping already, is it?"

Helma felt a rumbling sensation and looked up at the ceiling. But the sound came from outside, muffled by the snow. Before she could stand, a flash of light shot through the snow, through the room. The building shook and a tremendous boom shattered the morning. The windows shimmered and bulged.

Glory screamed. Everyone else jumped or gasped or froze.

"Oh, Faulkner," Helma said, already hurrying to the window where Glory still stood, gazing into white. As was her habit during any unusual or calamitous event, she glanced at the time. The clock above the circulation desk read 11:08.

"Is this the Big One?" George asked behind her. "Are we finally getting the monster quake?"

"It came from up there," Glory said. "Where they're building the new library."

Chapter 4

Fire in the Hole

"It was an explosion," Glory whispered.

"Now what hellish fury?" George said from behind Helma and Glory.

They all peered vainly through the windows for the source of the light flash. The snow blocked their view of anything but the most shadowy outlines. Whatever had happened was shrouded by white.

"Snow got into something electric and blew it up," Glory said.

"A transformer, maybe," George said, sounding doubtful. "We'll never find out in this whiteout. Just have to wait it out until the rumors fly, I guess."

"Do you think the new library blew up?" Glory asked, moving closer to George, as if he could shield her from further explosions.

George's shoulders straightened and he leaned over Glory, his voice deepening protectively. "All that exists of the new library so far is a partially scooped out hole in the ground."

"I'm going to find out what happened," Helma told them. Sirens shrieked close by but she couldn't tell from which direction they came.

"How?" George asked. "Call your ..." He glanced from Glory to Helma and finished weakly, "... friends."

"I have the proper clothing and equipment. I'll ski toward the northwest and if I don't come upon something extraordinary in ten minutes, I'll come back."

"Oooh, you're so brave," Glory said. Helma stepped back from her outstretched hand.

"This is a bad idea, Helma," George told her, frowning and stroking his beard like a contemplative professor. "It's dangerous out there. Deadly even."

"Helma's the most competent librarian I've ever seen," Glory went on, her eyes going dewy. "I have total faith in her information gathering skills. I know she can do it."

"Thank you," Helma acknowledged.

"Listen, Helma," George said. "This is *not* a good idea. *I* wouldn't go out wandering around in this."

"Where did you grow up, George?" she asked.

"Tucson. What's that got to do with ... Oh, because you grew up in the frozen reaches of Minnesota—"

"Michigan," Helma corrected. "I have had enough experience to respect weather. I don't take unnecessary chances. I may go no further than the end of our parking lot, just far enough to discover the problem, that's all."

George looked doubtful, but shrugged. "Okay, but slip my cell phone in your pocket."

"No thank you."

George Melville was a cynical but amiable man who seldom exercised, rarely exerted himself, and went softer with each passing year. But now a muscle in his temple twitched and his beard rose as he clenched his jaw. He reached in his pocket and pulled out a silver cell phone the size of a fat credit card. Without a word, he held it out to her, his face grim.

Helma understood when it was prudent to give way on inconsequential issues in order to complete a mission of consequence, so she took the phone, saying, "Thank you, George," despite having no intention of employing the tiny intrusive device.

The explosion had been too powerful for a transformer, Helma was sure of that. What it had been, she had no idea. George Melville was right: only a nascent hole in the rocky earth existed at the new library site. Nothing was present *to* explode. But the flash and bang had certainly come from that direction, only two blocks away. *Someone* from the library should investigate, someone responsible.

As Helma tucked her hair beneath her hat, Glory entered the workroom. "Here, wear this one instead." She held out her pink fuzzy hat with the fake cat ears and neon pom-pom.

"Thank you, but I prefer not to wear other people's personal clothing."

"People will be able to see you easier in the snow," Glory said, still holding out the hat.

Helma was about to repeat her assertion when she spotted a surprisingly generous light in Glory's eyes. She sighed and resignedly pulled off her own stocking cap. Her better judgment could be undone by the truly altruistic motives of people, no matter how she felt about them personally.

"Thank you," she said.

"You'll probably see the police out there," Glory said. "I hear sirens."

"If it's warranted, I may," Helma told her as she tucked her hair up again, this time under Glory's hat, which *was* luxuriously soft.

"I'll make sure there's hot coffee, in case he ... they, want to warm up here. Can you tell the chief I'll do that?"

"If he asks me, I certainly will," Helma assured her.

She was in danger of overheating in all her winter outerwear. "I'll be back shortly," she told Glory as she headed for the workroom door.

"Be careful," Glory called after her, and Helma turned back at the worried note in her voice. Glory stood with hands clasped to spandex, a frown between her brows.

"I always am," Helma assured her.

She had forgotten about the drift George said blocked the workroom door. There it was, as big as a car with snow blowing off its crest like sand from the knife edge of a desert sand dune. She was forced to walk through the library to the front doors, past all the patrons, carrying her skis over her shoulder. She felt all their eyes watching her. Someone, Jimmy Dodd, she thought, said, "Go, girl."

It was a relief to be outside, even in dangerous weather. Helma knelt on the cushiony white sidewalk and buckled on her skis, then took to the center of the street, her eyes squinted, all the better to watch for familiar landmarks. There was no traffic near the library. She skied slowly, skirting or plunging through drifts, stopping once to check her bearings.

And yes, the closer her approach to the new library site, the more flashing lights she spied through the swirling flakes, resembling Christmas tree bulbs shining through the old-time beautiful but deadly angel hair. Worse was the strange odor that grew stronger with each step in the icy temperatures: acrid, industrial. Her nose pinched with the sharpness of it.

Flashing lights pierced the snow behind her; she jumped at the whisper of tires through the soft white. It was too dangerous to continue skiing in the street. Using her poles, Helma felt along the street edges for the curb and stepped up onto it, making cautious parallel slides forward. Her cheeks grew stiff and she blinked hard to dislodge the snow clinging to her eyelashes.

Hunched shapes of running figures appeared in the snow. Questioning voices sounded like murmurs, now and then punctuated by shouts and orders.

When she judged she was a hundred feet from the site, Helma leaned against a tree trunk that felt curiously warm and removed her skis, leaving them propped there as she pushed through the snow. To her left, an obscured figure headed in the same direction. Both of them silently moved forward.

The site for the new library occupied a bank overlooking the bay. It had once held the offices of Harrington Enterprises. From that commanding location the family had begun, run, and ruined multiple businesses before the buildings burned in the 1940s. Vast forests timbered and milled, coal mines engineered and played out, fishing fleets dispatched. All gone now. All history.

The views from the new library would be spectacular: blue water to the San Juan Islands, and on clear days all the way to the whitecapped Olympic range on the Olympic Peninsula.

Helma shook out her hands, feeling her fingers sting with cold. The snow took on a gray cast and she squinted upward. Dust sifted down among the snow, as from a shaken rug. She supposed it was landing on her coat and on Glory's hat. Nothing could be done about it.

"Get back, please, ma'am," a man six feet away ordered. Helma hadn't seen him.

"Excuse me, but what happened?" she asked. He was official, but whether police or fire department, she couldn't read his insignia through the descending flakes. Snow clung to his shoulders like icing.

"Don't know yet," he said shortly and moved away from her.

Helma followed him. He donned a helmet and she recognized a Bellehaven fireman.

Wooden barriers were already being pulled from fire trucks and erected around the site. Helma neatly stepped around one and joined a group of figures.

"I've got the contractor," someone said. Helma

couldn't see his face but she easily identified the voice of Carter Houston, a police detective with the Bellehaven Police Department. They'd had association in the past, not always pleasant. "He said nobody was working. Shouldn't have been anybody in the hole."

"Had they been blasting?" someone else asked. "Explosives on the premises?"

Carter's voice mumbled into a cell phone and a moment later he announced, "No blasting. He said there wasn't anything down there to blow up."

"Well, *something* did," the first voice replied. "Damn snow. Can't see a thing."

"Think kids are at the bottom of it?"

"As big as that was, I sure as hell hope not."

"Excuse me, gentlemen," Helma said, "but was anyone injured?"

Silence fell. It was Carter Houston who finally answered in a weary voice. Perhaps weary and wary. "Miss Zukas, these *are* police barricades. The public, as always, is requested to remain on the opposite side of the barricades."

"This is the site of the new public library," Helma told him, "and in the absence of the library director, I represent the library."

She certainly wasn't lying. She didn't see any other library employees at the site. "What do you believe happened here?"

Carter spoke slowly, deliberately. "We do not know yet."

"Was anyone injured?" she asked again.

"Not that we're aware of. If you'll excuse us?" Carter

was persistently polite, always impeccably dressed. He stood only three feet from Helma, a round figure with a youthful resemblance to Alfred Hitchcock, wearing a buttoned leather jacket, his black scarf knotted like a tie, a Russian hat and zip-up boots assuredly covering his glossy black wing tips.

Helma didn't move, and Carter beckoned for the other men to follow him, away from her.

Suddenly, she remembered. Her breath went tight. "Is Mr. Harrington here?"

Carter stopped and turned back to her. "Harrington? Which one?"

"Franklin," Helma told him. "He left the library, saying he planned to check the site."

"In the snow?" Carter asked, just as she had.

"He's extremely interested in every step of the excavation. He's here so often the construction crew gave him his own hard hat."

Helma felt all their eyes piercing through the snow at her, alert. Her every word was suddenly vital. The air tensed with new urgency.

"How long ago?" Carter asked her, his voice hard.

"Twenty minutes." Helma had an excellent sense of the passage of time. "He said he'd return to the library afterward."

"He's probably already there," Carter said.

"I might have missed him in the low visibility," she agreed.

"Check the library," Carter ordered one officer, and to another he said, "Call his house. If he's not there, get somebody to check along the route. On foot."

While the police discussed Franklin, Helma stepped closer to the excavation and squinted down into it through the snow. Scattered lumps of brown earth were visible everywhere, anomalies in all the white, as if a child had thrown shovelfuls of dirt. A bulldozer sat against one wall of the excavation, the snow blown from its roof, more dirt stippling it.

"I'm sure you've already checked that bulldozer," Helma said. "And no one's inside."

"You're anticipating us, Miss Zukas," Carter told her. "Members of the fire department are preparing to go down now. They have to assess the ground's stability." Next to Carter, one of the policemen flapped his arms back and forth across his chest, stomping his feet.

A fireman stopped beside Carter. "Looks like the blast wasn't *in* the excavation," he said, "but about fifteen feet away on the north rim." He pointed to the north. Helma looked but couldn't see anything.

"But it blew debris into the hole?" Carter asked.

"That's right. It was a big blast. We're setting up a perimeter now."

"I'll be right there," Carter said. "Keep it clear."

"Will do."

Helma remained at the edge of the collapsed excavation site as the firemen secured ropes and began their descent. She would have chosen a route twenty feet to the left of theirs but conceded that the snow might be hiding some obstacle they could see and she couldn't.

"Watch that rock," a fireman above called to his descending comrade.

The flurries alternately covered the view, completely

hiding it before the winds swept the snow aside like a curtain and the scene was exposed like an old-fashioned fuzzy television screen.

"Carter said you spoke to Franklin Harrington?"

Helma turned to see Wayne Gallant approaching, wearing a Russian hat like Carter's, and she wondered if it was police issue. Snow dusted it so it appeared silver tipped. "I did. He's a morning regular at the library."

"Even on a morning like this?"

"He seemed to actually be enjoying the weather," she told him, recalling his shining eyes as he entered the library, his protestations that he'd experienced blizzards that had lasted for weeks.

"What brought him in this morning?" Wayne asked. He made a hand signal to one of the policemen, who nodded and disappeared in the direction of the police cars.

"He was checking last minute facts for a book he wrote about the Harrington family."

The chief nodded, distracted, and Helma felt an icy edge of doubt. "He wasn't at the library, or his home, was he?"

The chief shook his head. "No, but he's a pretty social fellow and might have stopped along the way. Sorenson's Coffee's open; maybe he's there. We're checking his route right now. He didn't mention meeting anybody? He left alone?"

Helma nodded. George had wanted to follow Franklin, and she'd discouraged him. She'd told him Franklin would be *insulted*.

"Don't worry," Wayne told her now. "We'll find him." One side of his mouth lifted in a grin. "Nice hat."

Helma touched her head. She'd forgotten Glory's pink fuzzy hat with its cat ears and pom-pom. "It belongs to ... " She looked at him, remembered, and finished, " ... someone else."

"I'm not surprised," he said.

He reached for her arm, preparing to steer her around a tumble of rocks, when a calm voice said, "Hey, Chief."

He stopped. The talk around them ceased. The voice came from beneath them, in the excavation. It was a quiet voice, filled with portent and sadness. Helma held her breath.

At first she could see nothing, then the shroud of snow capriciously cleared and she spotted a fireman standing in the ruined excavation, holding up an object.

It was a yellow hard hat. Helma could only read HARRI written across the brim, because the rest was obliterated by a dark substance.

Chapter 5

Games of Chance

Helma returned to the library an hour later. She skied back along the sidewalks, no joy in slipping through the snow, unmindful of the cold.

Franklin Harrington was dead. For years, since his retirement from the Harrington enterprises, she'd greeted him nearly every weekday morning. He'd read the papers, spent time on his historical research, exchanged pleasantries with the staff. He'd once correctly referred to the library as a "local treasure."

Death left Helma heavyhearted, any death, even the expected or that of the ancient. She recalled a quote she'd read somewhere: "Every time an old person dies, a library burns down." And a violent death ... She shuddered.

So her attention wasn't focused on the library world as she entered the building through the front doors, her skis over her shoulder, her eyes downcast. Over and over her mind played the scene of Franklin leaving the library—alone. And it had been she who'd let him go, who could have encouraged George to follow him, who might have saved his life.

"Oh my, I didn't recognize you."

Helma raised her eyes and suddenly felt as if she'd stepped onto a stage without her lines, late for her cue and facing an impatient audience.

The Chinese women, Jimmy Dodd, even the homeless man, all stared at her. Glory sat at the reference desk, holding a tissue to her red and blotchy face. George stood beside her, caught in the uncomfortable pose of trying to comfort her in a public place.

But the person who'd spoken, who now stood in front of Helma, was the library director, Ms. May Apple Moon.

Helma, who never stared and rarely showed dismay at the personal appearance of others, politely focused on Ms. Moon's face, still able to view her outfit from her peripheral vision.

Ms. Moon, who had recently crested the upper swing of her yo-yoing weight and was dieting her way downward again, wore furry mukluks with raffish laces that tied just below her knees. Helma had never seen her in pants, but now baby blue stretch pants aptly stretched across her lower body, and a blue sweater decorated with kittens barely reached her waist. Ms. Moon's wavy blond hair was damply flattened from wearing a hat.

"We heard it was a bomb," Ms. Moon said, her hands clasped against her chin. "And Franklin Harrington? Can that be true? In the library excavation?"

"An explosion of unknown origin is what they're calling it at this point, near the library excavation, not in it," Helma explained. "And yes," she added heavily, "Franklin Harrington."

Ms. Moon moved her hands to cover her heart, closed her eyes and swayed gently on her feet.

Helma had seen it happen before, when Ms. Moon took time out to contemplate the conundrums of life and death, and simply waited until Ms. Moon's bosom heaved and she opened her eyes. "Franklin Harrington," she repeated in tones of awe. "Gone on to another level of existence."

"Blown to kingdom come," George suddenly interjected, as if he couldn't help himself, then grimaced in apology.

Glory sobbed. "Every morning he came to the library, every day for years and years. I loved to help him, just loved to," and she held her tissue to her nose. "Oh, I'll miss him. For years."

Helma refrained from reminding Glory she'd been employed at the library for less than one year, and that she passed on anyone over the age of thirty-five to Helma if she was nearby, saying, "You have more in common with them: you speak their language."

Ms. Moon nodded somberly. "Franklin Harrington was an asset to the community—and the library of course." Suddenly, her eyes flew wide. "Oh," she said. "Oh. You don't think … "

Whatever she'd been about to say, she covered her mouth with both hands and hurriedly left the public area, heading toward her office and leaving George and Helma staring after her.

"Obviously, it just hit her like a bolt from the sky that Franklin's death might be a teensy weensy bit suspicious," George said to Helma.

Helma wasn't so sure. Despite what the staff—not she—referred to as Ms. Moon's "la la factor," Helma had witnessed the director being overcome by her pragmatic side in the past. Whatever had struck her just then *hadn't* been related to her abiding interest in the mysteries of existence.

"Murder?" Glory gasped, and George turned back to her.

As Helma passed the tables of Chinese women, unzipping her jacket, the excavation scene on her mind, Bonita Wu rose from her table and intercepted her.

"We women would like to play cards," she said, her eyes sinking in her wrinkled flesh, her mouth partly disappearing.

"I don't believe we have any playing cards," Helma told her. "Although the library does own several books and magazines you and your ... the women might enjoy. I can ... "

She was stopped by Bonita's stare. "We have our own cards," Bonita said. "I felt it was polite to ask you first."

"Of course you may play cards," Helma told her. "Please be comfortable here."

"May I ask who died?"

"Franklin Harrington," Helma told her. "The man who was here earlier."

"The elderly gentleman?" Bonita asked.

Helma nodded, thinking that Franklin was at least ten years younger than Bonita.

Bonita's lips parted as if she were about to speak, but then she closed her mouth tightly, causing it to disappear again, nodded once more, and returned to the women, who watched the exchange expectantly.

On the way to her desk, Helma shed her coat, folded the fuzzy hat and set it on Glory's desk, and was just unlacing her ski boots when she heard her name called.

"Helma." It was Ms. Moon. "Come here, please. I'm in my office." Her voice was filled with despair, so much so that Helma retied her left ski boot and hurried to Ms. Moon's office.

"Yes?" she asked, stepping inside and first glancing around the office for signs of a physical problem. Ms. Moon's crystals sat on her desk next to her metronome, and the walls were hung with her new collection of spiritually enhanced grizzly bears and whales with round humanoid eyes that gazed pleadingly at the viewer. The soft tinkle of bells issued from hidden speakers. Her drapes were pulled tight against the snowy day. Nothing was out of the ordinary except Ms. Moon's flushed face.

Ms. Moon gave a small nervous giggle. "It's been years since I've worn these pants, and the seams have weakened with time," she explained.

"I always carry a sewing kit," Helma assured her. "I'll be right back."

Ms. Moon held up her hand. "No, that won't work." She flushed even more. "You keep a spare sweater in your cubicle, don't you? May I borrow it, just for the day, or until the snow lets up and I can run home?"

Helma understood immediately. "To tie around your waist?"

The director nodded miserably.

"Of course. I'll get it."

When Helma returned with the sweater she kept in her desk drawer in appreciation of the unreliable heating system, Ms. Moon stood. Keeping her back turned from Helma, she tied it around her waist. Helma winced to see the sleeves tugged and knotted, reminding herself it *was* an emergency.

She had turned to leave when Ms. Moon cleared her throat. "About the explosion and poor dear Mr. Harrington."

"It's a terrible tragedy," Helma said, feeling the sorrow descend again, seeing Franklin walk out the library doors.

"Do you think … " Ms. Moon continued hesitantly, then paused.

"That it might be homicide?" Helma finished for her. "It's too soon to speculate."

"Well, yes, that too." Ms. Moon picked up her baseball-sized crystal and absently rubbed it against her upper lip. "But … the new library. What will this mean for our new library?"

"The explosion was actually *beside* the site," Helma assured her. "If there's any damage to the site itself, it can be reexcavated. Nothing has been built yet, the foundation hasn't been laid, nor even leveled."

"No, I mean because Franklin is gone. You know how contentious it was in the Harrington family."

"Not really," Helma reminded her. "I wasn't included in the negotiations."

"Believe me, it was. Del's a developer, you know. His son, too. They wanted to put condos there: the view. Franklin had the final say. But now that he's gone ... "

"But surely there's no question about the site now," Helma said. "The papers were signed long ago and—"

Ms. Moon shook her head. "They weren't. Franklin retained ownership until the project was more than half complete, that was his concession to his brothers."

"How can that be?" Helma asked. "I attend the library board meetings. I don't recall hearing that proviso. And I can't believe the city would go along with such a problematic agreement."

Ms. Moon rubbed her temples. "I know, I know. But how else were we ever going to get a new library? The bond failure, the city budget ... Then Franklin stepped forward with his offer. The library wouldn't cost the city a dime until it was fifty-one percent completed." She shook her head. "They loved *that*. Franklin wanted to maintain control until he knew there was no turning back. And he wanted the details kept private, which suited everybody."

"But you have the agreement?"

Ms. Moon looked up. "He wouldn't have backed out. Nothing was more important to Franklin than the Harrington legacy. He *wanted* this library. But his brothers—"

As if on cue to the portent of this news, the heating system groaned, metal screeched as if it were grinding together, and the constant hum of circulating air went dead silent.

Into that eerie stillness, Ms. Moon held her hands to her cheeks and moaned, "The library, my new library."

Chapter 6

Running Hot and Cold

Helma didn't know which dire situation required attention first: the absence of the ever-present hum that signified the heating system had just quit; or the distraught director slumped over her desk.

But since she was currently in Ms. Moon's presence, she dealt with that predicament first.

"It's too soon to worry over the disposition of the library property," she told Ms. Moon. "Franklin Harrington has only been dead a matter of minutes. Concerns for the property will come later. And certainly his brothers will respect his wishes."

Ms. Moon actually snorted, and Helma remembered a scene before the announcement of the new library site in which Franklin's two brothers Del and Rosy, had exited Ms. Moon's office red-faced and tight-lipped, while Ms. Moon serenely watched them leave, a smile of certainty on her face. George had claimed the closed office meeting had also been accompanied by shouting and whale song.

"They hate me," she whispered now. "They'll take the property away from me."

"Surely they—"

Ms. Moon looked up at Helma, interrupting her. "Will you help?"

Above them, pipes clanked and the heating system began humming once more, but before Helma could relax, it quit again with an ominous thunk.

"Will you?" Ms. Moon repeated.

"If there's a reasonable way I can help," Helma told her, glancing up at the ceiling. "I will."

Ms. Moon set aside her crystal. "That's settled, then." Her face lit with a relaxed smile. "Now, we should plan a way to honor Franklin and his place in local history." She pulled pencil and paper toward her.

"Ms. Moon," Helma cautioned, "we have pressing issues right now. The snow—"

"Everybody talks about the weather, but you can't do anything about it," Ms. Moon said cheerily. "Relax into this gift from Mother Nature, a fleeting rarity to be savored, don't you think?"

"A rarity, yes," Helma agreed. "But our heating system has also just failed. We must make arrangements for our stranded patrons, schedule repairs for as soon as technicians can reach us."

Once again, at that very moment, the heating system rattled back to life. Ms. Moon waved her hand in dismissal. "See, it's fine. If we had our new library—"

"I'll go help George and Glory," Helma said, fore-stalling Ms. Moon from dipping wholeheartedly into another premature lament.

The library felt cut off from the rest of Bellehaven. In a more fanciful moment, of which Helma experienced few, she might have compared it to being stranded on a cushiony planet of cotton, or floating through a thick fog. The explosion at the library site and Franklin's death felt remote, as if she'd dreamed them.

If only she had.

In the center of the library, George Melville and Jimmy Dodd stood near the Chinese women's tables, intently watching. None of them spoke. The homeless man had disassembled his pencil log cabins and was now distributing the pencils throughout the library, pointy ends down, two to each of his chosen loca-tions.

Helma saw piles of money: change and bills, both American and Canadian, in the center of each table. And gathered around the tables with their chairs pulled in tight, the women played cards, their attention zeroed in on their games. At her table, Bonita Wu shuffled her deck so swiftly the cards blurred like wings.

"I'm not just a pretty face," Jimmy Dodd was say-ing. "I work as a dealer between bus runs. I'll deal this table."

"I know how," George added. "I could ... " He glanced at Helma. "Well, maybe not."

"Gambling in the library," Helma said aloud. She glanced around the public area. No children were present. And it *did* give the women something to do, to calm the claustrophobic feel of snow and the pall of recent death. "But maybe today is an exception."

"Way to go, Helm."

"Helma," she automatically answered. She hadn't seen Ruth Winthrop, who sat at the third table, her hand resting on two cards. "Hit me," she told the woman dealing. And when the woman gave her a card, Ruth thumbed up a corner, looked at it and smacked her forehead. "I'm out."

Ruth rose to her full height, grinning. "Thanks, ladies. I'll be back after I score a few more pennies for the pot."

Ruth was in her stocking feet but still stood over six feet tall. In honor of the snowy day, she wore a yellow single-piece zip-up snowsuit that strained at the hips. Helma wondered where she could have ever found a suit long enough to fit her body. A striped scarf tied back her bushy hair at the same time it circled her neck.

"Ain't this something?" Ruth asked, and Helma was uncertain if she meant her clothes, the snowy day, Franklin's death, or the fact that full-scale gambling was occurring in the confines of the Bellehaven Public Library.

Helma and Ruth had known each other since they were ten-year-old enemies at St. Alphonse School in Scoop River, Michigan. They'd graduated into a disconcerting friendship that left them both weary if they spent more than an hour in each other's company. They'd coincidentally ended up in Bellehaven,

Helma for her first professional library job, Ruth following a musician lover who'd moved on without her.

"I thought you were painting," Helma said.

"I am. I'm just taking a break. I figured the library must be Storm Central, so I talked Paul into driving me here in his Jeep." She winked and popped a peanut from her pocket into her mouth. "You can't tell a Minnesota boy the weather's too bad for him to drive in."

"Where is he?" Helma asked, glancing around the library.

In Ruth's tumultuous love life, Paul was the only man Helma had ever seen her cry over. Paul was a reasonable, calm man with whom Ruth had absolutely nothing in common. After spending a disastrous year with Paul in Minnesota, she had returned to Bellehaven and her painting, which earned her an erratic life of financial highs and lows. "We're too deep under each other's skin," Ruth had told her when she announced that Paul was temporarily moving to Bellehaven. And now they lived in separate houses across the alley from each other.

"He's stuck in a snowdrift on the other side of town. I walked the rest of the way here." Her face went serious. "I heard the explosion."

Helma nodded. "One of our patrons, Franklin Harrington, was killed. He was here this morning."

"That's what George said. One of the triplets. The good one, as far as I'm concerned."

"You know Rosy and Del?" Helma picked up a Canadian quarter from the floor.

"I'll take that," Ruth said, holding out her hand. "Not intimately. Well, not that Del hasn't tried, and Rosy wouldn't. Big names in Bellehaven. But I tell you that lot can be a shady bunch."

"Franklin *did* donate the new library site," Helma reminded her.

Ruth gazed out the window in the direction of the site. "Yeah, prime real estate. Probably did it to spite the siblings. Maybe you can erect a statue of him in front of the new building. This probably wasn't an accident, right?"

"The police are investigating," Helma told her. She glanced over at Glory, who was staring at Ruth. Glory hardly reached Ruth's elbow, and was as mesmerized by Ruth as if she might be by an apparition. Ruth pretended not to notice.

"Perfect day for a murder. The killer probably dressed in white and simply melted into the flakes." Ruth raised her eyebrows. "Remember those stories about the Polish resistance fighters on skis in World War Two?"

"I believe those were the Norwegians," Helma told her. "The explosion could also have been a gas main weakened by the excavation."

"Which just happened to blow sky high from the weight of all those little snowflakes when dear old beloved Mr. Harrington wandered past. I don't think so. Check the brothers' whereabouts, that's my advice."

"I'm sure the police will," Helma told her.

Behind them, Jimmy Dodd said to someone, "Way to go," accompanied by the sound of jangling coins.

They paused as more sirens wailed from the direction of the library excavation.

"Late for the party," Ruth commented, looking toward the window. She unzipped her snowsuit a few inches. "Whew, it's hot in here."

"You could take off that snowsuit," Helma suggested.

"Can't. I don't have anything on under it. Oh, hey, can I borrow ten dollars?"

"To gamble?"

"To keep your visitors occupied. Think of it as a public service. I'll stop them from rampaging all over the library."

"I don't lend money to strangers—or friends," Helma explained to her, "and especially not for gambling."

"Ben Franklin would love you. But I bet George will," Ruth said, unzipping her suit even farther. "Hey, George?"

Glory approached Helma from the side, her eyes round. "Is it true?" she asked in a low voice. "Was it a terrorist attack?"

"Did someone in authority give you that information?" Helma asked her.

Glory shook her head. "But you know: an *explosion*. That could be terrorists, couldn't it?"

Someone less generous than Helma might believe Glory had a hopeful light in her eyes.

"There is no reason to believe that," she told Glory. "An explosion of some type killed Mr. Harrington, yes, but it's far too soon to speculate on the source."

"But nobody said it *wasn't* a terrorist," Glory persisted.

After George slipped two bills into Ruth's hand, he joined Helma by the reference desk. "Ruth's upset about her upcoming show," he said, watching Ruth sit down at a table, holding up the bills to the women like a trophy. "Have you seen her new stuff?"

"She's still painting," Helma told him. "I'll see her work at the opening."

"Don't count on it. I'm betting she'll back out. Our Ruth isn't happy about sharing the Penny Whistle Gallery's walls."

George was right. Ruth's exhibits had always been one-person shows, but her first show following her return to Bellehaven was scheduled to be a joint show, and Ruth hadn't taken it well.

"Did she tell you she was backing out?" Helma asked.

George cupped his hands around his beard and tugged in an exaggerated manner. "Just rumors."

"I prefer not to give credence to rumors," Helma told him.

"Yup, I know that. Glory said you thought we might have terrorists lurking around Bellehaven."

"No," Helma said emphatically. "I do not."

"I didn't think so, either," George said. "But you know how rumors start."

She definitely did. "Have you seen Dutch?" she asked George, looking over at the unmanned circulation counter.

"Saw him in the Fiction stacks a while ago. I can check out books until he comes back. Not that we've got any customers eager to take home a little light reading."

"I can do it, if we need to," Helma said.

George cleared his throat and rolled a pencil between his hands. "You know what they say about hindsight?" he asked.

"About it being twenty-twenty?" Helma said.

George nodded. "Franklin's death was a sad, damn thing, but it wasn't *your* fault, or *my* fault. Believe that, okay?"

Helma nodded, thinking it was *someone's* fault.

Chapter 7

An Invitation

The games were in full swing, sound effects provided by Ruth, contributed to now and then by whoever paused to watch. Bonita Wu and the women played silently, raptly, using their hands to signal their plays.

"You're killing me here," Ruth said, and the homeless man responded in such modulated tones, "Poor choice of words," that Helma looked up from the reference desk where she held her finger to the telephone number of the furnace repair people.

"Sorry, everybody," Ruth said with an airy wave of her hand. "He's right. This is a time to be sensitive about our verb images."

At least the telephones still worked. Helma studied the blowing snow, wondering if or when the power might fail them. The furnace company's line was busy.

The heating system still continued to operate, interrupted by rumbles and groans, despite Ms. Moon's assertions that the problem had repaired itself. Helma hit Redial every thirty seconds until finally a weary voice answered.

"Yeah?" the man asked.

"This is Miss Helma Zukas at the Bellehaven Public Library and our heating system is faltering."

"You and half the town. You got heat right now or not?"

"At the moment, yes, but it has stopped at least twice this morning, probably more."

"But it came back on, right?" Another phone rang in the background.

As was Helma's habit when dealing with trying situations on the telephone, she rose from her chair and stood beside the desk. "The library is a public institution," she informed him, "and we are currently entrusted with the safety of several members of the public who have no other means. We are dependent on this system, and by extension, on you."

A long sigh came from the telephone. "Okay, okay. We'll get over there when we can."

"I would naturally expect you to take care of the vulnerable before the library," Helma conceded. "Thank you."

"Yeah," he said, and hung up.

Glory strode from the workroom toward Helma, her face alight with curiosity.

"Your phone's been ringing, just *jingling* away, back there. Ms. Moon and I are discussing programming and it's been such a worry to us—ringing and ringing like that—so I felt I should answer it in case it was, you know, an emergency."

"And when you answered my telephone," Helma said, "did it prove to be urgent to *you*?"

"He wouldn't tell me," Glory said. She wrinkled her nose. "At first I thought it was Wayne, I mean, the chief of police, so I asked him if he had news about Franklin Harrington." She shrugged. "He didn't, so don't worry, it wasn't him."

"Please don't answer my telephone in the future."

"Oh, I know, I *know*." Glory held out her hands in imitation of helplessness. "I would *never*. That's why I came out here. I mean, don't you think Dutch should be able to see you sitting right here twenty feet away from his nose? I don't know why he keeps transferring phone calls for *you* to your *desk*."

Dutch stood at the circulation desk shuffling date due slips while he appeared to study the photocopier gently humming to itself across the room.

"I'll go tell him," Glory said.

"I will," Helma said. "Thank you."

"Well, okay. If you want to. I don't mean to interfere."

Glory followed after Helma toward the circulation desk. Helma stopped and turned back to her. "Was there more, Glory?" and waited until Glory shook her head and wandered back toward the workroom.

Dutch straightened his shoulders at Helma's approach, squared the date due slips by rapping them on the counter, then set them aside. "Ma'am?"

"I'll be at the reference desk, Dutch, should a telephone call come for me."

As if to punctuate her words, the phone rang. After Dutch greeted the caller, he said, "One moment, sir. I'll connect you," and Helma watched his index finger tap the first three numbers of her extension in the workroom.

She placed her hand over the number pad so he couldn't complete the number. "I'll take this call at the reference desk, Dutch."

He nodded and redialed the correct extension. Helma returned to the desk and picked up the phone on the second ring.

"This is Miss Zukas."

"Helma, this is Boyd. Are you all right? I heard you were at the excavation site. Franklin was a good man. He'll be a loss to this community."

"Were you there?" Helma asked.

"Yup. I walked over to see what was going on. I heard that round cop say a librarian had been there." He paused. "I figured it had to be you."

"It was," Helma admitted. "You knew Franklin?"

"Not well. He helped me with some train research."

Boyd Bishop was a widowed writer who wrote westerns he couldn't get published. He also had another, deeper secret that only Helma, in all of Bellehaven, was privy to. He had become a friend in the past few months.

"Some weather, huh?" he said. "Will you go out with me tomorrow?"

"Out?" Helma asked. "The buses aren't even moving."

"I have something I want to show you, and you can see it best during snow. I'll call you tomorrow with the time. Say yes."

Boyd was impetuous and enthusiastic. Helma hesitated. The weather, Franklin's death.

"What is it?" she asked.

"Something Franklin Harrington showed me."

"It's more appropriate for you to show the police than me," she suggested. From somewhere outside the library came the revving of a heavy engine.

"Nah," Boyd said. "Nothing like that. This doesn't have anything to do with Franklin's death. But it might give you an idea of the man's meticulousness."

Helma rarely participated in such vaguely formulated adventures. But she didn't refuse, hearing Aunt Em's voice say, "Nothing ever happens to people who say no."

"Tell you what," Boyd said cheerfully. "Think about it and I'll contact you tomorrow. Bring mittens," he told her before he hung up. "And dress warm."

Helma's hand hovered over the telephone. She was a naturally curious woman, and it *had* been two hours since the explosion that took Franklin Harrington's life. No, not yet. She pulled her hand away, and as she did, the pipes in the ceiling and those beneath the floor groaned with such a hopeless, slipping sense of mechanisms gone wrong that as the circulating air went dead once more, Helma knew that this time the heat would not be restarting itself.

In the ensuing silence, voices self-consciously stopped. Hands of cards froze, heads raised alertly as they waited for the system to recover and throb back to life.

But of course, it didn't.

"We're in for it now," George announced, gazing out at the snow. "It's not exactly balmy out there."

"No worries," Jimmy Dodd said from the table where he was dealing cards. "There's plenty of gas in the bus. We can always move into it if it gets too cold in here."

"We have coats," Bonita Wu said, her hand resting on two cards on the table. "We'll stay here."

Jimmy looked at the stacks of bills and coins in front of Bonita. "Sure, as long as you're winning, right?" And Bonita inclined her head toward him once.

"I've notified the heating repair company," Helma told them. She didn't need to raise her voice to be heard in the breathless room. "The very worst that can happen is we may be slightly uncomfortable until they arrive."

The homeless man shook his head. He had gathered unused bookends and built a U-shaped wall around a section of one of the nearby tables. "I came in to *get* warm. You should have installed a better furnace."

"Yeah," Ruth told him. "You'd think all your tax dollars would do a better job of it."

"I'm a homeless citizen of this town," he said, thrusting his chin toward Ruth.

"That makes you an oxymoron," she told him.

"Oxy poxy," he replied indignantly.

Without heat, it was prudent to block any drafts, so

Helma began closing doors to the study rooms beyond the Biography section. Then she dashed down to make sure that the doors to the empty and dark children's library were closed.

She paused there for a moment to view a drift that had grown outside the back door, its humped edge nearly to the door handle. The wind whistled through the metal sculpture of a reading child on the empty fountain. It was a lonely sound.

When she returned upstairs, Ms. Moon and Glory Shandy were waiting beside the reference desk, their faces stricken.

"Has something else happened?" Helma asked.

"Yes," Ms. Moon said.

"No," Glory said at the same time.

They fumbled their words over one another while Helma waited for them to sort themselves out, deciphering the single word that peppered both their tumbled sentences: "called."

"Oh, I didn't mean to," Ms. Moon said, and Helma winced as Ms. Moon stretched the sleeves of her sweater, still around her waist, tying them into a granny knot and then unknotting them.

"I thought it would be all right," Glory added, and Helma deduced immediately that whatever call had been made was Glory Shandy's idea. "I can't believe he didn't already know."

"Who did you call?" Helma asked Ms. Moon. "And what didn't he know?"

"Del Harrington," Ms. Moon answered.

"You telephoned Delano Harrington," Helma surmised, "and he hadn't learned yet that his brother had been killed."

Ms. Moon nodded, tying and untying. "We thought we'd just mention a tiny smidgen about the library site, to remind him of Franklin's wishes. I never dreamed the police wouldn't have informed him yet."

Helma gazed from one woman to the other, both of them looking like guilty but defiant children. Ms. Moon bit her lower lip, Glory twisted one of her red curls around her finger.

"It's only been two and a half hours since Franklin's death," Helma pointed out. "I'm shocked."

"Me, too," Glory agreed, vigorously nodding her head. "You'd think they'd tell his own brother right away."

"No," Helma said firmly. "I'm shocked you'd phone Delano Harrington a few hours after his brother's death to discuss *land*."

"It only made sense to put a word in for the library as soon as possible," Ms. Moon said, raising her chin.

"And besides," Glory added, "they didn't get along *that* well." At the expression on Helma's face she hastily added, "That's what I heard, anyway."

It was pointless. "And Del's response?" Helma asked.

"He called me a ... " Ms. Moon winced and Glory made "ooooh" sounds as she patted Ms. Moon's shoulder. "Names," Ms. Moon said. "He called me names."

"Delano was angry," Helma interpreted.

"Yes," she said simply. "Very."

Helma pictured it. Franklin might have been the oldest of the triplets, the son who'd inherited the final say in family matters, but Delano was the triplet who'd reportedly inherited the ambition that drove the early Harringtons to create their empire. He was a developer, an unsuccessful mayoral candidate, a man who people treated cautiously. She had adequately answered his questions at the reference desk, and he sometimes asked for her personally. Always businesslike, he had little patience for chitchat.

It was unlike Ms. Moon to confess a failure or report a personally embarrassing moment, especially to one of the staff, and most especially to Helma. There was more; she could feel it.

"The heating system has quit," Helma began.

Ms. Moon adjusted Helma's sweater at her waist, and still looking down, said, "Del likes you."

"I have assisted him on a professional level," Helma told her. "I suspect he respects my skills but I doubt he has a single personal feeling toward me."

"He likes you," she repeated.

The phone on the reference desk buzzed, signaling a call being transferred.

"Excuse me," Helma told Ms. Moon and Glory, and waited for them to move away before she picked up the receiver.

"This is Carla at city hall. Thanks for taking in the busload this morning. I'm sorry my call was so panicked. Hardly anybody's here and the phone just would *not* stop." Helma recognized the voice of the same woman who'd called to ask if the library was open, before Bonita Wu and the Chinese women's arrival. "Are they having any problems?"

"None that I can see," Helma said, glancing over at the intently playing women, most of them with coats draped over their shoulders against the cooling room. There was no point in mentioning the failed heating system.

"Good, good. The last thing we need is some kind of international incident. It's utter chaos over here."

"With Franklin Harrington's death," Helma said, preparing to ask for the latest information on the explosion.

"And now Randall."

"Randall?" Helma asked.

"Yeah, Randall Rice."

"Randall Rice, the city finance commissioner?" Helma repeated.

"That's what the police are saying," the receptionist told her. "They didn't see him right away because of the snow. He was under a tree and somebody spotted that crazy plaid jacket he wears. He can thank his own bad taste for being discovered."

"He's alive?" Helma asked.

"So far."

Chapter 8

Strange Partners

"Why was Randall Rice at the excavation site?" Helma glanced out the window in the direction of the hospital. That must have been the belated sirens they'd heard—an ambulance rushing Randall to the hospital. Nothing was visible, not even the parking meters.

"Don't know," Carla the receptionist told her.

"Was he with Franklin Harrington?"

"Don't know that either." A pause. "But he must've been, don't you think?"

After distracted goodbyes, Helma hung up. Randall Rice. A man so renowned for his financial acumen that the city had designed an unelected position just for him: finance commissioner, which he'd held in a vice grip for nine years. Helma had heard him referred to as a money czar, a numbers maniac, and worse. She'd answered phone questions from him, and each time he'd called, he identified himself in a deep reverent voice as, "Finance Commisioner Rice here."

"You look like you've been slammed for overdue fines," Ruth said. "What's happened?"

Helma gestured toward the telephone. "It's not official yet—I don't believe it is, anyway—but the police receptionist said Randall Rice was found near the excavation pit. He's at the hospital."

"Our esteemed city finance fascist?" Ruth said. "The guy with the paunch and comb-over?" Her eyes gleamed, and not with tears. "Oh my, what a shame that is."

A few years earlier Ruth had challenged the city's scheme to tax all Bellehaven artists who actually had the good fortune to make money. In a memorable city council meeting, she and Randall Rice had exchanged an escalating series of comments, he implacable, and she pulling herself taller and becoming fiercer by the moment, until suddenly, in exasperation after Randall said, "You're not seeing my point," Ruth had dropped back to her seat, saying, "And you can't make yourself tall enough to see mine," causing him to flush a hot crimson. He *was* slightly below average in height, and by Ruth's standards that put him beneath her radar.

"Were he and Franklin buddies?" Ruth asked.

"I don't know. They both had an interest in history."

Like many people who consider another person their enemy, Ruth had an abiding interest and knowledge of hers. "The Rice man's interest in history was in renovation so he could get his name on a plaque or something. All for the good of his teeny-weeny image." And she held her fingers an inch apart.

"And Franklin's interest revolved around his family's history."

Ruth shrugged. "Somebody saw Randall and just didn't like the way he looked so they blew him up. He was the type who'd piss off the worst criminal." She paused and the gleam left her eyes. "Yeah, but Franklin, now … he was a good guy."

"Random crime is rare in Bellehaven," Helma explained, "and statistics prove that crime rates drop during severe weather."

"So this was a murderer who came from a place that has four seasons, somewhere life goes on when the snow falls. It could have been a disgruntled Bellehaven taxpayer."

"I wonder if the police—"

Ruth turned her head and glanced at the women playing cards. "Hey, don't start without me. I still have four dollars."

Helma's hand was on the telephone when the homeless man hesitantly approached her. He'd smoothed his overlong hair and tucked it behind his ears. "Will the police know if I use a computer?"

"There aren't any police in the library," Helma told him. She subtly leaned back from a strong odor reminiscent of the commercial area of the harbor.

He dropped his voice. "No, I meant can they tell, through the air?"

"I don't believe they have that capability."

"But you're not sure, are you? You don't know what I know." His voice rose. "There are secret things they can do we don't know they can do. We have no idea." He spoke in a volume that bordered on shouting. "We're in the dark."

The women looked up as the man shifted from foot to foot. Dutch stepped away from the circulation desk toward them. Helma recognized an escalating situation. She dropped her own voice, having learned that many people naturally followed suit.

"You're right," she whispered, leaning forward and cutting him off.

He stopped, startled, and dropped his hand, his mouth gaping. "I am?"

She nodded gravely. "You are. We never *can* know what other people will do. It's impossible. You're completely correct."

He stopped shifting; his forehead smoothed, and he nodded, too, before whispering, "What is the safest strategy?"

"Either I or another librarian will be on duty, right here at this desk," Helma told him, touching her index finger to the reference desk top. "You'll be safe. Go ahead. You may use the computer."

"Thank you," he whispered, his face shining in gratitude, and looked both ways before darting toward the banks of computers.

Helma then used the librarians' computer at the reference desk to pull up Franklin's address, intending to see if the two men lived near each other. She knew Franklin had a library card. Randall's calls to the reference desk were usually for statistics, market quotes, and addresses.

Franklin Harrington lived in the historic Harrington house only a few blocks away, just as she'd thought. Randall Rice did not have a library card. Frankly, she was surprised and had to resort to the phone book to find his address. And there she discovered another surprise. Randall Rice lived outside the city limits. Not far outside, true, but still beyond the legal boundaries. By rights, he should have been phoning the county library with his reference questions, not the *city* library.

"Look," Jimmy Dodd called out. "It's letting up."

Snow still fell, but yes, the sky was definitely lighter and the flakes appeared gloppier, their trajectory straight downward instead of floating and swirling, as if they were growing heavy as snow warmed into water. But unless there was a sudden warm wind, a chinook, it would still be at least tomorrow before the streets were passable. There wasn't much choice for the citizens of Bellehaven but to wait it out.

Chapter 9

In the Deep Freeze

Through the gauzy white, Helma could now decipher the casino bus with its still-blinking lights parked at the library curb, and beyond it, the outline of the courthouse and police department. A four-wheel-drive vehicle inched slowly up the drifted street, its emergency lights flashing.

The first flush of crisis and chaos was coming to a close and would soon be properly replaced by a planned, coordinated, and organized response. Hilly streets would be graveled, sidewalks shoveled, stores reopened, schools back in session.

Order would prevail, as it should. Still ...

"Looks like we might get out of here before the food runs out," Jimmy Dodd said.

"Or my money," Ruth said.

Maneuvering his handful of cards, Jimmy zipped up his coat, adding, "Or freeze to death."

Bonita Wu raised her head and squinted out the window. "In one hour, we'll leave," she said, and returned to dealing cards to the women at her table.

"Gotcha," Jimmy said.

"It's advisable that you wait until the police give the go-ahead," Helma cautioned, thinking Jimmy was right again: it was definitely growing colder in the library. She wished for her extra sweater but it still hung around Ms. Moon's hips. The sleeves would probably be too stretched for her to wear, anyway. So instead she retrieved her coat from her cubicle, walking swiftly past Ms. Moon's office, where she glimpsed the director hunched at her desk, speaking in a low voice into her telephone.

"If we can get out of town to the northwest," Jimmy was saying as Helma sat down, "there'll be less snow near the casino." Without the murmur of the furnace, voices traveled in the library. He added, "It's closer to the water."

With her eye on the card play, Bonita nodded. "If we do not arrive at the casino before five o'clock, we will be honored to accept an offer to spend the night at your hotel. Courtesy of your tribe, of course."

Jimmy peered at his watch, then outside and back at his watch again. "Before five, huh?"

No one else entered the library; no one approached the desk for reference help, although the phone rang several times, which Dutch answered again and again, either saying, "Yes we *are* open," or, "It would be more appropriate to call 911."

Helma's fingers grew clumsy with the cold. She

pulled her coat sleeves over her hands, and sensing someone standing in front of the reference desk, looked up into the ruddy cheeks and troubled eyes of Wayne Gallant.

"Excuse me," he said. "Can I talk to you about Franklin Harrington?"

"Certainly," Helma said, standing. "I heard about Randall Rice. Do you know his condition?"

"He's in the ICU, that's all I know right now." He removed a small notebook from his inside coat pocket. He was intent on police business and his face was impersonal, calm and determined. "Can you lead me through, as much as possible, a minute-by-minute description of what Franklin did this morning?"

Helma nodded and walked with him toward the front doors. "Franklin entered the library as soon as the doors were unlocked. As I told you earlier, he said he was checking last minute facts for the family history he'd written."

"Could you tell anything about his state of mind?" the chief asked.

"He was jovial," Helma told him. "He may have been a little more ... excited than usual—but we all were because of the snow."

She showed him the microfilm machine where Franklin sat. "He looked at microfilm for about forty-five minutes."

"Did you help him?"

"No. Franklin had used the machines for years; he was very capable." She glanced around and didn't see a spool of microfilm or a rectangular white box above the microfilm cabinets. "He even refiled his films, although we did ask him not to."

"Did he mention the library site?"

"Only that he planned to walk by to see how it was faring in this weather, and then return to the library. He said he'd be back in fifteen minutes. I warned him about the cold." She didn't mention that if she hadn't discouraged George, he might have followed Franklin out into the snow. She remembered the elegant old man's smile and felt the familiar stab of sorrow, compounded by personal regret.

At the sound of clicking coins, Wayne glanced over at the three tables of women intent on their card games. "Did he speak to anyone else?"

Helma thought. "Several people, in passing. We all mainly discussed the snow. There wasn't anything else that seemed important enough to discuss, actually."

Glory walked into the public area from the workroom and circled Wayne and Helma like an errant satellite, casting glances their way.

Wayne left Helma and spoke to the Chinese women, who shook their heads when he asked about Franklin, then the homeless man, who tried to block the chief's view of his computer screen. Helma heard him say, "I didn't talk to him and I've fixed everything bad I ever did in my whole life." Glory edged closer and Wayne Gallant waved toward her but returned to Helma.

"It's cold in here," he commented.

"The heat's off," she told him. "I've phoned the repair company."

He nodded.

"I heard the explosion," Glory said eagerly, stepping up beside Wayne. "There was a bright light." She gave a shivery shrug. "I was so scared."

"I'll be back to talk to everyone tomorrow," Wayne told Glory. "I have business at the station right now." He nodded and waited until Glory moved toward the Internet computers before he spoke again.

"Anything else?" he asked Helma.

She repictured the morning, the confusion with the arrival of the busload of women. "Franklin did use the telephone."

"Do you recall the tone of the conversation? Who it might have been?"

"I respect our patrons' privacy," she told him.

Finally, he switched his focus to Helma, *really* looking at her. One corner of his mouth raised and he regarded her, waiting.

"I wasn't listening," Helma made clear, "but his voice did remain pleasantly modulated."

"I see. Thanks."

"Do you believe he and Randall Rice were together?" she asked.

"In some fashion, yes." An eyebrow raised. "Word moves fast in this town."

"Was it a gas explosion?" she asked straight out. It was too cold to waste time working her way to the subject.

"We're still investigating the cause," he told her.

Helma's long association with both Wayne Gallant and the Bellehaven police enabled her to understand certain nuances. "Then you suspect another cause."

She remembered Glory's fears and dropped her voice. "Not terrorism?" she asked, and was relieved when his mouth opened in surprise.

"One last question," Wayne said, closing his notebook. "Did anyone leave the library just before the explosion? Was everyone still here in the public area?"

"As far as I know. We all ran to the windows when we heard the blast. My attention was on that." Helma pointed to the picture window where they'd peered vainly into the falling snow. "I understand why Franklin had gone to the excavation site—he had an abiding interest in the project—but why was Randall Rice there?"

As soon as she said it she realized her question should have been framed more discreetly. The chief's eyes shadowed and an expression she knew so well— "police business"—settled on his face. He tucked his notebook back into his pocket. "I'll prod the furnace repair guys, but in the meantime I think we'd better vacate the library building before it gets any colder in here."

Chapter 10

Heading Out

Even in the midst of a death investigation and a dangerous storm, once the chief made a few phone calls, things began to happen.

A police car was pressed into leading the casino bus to a hotel. Jimmy set his jaw, and Bonita Wu's eyes disappeared in a frown as the policeman, Officer Young, explained how they should follow him to the Oxbow Hotel in south Bellehaven.

"We need to be on the northwest side of town," Jimmy insisted.

"Why's that?" Officer Young asked, his own eyes narrowing.

Jimmy bit his lip, glanced at Bonita and said to the policeman in a low voice, "Feng shui. If they aren't on the northwest side of town," he made throat cutting motions, "I'll be stuck with a busload of raging women positive they're about to die. Have pity, I beg of you."

Officer Young looked skeptical. Bonita tottered forward, suddenly appearing autumn-leaf frail and so ancient the policeman himself reached out his hand to steady her. "Is very bad," she said in an aged high-pitched squeak, her low voice and perfect English mysteriously absent.

"I don't know," the policeman said, shaking his head at Bonita and Jimmy. Helma doubted Officer Young could take time to assure the bus *stayed* at a hotel, and once Jimmy was at the edge of town he'd continue driving northwest to the Nettle casino, doubtlessly reaching it before the crucial hour of 5:00 P.M.

"You can take me home as well," Ms. Moon said, and Bonita's eyes gleamed. "I live on the west side of town."

Beside Helma, Ruth muttered, "So much for the captain staying with her sinking ship."

"Me, too," Glory added. "I'll go with you."

Ms. Moon smiled at Bonita Wu, and folding her hands in a prayerlike tent at her waist, she bowed to the elderly woman and said, "I have always admired the religious philosophy of your people."

One of Bonita's eyebrows may have raised; it was difficult to tell on her ancient face. She said nothing. Ms. Moon smiled serenely.

"I'll drop you off at the mission," Officer Young told the homeless man, and Helma realized the decision was set; the Promise Mission for homeless men was also on the northwest side of town.

"Will they make me pray?" he asked, wiping his

sleeve across his face. "I don't need to pray anymore; I can fix it myself."

"We might still have room in the jail," the officer told him.

"Okay, okay. I'll go quietly."

Ms. Moon considered the homeless man, then said brightly, "I get carsick so I'll have to sit up front. You two ride in the back."

The chief's cell phone chirped and Wayne stepped near the atlas case to answer it. Helma was not listening; she'd only moved to realign a row of gazetteers slipping sideways, as soft-covered, oversized books tended to do. All she heard him say was, "Okay, I'll take care of it."

He closed his phone, turning as he slipped it into his pocket, and grinned when he saw her sliding a bookend against the gazetteers. "I have to leave but Mark will be back for you and the others."

"Has anything happened regarding the deaths?" Helma asked.

His grin widened. "Wait here until he gets back."

"I have my skis," Helma told him.

"I'd rather you rode with him. Once the four-wheelers get out there, the streets will be too dangerous for pedestrians."

"The snow has let up," Helma said. "Visibility has improved."

"He'll take you and Ruth home," Wayne repeated.

"I'm able to—"

Suddenly Ruth was standing between them, bright yellow, hands out flat toward each of them in her exaggerated way as if she were separating boxers. "Aye aye," she said, saluting Wayne, and to Helma, "Whaddaya say? Let's go home with the nice policeman."

Wayne touched his head as if he wore a fedora. "Excellent. We'll talk later," and he hurried out of the library while beside Helma, Ruth hummed the refrain from the William Tell Overture.

When Ms. Moon was rebundled in her winter clothes and ready to leave, she broke away from Glory, Officer Young, and the homeless man, all standing by the front door. "Wait," she told them. "I forgot something. It's vital."

Outside, the women had boarded their bus. The engine revved, exhaust shadowed the pure white snow, and windshield wipers snicked across the glass, piling the snow into slabs. Jimmy Dodd had knocked most of the snow off the bus sides and roof with a broom from Jack the janitor's closet.

"Here," Ms. Moon said, thrusting Helma's sweater into her arms. But that wasn't all. Enclosed in the sweater was an object the size of a ream of paper.

"What is this?" Helma asked.

Ms. Moon, who was never quite sure about Ruth, looked at her meaningfully, and Ruth took two steps away and pointed her index fingers into her ears. Ms. Moon dropped her voice. "My files from the new library site: negotiations, my observations and dreams, information on the Harringtons, applicable communiqués."

"Why are you giving them to me?" Helma asked, holding the sweater and its bulk in front of her, out from her body.

"Because I've decided you're the one," she said in the ardent voice of a woman bestowing a coveted award, touching the air around Helma with a mittened hand. "Because of your thoroughness, your association in the community, and your excellent relationship with the Harringtons. Why, if it hadn't been for you championing our cause with Franklin, he might never have given the library site to us. Because of all that ... " She smiled until her gums showed, then continued.

"I've placed *you* in charge of arranging for the library site to remain exactly as it is."

"That is not my—" Helma began.

"Tut tut," Ms. Moon interrupted. "Don't be modest. I've already cleared it with the mayor and the library board."

"I ... " Until that moment, Ms. Moon had never mentioned Helma's small role in Franklin's bequest of the library site. Even to Helma, she'd said the new site was due to "*my* fortunate association with the esteemed Harrington family."

Ms. Moon held up her hand. "No need to thank me. I have complete faith in you. Complete. Besides, Del likes you. Bye now." And she hurried after Officer Young, the homeless man, and Glory, leaving Helma holding the bag her sweater made around the files.

Helma set the bundle on a nearby table and unwrapped it to expose a thick folder. Papers stuck out of it in every direction. All sorts of paper: colored, typed, stationery. She glimpsed Ms. Moon's distinctive loopy handwriting in a multitude of colored inks.

"What's that?" Ruth asked.

"Ms. Moon gave me her notes on the library site. She asked me to represent the library in the site's final disposition."

"Which means she's botched it big-time," Ruth said. "We're talking about the hole in the ground, right? I thought it was a done deal." She poked a finger at the folder and the papers sticking out of it. "What a mess. Save it for another day."

"I'll take it home in case the library's closed tomorrow," Helma said, tucking papers back into the folder and sliding it into her bag.

"Ding ding," Ruth said. "That's the sound of alarm bells going off." She shrugged as Helma closed her bag over the folder. "Masochist."

Ruth and Helma sat in the foyer and waited for Officer Young to return, Ruth muttering darkly over an art magazine, saying every once in a while, "Poseur," and Helma taking the opportunity to create a timeline of the day's events

Dutch, the only other staff person in the library, tidied up: changing stamps to tomorrow's date, turning off computers, realigning the tables and chairs disarranged during the card games. Now he walked back and forth in the empty library. A frown disturbed his normally military-calm features. Helma watched him, curious.

"Is that our ride?" Ruth asked, pointing out the window. "He's back awful fast. Ooh, look. We get the flashing lights."

The police car's lights *were* flashing. The wind had momentarily stopped. Helma gathered up her bag while Ruth pulled on mittens that looked as huge as bear paws. "I'll sit on that hard seat in the back," she offered. "I've had experience. You can sit up front with the gun."

Helma glanced back at Dutch. He walked once more past the main windows, then stopped and stared outside, not noticing that Ruth and Helma were preparing to leave.

"Go ahead," Helma told Ruth. "I'll tell Dutch our ride's here."

"Well, hurry it up or I'll grab the front seat."

Helma approached Dutch cautiously, clearing her throat to announce her presence. He didn't move.

"Dutch?" she said softly.

He jumped and spun toward her. Helma stepped back.

"Ma'am?" he said, but his eyes swept past her, behind her, around the library and back again, his forehead deeply creased as he peered into her face.

"It's time to go home," she told him.

He nodded once and looked back out the window. Helma knew he hadn't really heard her.

"Dutch?" she said again, and he shrugged his shoulder as if a biting insect had buzzed him, but didn't look her way.

Helma stood tall and cleared her throat once more. In her silver dime voice, she ordered, "The police are here to take us home. Get in the car, sir."

Dutch turned on his heels. "Ma'am," he said so sharply it sounded like a bark, and followed her from the library building.

Chapter 11

The Long Ride Home

"Oh, look," Ruth said, standing in the snow beside the back door of the police car. "The chief sent one of his big guns for us."

Helma opened the passenger door and saw not Officer Young at the wheel but Detective Carter Houston. He still wore his black Russian hat, and his round smooth face was solemn. He'd fastened his seat belt so that there were no wrinkles in his black coat.

Carter nodded as they climbed inside: Helma in the front, Dutch behind Carter. Ruth, smiling widely, sat behind Helma. Carter Houston's lack of humor made him irresistible to Ruth. The car smelled of disinfectant.

"So tell me, Carter," Ruth said when the doors were closed. "How is it you can be spared to play taxi driver in the midst of an investigation into mysterious death and maiming?"

"Fasten your seat belt, please, Miss Winthrop," Carter said. He gazed in his rearview mirror at Ruth, his hand poised above the gear shift.

"Whatever you say. Is that your grandmother's hat?"

Carter pulled the cruiser away from the library, snow crunching beneath the tires. Helma peered back at the dark library building. They'd been the last to leave, and she wasn't one to wonder if she'd forgotten to adequately secure the doors. She rarely performed any act without noting at the time that it had been accomplished successfully.

Carter drove slowly. He'd had occasion to visit both Helma's and Ruth's residences and knew where they lived. They passed a skier cautiously stepping over a mysterious shape. Two dogs loped up the snowy street in front of them, then veered into the trees near the museum.

"The chief said you were the last to speak to Franklin," Carter said to Helma. He didn't turn to look at her, but continually scanned the winter scene in front of them, both hands light on the steering wheel.

"The last person in the library, at least," Helma corrected. "Do you believe he and Randall Rice were on their way to the new library site together?"

"Did you ever see the two men in each other's company?"

"No," Helma told him.

"I did," Ruth said from the backseat.

Carter's eyes imperceptibly narrowed and he looked in his rearview mirror again. "When was that?"

"Once at city hall. I was paying—well, I was actually begging for clemency—a parking ticket. You guys are just too, too eager at slapping those babies on windshields. I'd dashed into Sorenson's, grabbed a coffee and dashed out, and there it was on my windshield like a giant scarlet letter."

"Franklin and Randall?" Carter reminded her.

"Oh, them. I saw the two of them standing in the hallway talking, that's all."

"Were they friendly?"

"Couldn't say. They were just talking. Randall had probably figured out some rotten scheme to squeeze another seventy-six cents out of Franklin."

"Then your impression was not friendly?" Carter persisted. He kept taking swift glances into his mirror.

"I didn't say that, Carter. Don't shove words down my throat. Is *anybody* truly friendly with that weasel? You know what I heard his hobby is? Coin collecting. Is that fitting or what? Lord of Money."

"Dutch?" Carter asked. "Did you ever see Franklin and Randall together?" Helma could tell from the way Carter twisted his head that he couldn't quite catch Dutch's reflection.

Dutch sat peering out the window, his face averted from the interior of the car. He didn't move his head, his hands clasped between his knees. "No," he said simply.

"Carter," Helma said, turning more toward Carter. "Did Wayne Gallant *request* that you drive us home? Are your questions part of the investigation?"

"Oh, Carter," Ruth cooed. "Are you playing at undercover cop?"

Carter's face flushed but his expression didn't change. "I am *always* a detective," he said stiffly. "And may I remind you I *am* currently on duty?"

"That must be what always makes me want to spill my deepest, darkest secrets to you, then," Ruth said. Helma heard her yawn.

"I didn't see anything unusual about Franklin's visit this morning," Helma said, feeling the smallest touch of sympathy for the dogged detective. "Except for the weather, of course."

Carter nodded. He leaned closer to the dashboard, listening to something in the incessant chatter of the police radio. Helma caught words like, "roll over," "collapsed roof," "shelter," and "unnecessary speed."

Suddenly, the sun broke through and the world glinted, gleamed, and sparkled with such intensity that Helma felt an ache deep behind her eye sockets. And just as quickly the sun disappeared and the scenery returned to silver gray.

"Did you know Franklin Harrington?" she asked the detective.

"Not personally," he said.

Ruth leaned forward, straining against her seat belt. "Who do *you* think wanted to blow him and Randall sky high?" she asked.

"We don't know yet that anybody did," Carter replied easily.

"Yeah, stick with the party line," Ruth said, blowing out her lower lip. "I bet the only accident was that

Franklin happened to be in the way when somebody went after Randy Rice." She looked smug for a moment, then added, "Not that I'd wish any explosions on Randy Rice, of course."

Helma had a view of Dutch, who still sat as still as stone, still staring out the window.

"Where can we take you, Dutch?" Helma asked.

Dutch slowly and smoothly turned his head toward her. "Drop me at the corner of Cedar and Eighth," he said. "Just a couple of blocks from here."

Cedar and Eighth was situated between downtown and the southeast side of Washington Bay. Condos stood on the southwest corner, a converted Victorian on the northwest, and on the other corners a vacant lot and an architecturally restrained two-story apartment building built in the seventies. A desultory string of partially burned-out Christmas lights hung in one of the building's windows.

"Thanks," Dutch said as he climbed out of the car. He stood on the corner while they pulled away, and Helma watched in the passenger side mirror to see which building Dutch entered. But two blocks down the street, when he faded into the snow, Dutch still stood on the corner, hatless, facing away from the departing police car.

"Old Dutch didn't want us to see where he lived," Ruth said, looking out the rear window. "Secretive fella, isn't he?"

"Private," Helma amended, noticing that Carter was also watching Dutch in his rearview mirror.

"Takes one to know one. I bet he lives somewhere

else altogether," Ruth went on, turning toward the front. "Have you ever met his wife?"

"I'm not aware he's married," Helma told her.

"The curse of the library world. He probably lives in a one-room apartment above a smoky bar downtown."

"Smoking is prohibited in publicly accessible buildings in Washington state," Helma reminded her.

Ruth rolled her eyes. "Don't you recognize when something's said for affect? Look at that." She pointed out her window, and Helma looked into a stand of cedar trees where tree limbs were springing upward and dropping their layers of snow so it scattered and fell to the ground like drifting leaves and feathers.

"It's warming up," Helma told her.

"Too bad."

"Can't happen soon enough," Carter said with uncharacteristic openness. He expertly steered around another snow-covered car and stopped by the side of the street in front of the Bayside Arms. "I don't think I'll drive in," he told Helma, pointing to the drift that knifed across the parking lot. No tire tracks marred the smooth plain of snow.

"Wait. I'm getting out here, too," Ruth said. "Not that I don't want to spend another scintillating few minutes with you, Carter, but nothing's going on at my house except for my paint drying."

A gust of wind off the bay smacked against Helma as she stepped out. She caught her breath and clutched her bag to her.

Around them, as she and Ruth waded through the

snow to the apartment building, snow slid from roofs and dropped from trees, cratering the white ground.

Since snow shovels were a scarce commodity, Walter David was using a broom to clear the sidewalk. He grunted as he pushed a built-up load off the curb, looking up as Helma and Ruth trudged toward him, then followed them into the lea of the building by the staircase. He wore a purple UW Husky cap pulled over his ears and two sweaters, no coat.

"The police brought you home," he said, his pink-cheeked face solemn. "I heard about Franklin Harrington."

"Did you know him?" Helma asked. Walter was one of the few Bellehavenites who hadn't come from somewhere else, who'd lived in town his entire life. He frequently had insights into Bellehaven life before its recent growth spurt.

Walter nodded. "Some. His daughter Frances was a year ahead of me in high school."

"Fran Harrington is Franklin's daughter?" Ruth asked. "I didn't make that connection before."

"Do *you* know Frances?" Helma asked Ruth.

"Only by sight. I dated one of her wasbands."

"Wasband?"

"Ex-husband. There were two."

"Yeah," Walter said, idly swiping at an edge of snow that had blown close to the stairs, leaving a row of broom-straw tracks. "Fran was one of those girls that guys like me only dream about. I knew, or know, all of the Harringtons a little. Hard not to when they're one of Bellehaven's major league families."

"Helma here has been charged with placating the whole bunch of them," Ruth said. "You can give her a few tips."

"Over the library site?" Walter asked. "I heard rumbling about that piece of property months ago. If the library hadn't got it, Del and his son's fancy shmancy condos would already be built, I bet."

"Franklin was very foresightful with his bequest," Helma said before Ruth could engage in any more Harrington or land development conjecture—or in her own role in the new library site.

Ruth pointed to Walter's window, where Moggy sat on the sofa back looking like his white Persian face was mashed against the glass. "Drop Moggy in the snow and you wouldn't find him until Spring."

Walter frowned at Moggy as if he were in imminent danger.

"Ruthie, Helma." It was TNT, the retired boxer who lived next door to Helma. Even in the snow, he wore his usual gray sweats, only in bulky layers with a stocking cap and old-fashioned buckle boots jangling as he paced up and down the sheltered stairs and the length of the building, a poor substitute for his everyday jogging and sparring. "I heard the explosion," he said, gazing through the occasionally falling flakes toward town. "Thought it was an earthquake at first. I heard Randy Rice got it, too. That right?"

Helma nodded. "He's in the hospital, critically injured. They were too close to the explosion, both of them."

"Damn shame. Randy spends time at the gym. Can't

box for beans, though. Got no legs." TNT shook his head, bad boxing as regrettable as injury and death.

"Bad weather to die in," Walter said, and TNT gravely nodded.

Helma left the two men to their soulful musings and climbed the stairs with Ruth at her heels.

Her phone was ringing as she unlocked the door of her apartment. It was her mother.

"Nobody answered at the library," her mother said breathlessly after Helma said hello. "I heard there was an explosion. Are you all right? Did the library blow up? I nearly fainted. And Franklin's dead, I heard. I can't believe it. And I'd already asked him to speak about his new book. I planned a congratulatory reception right here in the rec room for him, with a carrot cake and balloons. Polly Wright made the cleverest bookmarks with a picture of the first Harrington on it—in sepia. I don't know what I'll do now."

Following a lengthy and somewhat acrimonious campaign, Lillian, Helma's mother, had been elected the new program director for her retirement complex: the Silver Gables. Lillian and Helma's Aunt Em, both Michigan transplants, shared an apartment there, excessively proud of the complex's racy reputation among the retired set.

"I'm fine. The explosion was near the excavation site of the new library. The library's heating system failed so we closed."

"How did you get home, dear? The roads are impassable. Well, for most people. *I* could drive them, I'm sure. Your father always said I was the best winter driver he'd ever seen. Just forget you have brakes and a gas pedal, that's my secret. Who brought you home?"

"The police," Helma said, and immediately regretted it, hearing her mother's gasp of pleasure.

"Oh, that dear, dear man. He must have been worried sick about you, even in the middle of murder. Isn't that sweet?"

"They haven't declared Franklin's death a homicide, Mother," Helma said, and behind her Ruth snickered.

"Oh, but Shelley Burns's niece Barbara works at the post office and she told Shelley that it was murder."

"I'm not sure a post office employee would be an authority."

"Well, *she* delivered mail to the mother of an intern at the police department who had it straight from her daughter. Franklin—and that other man … "

"Randall Rice," Helma supplied.

"Yes, that's him. The rumor here is," Lillian dropped her voice, "that Mr. Rice had enemies, plenty of them. He was the target. Franklin was accidental … oh, what's that term? You know, collateral damage. He was a beautiful man, simply beautiful. Just ask Em. Nobody would want to kill Franklin. We all just loved him."

"How's Aunt Em's cold?" Helma asked.

"Better. She's in the bathroom right now breathing Vicks inside a tent over the sink. You know Em. No medicine, not even a flu shot. She's lucky to be alive."

Helma had no sooner hung up, rushing the conversation to an end at the sight of Ruth rummaging through her cupboards, when her phone rang again. She gazed at it, reluctant to pick it up.

"Caller ID is worth the money," Ruth said as Helma finally answered on the fourth ring, expecting her mother with an additional tidbit she'd forgotten to tell her. Often it was news from their old Scoop River, Michigan, newspaper and began with, "You'll never guess who died."

"Miss Zukas, this is Delano Harrington, and as soon as this damn snow melts I expect to talk to you."

Chapter 12

Opening a File

"And the subject you wish to discuss?" Helma asked Delano Harrington. She waited politely while he sputtered, possibly from colds older people were susceptible to this time of year.

"What else?" he answered, each syllable dropping like a stone. "The property my brother simply waltzed in and handed over to you people."

This did not seem to be the moment to offer sympathy to Del for the loss of his brother. "If by 'you people,'" Helma said, "you mean the citizens of Bellehaven, your brother exhibited great generosity and civic responsibility. Thousands of people will be grateful to Franklin. And the Harringtons," she added.

He paused for the briefest moment, and went on. "Yes, well a library was never the intent for that land. If Franklin hadn't been born first and fallen into the clutches of that woman, this wouldn't be an issue."

"And who are you referring to as 'that woman'?"

"Your appropriately named director, that's who. Why do people with their noses stuck in books need a *view*?"

"Where would you like to meet?" Helma asked.

"Right here. Tomorrow. This ridiculous snow will melt by then. There's no sense to it. You come here. I'm old; I don't need to go out."

The invitation to meet him on his own territory didn't sound like a privilege, more like a threat. "I'm afraid I don't know your address," Helma told him.

"The Harrington house, where else? The entrance that faces Kulshan. Ten-thirty. Sharp."

"If the weather—"

"I already said it would melt. I've been around long enough to know that."

"I'll be there," Helma told him. "And I'm very sorry about your brother's death. He was a gentleman."

"He was a fool," Del said curtly, and hung up.

"What was *that* about?" Ruth asked as she pushed aside the bottled oils in Helma's cupboard.

"Franklin's brother wants to discuss the library site."

"Which one?"

"There's only one library site," Helma told her.

"No. Which *brother*?"

"Delano. If you're looking for alcoholic beverages, I don't have any. There's orange juice and cola in the refrigerator."

Ruth closed the cupboard door and opened the refrigerator, draping herself across the door. "Got any bottled water?"

Helma shook her head. "Bellehaven's water is adequately purified. It won the State of Washington's Clear Water Award two years ago."

"Clear ain't pure. It comes out of a *lake*, Helma. People swim in it and stuff."

"And then it's treated. Many bottled water companies fill their bottles with city water that's been treated."

"Bottled water *looks* nice," Ruth insisted. "You know, all those sparkly plastic bottles."

"It's a delusion."

"I embrace my delusions. Leave me alone. Kitty kitty."

Boy Cat Zukas glanced up from his basket and yawned as if his mouth were able to unhinge itself like a snake's. Then he uncurled himself and stretched in such a boneless manner that Helma had to look away.

Ruth picked up Boy Cat Zukas and swung him onto her shoulder. "Watch out for Del Harrington's hearty har har demeanor. It's a front."

"He didn't sound very hearty just now," Helma told her. "But then his brother died today." Distracted by the snow, Helma hadn't put her laundry in the washing machine that morning, and now she took a moment to do it.

"No love lost between the Harrington brothers," Ruth said, following Helma to her washing machine in the hallway. "They were definitely not three peas in the pod."

"How well *did* you know the Harringtons?" Helma asked as she pulled a white sock from the pile of blues and greens.

"I only met Franklin a couple of times, but Del thought he was some kind of an art critic once, back when his wife was still alive—or maybe he was just attracted to *my* art. Or my body. Rosy oozes charm, loves all things good. I suppose his life was a scandal once, but now he's considered an old dear. Del can be a little scary. Why are you turning all your clothes inside out?"

"It protects the color and exposed fabric," Helma explained. "Fewer snags."

"Really? Sounds like one of those old feel-good tales, like burnt toast doesn't have any calories."

"Why does Del scare you?" Helma asked, closing the washer lid and turning on the machine.

Ruth shrugged and Boy Cat Zukas gave an irritated yowl from her shoulder. "I don't know. He has, what they call in novels, hooded eyes, like behind them he's speculating where to stick the knife to get the best blood spatter patterns."

"That's very sinister, Ruth," Helma said.

"Ask people he's done business with," Ruth suggested.

"I'm meeting him tomorrow at ten-thirty. Sharp."

Ruth snorted. "Old Del's obviously not prostrate with grief over the demise of his number one brother. Is he sending his private snowplow to pick you up?"

"He claims the snow will be melted by then."

"Yeah, darn." She sighed. "It probably will be. Everything back to dull normal."

While her laundry churned, Helma pulled Ms. Moon's folder of the Harrington site from her bag and opened it on her dining room table.

"Studying up?" Ruth asked as Helma lifted the first page.

"I need more background information on the library site if I meet with Del tomorrow," Helma told her, not exactly trusting that Del's weather predictions were correct.

"Like I said, you can bet it's an unholy mess, both the situation and," Ruth pointed to the tumble of papers, "the Moonbeam's papers."

Helma didn't know why Ruth was still there. Usually Ruth viewed visiting her as a punishment in confinement, and by this time would have been grasping at any excuse to flee her apartment for her own unorganized life.

"How many paintings do you still have to finish for your show?" Helma asked her.

Ruth ran both hands through her hair, bushing it out. "Oh God," she moaned. "Too many, way too many. I'm not going to make it this time, I just know it. I don't know why I do this stuff."

Helma was used to this lament before one of Ruth's shows. If she reassured Ruth that, yes, she *would* make her deadline, it only made Ruth mad, and she'd rail that *this* time was different; she'd lost her talent; there wasn't time to finish; the paintings she'd done were amateur at best; they "sucked"; nobody'd buy a single canvas anyway.

"Maybe you could cancel the show," Helma suggested. There was also no point in saying that despite Ruth's chaotic work habits, she'd never known her to miss a single deadline.

"Are you crazy?" Ruth snapped. "Besides, that's not the problem. Do you know the last time I *shared* a show with another artist?"

Before Helma could answer, Ruth spat out, "Grade school. Friggin' fourth grade. My work stands alone. You have to view it as a whole to appreciate it, not see it mixed together with some beginner wannabe's renderings. Who ever heard of an artist named Shiny Waters?"

"Is Shiny Waters a beginner?" Helma asked.

"Yeah. The gallery owner's cousin or something," Ruth said morosely. "Obviously one of those types who believe you have to come up with the cute name before you come up with the work. Shiny Waters, hah! I can't bear to discuss it anymore," she ended dramatically.

So while Ruth picked up magazines, then wandered to the window and made rude comments about the snow or played with Boy Cat Zukas in a poking way that Helma thought was cruel but caused Boy Cat Zukas to purr in a rackety barrage, Helma leafed through the stack of paper in Ms. Moon's Harrington file.

At first she couldn't make sense of it. The papers weren't in order chronologically or by subject matter. Here were notes from a phone conversation between

Ms. Moon and Franklin with hearts and penguins doodled in the margins. Here was a computer printout with the biographical facts of the brothers. And here—she was positive its inclusion was accidental—was a page covered with sketches of library logos with various fonts, nearly all with the designation, "May Apple Moon, Director," incorporated in such a way that the words appeared unextractable.

Helma was frankly surprised by the breadth of Ms. Moon's notes. The director wasn't normally so thorough. It was as if she were documenting the exchanges and negotiation at the level of a government official who feared he or she might be investigated. Every phone call, every meeting, every thought.

Suddenly Ruth whooped, and Helma looked up to see her waving a sheet of paper covered with Ms. Moon's handwriting. "I bet she didn't mean for you to see *this*."

"Ruth, these are confidential papers." She held out her hand for the sheet.

"Uh-uh, this is too good," Ruth said, holding the paper closer to her body. "Listen to this. And honest to God, I'm reading it word for word."

"Ruth ... " Helma repeated.

"'Franklin,'" Ruth read. "'Widower. One daughter, Frances.'"

"I know that," Helma said.

"Yeah, but not this." Ruth held up the page and intoned, "'Frances. Fortyish, mental lightweight. High fashion awareness.'" Ruth ended in a cackling giggle.

Helma frowned and held out her hand. Ruth handed

her the page with a flourish. "High fashion awareness"? And "mental lightweight"? The number forty
likely referred to Frances's age.

But there was also a reference to Delano's son, Delano, Junior. In purple ink beneath his name and after
his age, forty-seven, was written: "Money grubbing
developer."

Helma turned the paper upside down and set it on
the table, appalled. Ms. Moon had written a file that
included *gossip*?

"This is gossip," she told Ruth.

"Maybe," Ruth said, still snickering. "But she also
hit those nails squarely on their pointy little heads.
Frances is all flash, no smoldering flame of fire, and
Del Junior has a lifelong affair with the green stuff.
He'd probably sell his own ... or maybe blow up his
own ... well, you get the idea. He and Daddy Del are
partners. Build higher, build bigger, pay less."

"I can't put credence in hearsay," Helma said, tucking the paper into the Harrington family stack of papers, out of Ruth's reach.

"I have a whole new respect for the woman," Ruth
said.

When Helma was finished sorting, she had four neat
piles of pages in chronological order because, curiously, Ms. Moon had remembered to date every sheet.
She pulled four manila folders from her home files and
labeled them: HARRINGTON FAMILY, NEGOTIATIONS, OF-
FICIAL DOCUMENTS, and for Ms. Moon's musings over
library logos and slogans, NEW LIBRARY EPHEMERA.

Ruth clicked through the TV channels, mumbling,

"Boring," at news shows, "Chick flick," at a romance movie, and when she passed a movie with guns and a car chase, commenting, "Dick flick."

Finally, as Helma tucked the newly labeled folders inside a larger closable file and set it aside to read after dinner, she asked Ruth, "Is there something else on your mind?"

"Not really," Ruth answered.

"Coincidentally?"

Ruth shrugged and turned off the television. "I'm low on inspiration. You know Franklin's death?"

"Yes?" Helma said cautiously

"What if I painted it?"

Chapter 13

Ms. Moon Takes the Phone

"Paint Franklin's death?" Helma asked, pushing aside her Harrington folders and clearing the table in front of her. "Ruth, that's tasteless."

"No, it's topical. And it would blow Shiny Waters right out of the ... gallery. Nothing gruesome," Ruth assured her. "At least not too. No unattached body parts. Maybe just a hint of Randall Rice through the smoke." She held her hands squared, picturing it, then dropped them and looked at Helma. "You're thinking I'd be using a tragic situation in a misguided scheme for personal advancement, aren't you?"

"That's an accurate assessment," Helma told her, remembering the eerie silence as the fireman held up Franklin's darkly stained hard hat.

Ruth puffed her cheeks, then blew out the air in a rush. "Yeah, not up to my usual high moral standards. Have you considered the intended victim wasn't Franklin, but Del or Rosy, and in the snow, the murderer couldn't tell which Harrington he was seeing? I mean, maybe the library setting was a total coincidence."

"Their resemblance has probably lessened as they've aged," Helma said. "And Franklin is definitely the brother associated with the library site."

"Triplets before fertility drugs," Ruth mused. "And born to the town's wealthiest family, too. They must have been in the limelight their whole lives. Can't be too many secrets to uncover." She reached toward the file. "Let's go through these. I bet the Moonbeam has a few more succinct comments."

Helma placed her hand on the folders. "This is library property, Ruth. Ms. Moon has entrusted her files to me."

"Palmed off on you, you mean. Believe me, she hasn't told all." She shrugged. "Suit yourself. But I bet our loyal chief of police would be interested in some of that stuff."

"Ms. Moon is inclined to divulge all she knows," Helma assured Ruth. "And if Wayne believes the personal habits of the Harringtons or Ms. Moon's notes on the library site relate to Franklin's death, he'll request copies from her."

"Go ahead. Keep making the guy work for every inch forward."

"He *is* the chief of police," Helma said. "He knows what's more relevant to the case than I do."

"Now there's a declaration I find hard to stomach.

Don't you miss the way you guys used to get all cozy over gory murder details?"

Luckily, at that moment Ruth was distracted by Boy Cat Zukas swiping at her dangling earring and missed Helma's unintentional nod, forestalling any further conversation regarding Helma Zukas and Bellehaven's chief of police.

Ruth stretched and Boy Cat Zukas leapt from her shoulder to the floor, landing neatly on all four feet, without even a thump. "I'm getting hot in this getup," Ruth said, idly zipping and unzipping her yellow snowsuit, "and I doubt you have anything that'll fit me, so I guess I'll wander home through this white wasteland and get back to work. Maybe I'll paint something in shades of white to commemorate the day."

"Phone Paul to come get you," Helma suggested, rising herself, not dissuading Ruth from going. Ruth rarely sat still very long, some part of her body in motion or in preparation of motion. Concentration was a challenge in Ruth's presence.

"Nah, I think I'll walk. Take a little mental trip to the land of our youth."

"Let me know when you get home," Helma suggested.

"Not likely," Ruth said as she shoved her feet into her boots.

When Ruth opened the door to leave, Helma heard the scraping of a shovel against concrete. Yes, the storm had ended. She returned to the dining room table and pulled Ms. Moon's newly organized folders from the file.

There was no signed agreement in Ms. Moon's files that supported her claim that Franklin would pay for the first fifty-one percent of the new library's cost. There *were* notes in another hand, perhaps Franklin's, and numbers, too, but nothing official.

It was curious there wasn't any type of document, since Ms. Moon had included detailed color schemes for her new office, including paint names like "Summer Soother" and "Leisure Walk," with a trim color of "Acquiescence."

Helma tapped Ms. Moon's office dreams with her index finger, then rose and dialed her home telephone number, which she'd committed to memory a few years earlier when Ms. Moon had remained at home with a headache during a particularly messy audit.

"I've been going through your files regarding the new library site," Helma told Ms. Moon. In the background she heard what sounded like a television game show.

"I just knew you were the right person to give them to," Ms. Moon said.

"I'm unable to locate the agreement documenting Franklin's offer to bear fifty-one percent of the library's cost, or for that matter, any signed paperwork on his gift to the city."

"There are notes," Ms. Moon said, and Helma heard the cautious undertones in her voice.

"Mainly in your handwriting," Helma said, and when Ms. Moon didn't respond, she guessed, "There never was a documented agreement, was there?"

"Of course there was." Ms. Moon's breathing accelerated. "In a manner of speaking. It just wasn't on paper. It was a 'gentlemen's agreement.'"

"That doesn't constitute an agreement in the legal sense," Helma told her.

"It would be beneficial to the project if you met with Del right away," Ms. Moon said. "He seems the most ... uncertain. But Rosy will be supportive, I'm sure." She paused. "I know you agree the sooner my ... I mean, *our*, library's site is secured, the better."

"Del phoned me an hour ago," Helma said. "You—"

"No need to thank me," Ms. Moon cut in. "I just called him to facilitate your progress. When will you be meeting with him?"

"Tomorrow at ten-thirty."

Ms. Moon laughed her tinkling laugh. "I finally bow to your skill and intuition."

Helma stiffened. In her experience, praise from Ms. Moon was not a precursor to advantageous events for the receiver.

"I've been aware for years how you've been involved, whether accidentally or purposefully, in certain ... crimes in Bellehaven. You have associations in law enforcement."

"And?" Helma asked.

"And nothing. I just want to help you fulfill your mission, that's all."

Helma waited, straightening the pens and pad of paper beside her telephone.

"Of course," Ms. Moon said after a small chuckle, "when you *do* talk to Del Harrington, I know you'll impress upon him how I—I mean *we*—love that site. The vibrations there ... " If she could have seen through the phone lines, Helma knew Ms. Moon would be shaking her head in wonder. "And I know how grateful he'll be to know you're interested in the solution to his brother's death. It's the perfect pairing."

A chickadee briefly lit on Helma's snow-covered balcony railing. Boy Cat Zukas rose from his bed in a flash and stretched himself upright and flat against the sliding glass door, emitting a curious clicking sound. The bird paid no attention.

"I've always admired how your first concern is the library," Ms. Moon went on. "If you need to take extra time, we can arrange it. Don't worry about anything except the library site. Devote yourself to that. Thank you and goodbye."

Ms. Moon hung up, leaving Helma still poised to speak. All this in motion, and the last policeman probably hadn't left the explosion site yet.

Twenty minutes later Helma's phone rang again, and this time she was happy to hear Aunt Em's voice.

"*Labas*, Wilhelmina," she said. Her Lithuanian accent had thickened, as had her voice, as she'd reached and passed her eighty-eighth birthday, and it was now compounded by her cold. Aunt Em was Helma's father's oldest and last surviving sibling. She'd lived the longest and had witnessed the births and deaths of all her brothers and sisters. Sometimes she wistfully said, "I wish they were here so I could tell them."

Helma closed her eyes to listen, concentrating on distinguishing Aunt Em's words. "Your mother said you're helping your policeman with Franklin's murder."

"She did?" Helma asked. The only reference to Wayne Gallant she recalled was her mother's assumption that he'd given her a ride home.

"Franklin sat with me at the Senior Christmas Dessert Bash last year. Your mother told me to tell you that. A gentleman; he was, too. He didn't say anything to me a lady wouldn't want to hear." She sighed. "Mandagus." Polite.

"Everyone liked Franklin?" Helma asked.

"Oh yes." She lowered her voice, and Helma had the distinct impression Aunt Em's hand was cupped around the mouthpiece. "But the other brother, my my."

"Delano?" Helma asked.

"The same. I came up here so I could tell you."

"Up where, Aunt Em? Where are you?"

"On floor number eight. I took your mother's cell phone and climbed to the top of the building for better receiving. So I could whisper."

"Did you know Delano, too?" Helma asked, picturing Aunt Em standing by a window in the hallway talking to her. Even in her apartment, Aunt Em always spoke on the telephone standing as close to a window as possible.

"Not him, *her*."

"His wife?"

"No no no," Aunt Em said. "*Her*. She lives *here*, in our building."

"Who?" Helma asked.

"Del's *other* woman," Aunt Em whispered. "For years. Everybody knows."

"Aunt Em … "

"You come here. I'll show you." She raised her voice to normal levels, as if someone was walking past her. "And what are you doing, dear?"

"I was about to take a bath."

"Good idea in this cold. Hot water. Hot water is one of the greatest pleasures in our life. Long ago, we didn't have it so easy, not in Lithuania." She pronounced it "lit-wane-ya." "But now hot water is a gift. It is sens … " Aunt Em struggled for the word. "Sens … "

"Sensible?" Helma supplied.

"No, Wilhelmina. I mean, sensuous."

Chapter 14

Meet the Harringtons

After years of living in the Pacific Northwest, Helma understood the subtleties of weather. The slight pressure in the ears of a dropping barometer, the dry lips of unusual aridity, the "thick" sensation of humidity.

And so when she opened her eyes on Thursday morning, she knew before lifting her head from her pillow that the temperature had risen and the dripping sound from outside was not falling rain but melting snow.

Helma parted her bedroom curtains and gazed outside. It was still dark but the early morning glowed with the remaining snow. Ghostly humps lined the bare streets and slid off car roofs to the ground. Traffic whooshed past, traveling wet pavement, the engine of the city bus groaned as it climbed Garden Street.

Movement caught her eye and she spotted Walter David wielding a broom to push snow from the Dumpsters. From the way he leaned into the broomstick, it was apparent yesterday's beautiful feathery snowfall had turned into a heavy, wet nuisance.

Good snowball snow, she thought. Not that she'd ever been much for crafting snowballs. There *had* been that time her cousin Ricky had filled her school bag with snow while they waited for the school bus. Naturally, she'd scooped it out immediately to protect her school books and couldn't help it if during the scooping some of the snow had matted into a sort of projectile.

The explosion and death of Franklin Harrington shared the upper half of the *Bellehaven Daily News*'s front page, its headlines only slightly smaller than the headline written by the newspaper's new headline writer, who had a penchant for alliteration: BLIZZARD BLANKETS BELLEHAVEN.

Little was contained in the article that Helma didn't know. Randall Rice clung to life. No details on the source of the explosion. Franklin was lauded, as was the Harrington family and its long history of commerce in Bellehaven. Only Franklin's two brothers, Delano and Roosevelt, survived Franklin's generation. One nephew. Franklin had been a widower for over thirty years; one daughter, Frances. His death was a loss to Bellehaven. The library wasn't mentioned.

Gillian Hovel on the morning TV news had nothing new to say on the death of Franklin. She announced that all county schools were closed "for cleanup," all city offices were open, "with skeleton crews," and she was happy to be warm and toasty in the TV station newsroom. She warned that due to the melting snow overloading the drains, a sinkhole had opened at the corner of Fifth and Barrywood. "Barricades are up," she advised, then added with a wink, "but you watch out now, hear?"

Sinkholes weren't uncommon in Bellehaven after heavy rains. Over a hundred years ago, coal mines had tunneled beneath the land that now comprised the city and occasionally the earth readjusted itself by drooping or collapsing, once trapping a man in his SUV who was heard to say just before he gunned his engine and roared into a sinkhole, "Heck, I've driven across rivers deeper than that."

So Randall was still alive. Randall held the key to Franklin's death. Neither Gillian Hovel nor the newspaper had said whether Randall was conscious; maybe the police had already spoken to him.

Boy Cat Zukas only stared at Helma from his basket when she opened the sliding glass doors to her balcony, which she'd already swept clear of snow. Usually he slipped away immediately, as if he'd been held hostage instead of having sulked and stared and pressed himself against the glass to be let inside the evening before.

"Go, cat," she commanded. She didn't believe in bribery. Nor did she maintain cat facilities in her apartment, so there was no alternative but for Boy Cat Zukas to evacuate the premises.

After ignoring her commands twice more and only

yawning when she closed the door as if he'd won, Helma donned gloves and bodily picked up the wicker basket. As soon as it was six inches off the floor, Boy Cat Zukas hissed, leapt down, and strode onto her balcony, tail held high.

She closed the door and the cat jumped on the railing, balanced in a scrunched-up lump, and stared gloomily in at her.

At 7:52, Helma glanced once more onto her balcony at the vision of feline dejection, then picked up the Harrington file and left her apartment.

Although street conditions had returned to near normal, Helma drove across town with her foot poised and eyes wary. Traffic was light but slower than usual. The buses were crowded. Drivers leaned over their steering wheels, squinting suspiciously at other cars.

And everywhere, shoveling and sweeping and scraping, the scenery monochromatic: white and gray instead of green and gray.

Dutch briskly nodded to Helma from his post at the circulation desk. He still wore his hat and coat. She paused and listened. The library was silent, the atmosphere stale. She removed her gloves. There was no doubt: the air was frigid.

She turned to Dutch, who nodded. "The furnace part's supposed to come in this morning. They say they'll have it fixed this afternoon."

"We can't serve the public in these temperatures," Helma said. "Is Ms. Moon here?"

Dutch nodded his head toward the workroom and Ms. Moon's office.

Before Helma reached the partially closed door, she heard the director's voice, and Glory Shandy's as well.

She tapped on the doorjamb and their voices went silent.

"Come in," Ms. Moon called. "But hurry. Don't let the heat out."

Helma pushed open the door and entered. An electric heater glowed in the corner and the temperature was twenty-five degrees warmer than the public area.

Glory sat opposite Ms. Moon's desk, drinking from a ceramic cup she cradled with both hands. Between them on the desk sat a plate holding a maple bar cut into several bite-size pieces.

"Why, Helma, I didn't expect you this morning," Ms. Moon said, licking her fingers. "I thought you'd go directly to the Harringtons for that very, very vital discussion."

"May I speak to you?" Helma asked, then turned toward Glory, who jumped up from her chair as she seized a heavily frosted piece of maple bar.

"Oh, oh, I didn't mean to interfere. I'll leave you two alone. Bye-bye."

"Don't forget your cup," Helma reminded her.

"Isn't this cozy?" Ms. Moon asked Helma, waving her hand around her office after Glory left.

"It's definitely warmer than the public area," Helma conceded.

"It's a lucky thing most people come to the library

in coats," Ms. Moon said. She touched another piece of maple bar, then snatched her hand away from the plate, empty.

"It still isn't adequate heat," Helma told her. "It's wiser to close the library until the heating system is repaired."

"But don't you believe this is a critical period for our image? Exposing the public to our inadequate HVAC system will encourage interest in our new library."

"It will also encourage complaints," Helma pointed out.

"Do you think so?" Ms. Moon beamed. "That would be perfect."

"It's fifty-two degrees in the library," Helma told her. "School's been canceled, so we'll have an abundance of children today."

Ms. Moon waved her hand. "Children generate their own heat. The more children we have, the warmer it will be." She smiled. "Are you ready to meet with Del Harrington?"

"You are the better choice for this meeting," Helma said. "You have the history, the experience ... "

Ms. Moon touched the tip of her finger to the belly of a frog Buddha on her desk. "No, the currents are flowing seamlessly. It's remarkable. So smoothly *any-one* can tell this is the intended path, a passage to understanding and success. You. The Harringtons." She shook her head. "And you the last one to see Franklin alive."

Helma Zukas was not a woman to be swayed by the unexpected appearance of guilt, but she felt a dark surge of regret—yet again—for the way Franklin had left the library and gone to his death.

"Just perfect," Ms. Moon repeated.

Glory waited beside Helma's cubicle, twisting her hands together. "I need to ask you." She spoke in dips and dabs, her voice high-pitched, as if she were nervous, but her eyes remained cool, considering Helma. "Yesterday. I wasn't listening. Really. I just heard. I mean, I *didn't* hear."

"*What* didn't you hear?" Helma asked.

Glory blocked the entrance to her cubicle. She bit her lip, then dropped her voice to a whisper. "You didn't tell Wayne Gallant about Dutch."

Helma glanced around the workroom. No other staff member was present. "I'm not sure what you're talking about."

"Dutch was *gone* when the explosion … exploded. He didn't come back until just before you did."

"Are you certain?"

Glory vigorously bobbed her head. "I was looking for him in case any of the women got hysterical. I couldn't find him. Not anywhere. Should I tell the police?"

Helma couldn't say what made her do it. She had no reason, no knowledge, and at that moment, no motive.

"Oh," she told Glory, lightly touching her own forehead, "I forgot. You're talking about Dutch's unsteadiness."

"Dutch was sick?" Glory asked, frowning.

"He was still uncomfortable when the police took him home." She didn't confirm or deny; she related the truth. "You missed the conversation because you and Ms. Moon had already left. You were gone," she added. "But Dutch and I were with the police so I was aware of it."

"Oh," Glory said, her lips forming a perfect O, clearly disappointed. "I didn't know that," and she wandered off, a thoughtful look on her face.

Helma gave herself forty-five extra minutes before her appointment with Del Harrington and left the library by the workroom door. She had two objectives, both of which she intended to accomplish with the least amount of observation. Not *secretly*, but privately.

The hospital was only a block away but she drove her car instead of walking and parked in a space that straddled a long ridge of dirty snow.

Long ago, Helma Zukas had learned that those who moved as if they had the right and the power were rarely challenged by those who should know better. So now she walked through the automatic doors of the hospital, nodded to the elderly smocked volunteer at the reception desk, and kept on walking, her eyes focused on a point that was just beyond the view of those she passed.

She had been in the hospital under dire circumstances in the past and knew exactly where she was going. She removed a small notebook from her purse and held it in front of her, glancing at random blank pages. Down a hall to the left, through another set of doors, past the nurse's station, to the somber hallway of rooms with glass walls. Machines softly buzzed and beeped, monitors glowed with graphs and red digital numbers.

If someone had stepped in front of her and asked where she was going, she would have apologized and turned back. If anyone had said, "Excuse me?" she would have admitted she shouldn't be there and left. She truly would have.

R. RICE was written on a white board outside the room at the end of the ICU hall, with an incomprehensible list of medical shorthand beneath it. Helma stopped and looked in through the glass wall, noting that the glass was sparkling clean. Not even a fingerprint.

Randall Rice lay in the midst of pale blue and white, connected to tubes and monitors. He didn't move. She could only see a partial profile since bandages covered one side of his face. No one else was present. Beneath the single metal and Naugahyde chair near his bed lay a pair of women's black boots, as if they'd been distractedly kicked off and forgotten.

His solitude at the end of the hall, the lack of activity in his room, gave Helma a sense of bided time. She swallowed and took a deep breath.

"May I help you?"

She turned to face a young but weary-faced nurse who carried a tray holding a syringe and medication. "No," Helma told her. "But thank you. I was just leaving."

Next, she drove two blocks closer to Washington Bay,

to the excavation site for the new library. Yellow police tape, broken and sagging, kept her from parking on the same side of the street, so she made a U-turn and parked in the opposite direction, beside an old-fashioned pay phone with graffitied windows and an empty black phone book holder.

A freestanding metal fence had surrounded the site from the first ground-breaking shovelful, hefted by Franklin Harrington himself, and now it lay flat on the ground along two sides. The snow on top of the downed fence had melted over the steel and the last vestiges remained in geometric humps and shapes.

Helma followed the most trampled trail of icy footprints, which led along the eastern edge of the excavation. She didn't see anyone else but the state of the ground showed that the police had spent hours going over the scene. Yellow tape and markers, both along the rim and in the pit, ground-out cigarettes, long scuff marks.

She sniffed, trying to catch the chemical odor she'd smelled the day before, but it was gone. The bulldozer remained in the same position in the pit. Tracks led toward a stand of trees at the north edge of the site where more yellow tapes were tied between the trees.

Where Randall Rice was discovered. Helma stood outside the tape and just looked. A few tree branches had been broken, either from the blast or the recovery. Again, trampled and scarred ground. This, the whole site, felt a desolate place. She stood where the library's main entrance was planned, trying to visualize eager readers and children approaching the front doors.

"Are you with the police?"

Helma turned to face a man in a yellow hard hat like the one Franklin had carried. "No," she told him. "I'm with the library."

He nodded. "A tough thing."

"Are you the contractor?" she asked. He was a heavy man with an exhausted face and stubbled cheeks. He carried a pair of rough canvas gloves pressed between his elbow and side.

"Yeah. I don't know what in hell happened here. It's just a damn shame. Puts a stop to everything."

"Including life," Helma said. "Franklin was here often. You gave him a hard hat."

He shook his head slowly, back and forth. "Had to, for his own safety. Every time we turned around, there he was, on our ... tails, keeping track of how much dirt we'd dug, how the machines were running. I tried to tell him he was breaking every safety rule on the books, but he was all hot to get involved, like a kid with a new building set. I know damn well he came around when nobody was here. God save us from retirement."

"Did Randall Rice visit the site, too?"

He shrugged and rubbed his chin. "Don't know him by sight, only reputation. I never saw anybody with Franklin, but he could've been here. People like to watch buildings go up."

"But the explosion wasn't due to the construction activities?" Helma asked, and the man blanched.

"There was my first nightmare, that we'd clipped a gas line, and bam. But no, the cops found some kind of amateur getup that blew up over there." He waved a hand toward the trees. "Damn powerful. If it was a prank, it was a wicked one."

"When will you resume the excavation?" Helma asked. She glanced at her watch. It was time to leave for her appointment with Del Harrington.

"Between the cops and the Harringtons, it's all on hold now. I had to let the crew go." He gazed from the trees down into the silent pit, already forgetting Helma. "What a mess."

The Harrington family home sat at the edge of Cedar Falls Park, once Harrington grounds, then presented to the city by an earlier cost-cutting Harrington tired of paying for its upkeep.

The park, once considered a white elephant, had become so sacrosanct that the decision to replace its antiquated outhouses with actual restrooms had caused a near riot at a city council meeting. "If you put better restrooms in that park," one woman had shouted in bitter anguish, "you'll just be encouraging more people to use them."

Helma was four minutes early, exactly as she'd planned. She parked her Buick in the circular driveway that had already been shoveled, and was now lined with little sculpted walls of snow.

The Harrington house looked as if it could comfortably hold a family of ten or twelve. It stood three and a half stories high, with scalloped roofs and timbered walls. Old landscaping of giant rhododendron bushes and the largest monkey puzzle tree in the state embellished the grounds.

An older man, distinguished looking but in work

clothes, opened the front door as she climbed the steps. The words "faithful old retainer" jumped into Helma's mind. Servants in Bellehaven? He was white-haired, with one drooping eye and the other squinted at her suspiciously. He held the door handle, blocking her entry.

"I have an appointment with Mr. Harrington," Helma told him. "He's expecting me," she added when the man continued to squint at her. "At ten-thirty. Sharp."

"That right?" he finally asked. "Then you'd better hop to it. That old coot's a pisser, if you know what I mean and don't mind my saying so, when a guy can't help but be late."

He shook his head and bent down to pick up a green metal toolbox that had been hidden by the open door. "He calls me at four in the morning because his furnace is 'making funny noises.' Everybody's furnace is busting a gut with this weather. And I was up all night fiddling with the library's piece-of-junk furnace. Everybody's gotta have it this very second. Nobody's willing to wait anymore."

"Were you successful?" Helma asked.

"Just a squirrel trying to get warm, that's all."

"I mean with the library's furnace."

"Hah. Like putting a Band-Aid on a slashed throat. Had to order a part, but even that might not do it. Nobody sneezes, it might work for a while. 'Course, I didn't tell that librarian that. You ever met that woman?"

"I know the director," Helma said noncommittally.

He shook his head. "Nah, the other one. Zipper, or

Zucchini, something like that. Talk about demanding. She and the guy in this place should get along like bugs in a rug."

"Thank you," Helma said, and brushed past him into the foyer of the house.

Every Christmas the Harrington house was decorated with boughs of cedar, holly, and Victorian ornaments, then opened to the public for holiday events. Helma had never participated, but looking around now at the sweeping staircase, the wood paneling and Victorian furnishings, she agreed it was the perfect venue for hot cider, frosted sugar cookies, and a few stanzas of "Deck the Halls."

Nonholiday, it was obvious no one actually *lived* in these huge cold rooms, and she wondered if they ever had. "Hello," she called out in a modulated voice.

The house felt cavernously empty, and since it was obvious no one had heard her call, she went searching for Del Harrington, carefully observing each room she passed through, ever aware of the way out, as was her habit.

Parlor, dining room, second parlor, then up a half flight of wide and gleaming wooden stairs, keeping to the narrow Persian carpeting in the center of each step, her tread silent, one hand to the cool and polished banister.

She stopped when she heard voices, tipping her head to ascertain their origin. Paintings of Northwest scenes, all gloomily reflecting the wet and desolate style of the cabin-fevered, hung in the stairwell and hallway.

One might have expected a floor board to squeak

and announce her presence. But she stepped cautiously across uneven flooring, past two closed doors, until she stood outside a third door, its lintel ornately carved, the brass doorknob level with her breast.

She disliked disturbing anyone unnecessarily, so she paused, silently listening while the voices beyond the door sorted themselves out.

Two men, one older or at least rough-voiced, and speaking with more authority. The other voice tinged with exasperation, even a touch of querulousness.

"It's obvious," the younger voice said. "I don't see why you have to talk to anyone else."

"Perception is the ruling factor. When you have as much experience as I have, you'll understand that."

"When I have one foot in the grave, you mean."

The older man laughed. "Could be. We may not 'get it' until we're ready to die."

"Don't go all Buddhistic on me."

Helma raised her hand and lightly rapped on the door. Silence, then the sound of furniture and footsteps, and in a moment the door opened.

The man in the doorway was middle-aged, with startlingly black hair combed sideways across his forehead. He looked fit, if slightly ... not overweight, but *thick.*

"We didn't hear you knock," he said with a touch of accusation.

"The furnace man let me in. I'm Miss Helma Zukas and I have an appointment with Mr. Harrington."

"Ah, the librarian," the older voice said, and behind the younger man a close copy of Franklin Harrington rose from a chair. He may have been only a few minutes younger than Franklin but he appeared years younger, still vigorous, straight-backed. And yes, harder, without Franklin's crinkled warm eyes. "Come in."

This was where the living of Harrington house took place: in this more updated, used-looking space. Newspapers were piled at the end of a coffee table, empty coffee cups, bright paintings, and modern furnishings.

Helma felt both men's eyes examining her, taking her measure, and she gazed back just as frankly. They waited for her to speak and she obliged them.

"I'm here at your request, Mr. Harrington, to discuss the building site your late brother gave to the library."

Del's eyes flashed and his jaws tightened but he said in what she guessed Ruth would call his "hearty" voice, "Hold on there, little lady. Before we get down to brass tacks let me introduce you to my boy here. Delano, Junior. We call him Jay, short for Junior, just like you'd think. Not very original, are we?"

Jay nodded and shook Helma's hand, stretching his lips until his teeth showed and cheeks furrowed. "Nice to meet you," he said as she pulled her hand from his grasp. "You're Hilda?"

"Helma, but you may call me Miss Zukas."

He leaned toward her, still smiling, even chuckling, but his eyes coolly appraised her.

Del Harrington slapped his thigh. "That's telling him. He thinks he's a young Luther."

"Lothario," she automatically corrected, and Del laughed. Helma realized she'd been set up.

"See, Jay, she sees it in you, too. Called you a Lothario, you heard her."

"I'm sorry for your brother's death," Helma said, redirecting the conversation.

Del nodded, momentarily sobered. "Yeah. You get older, you know your time is coming, but that's not the way you expect to go."

To Helma's left, Jay made motions with his hands like an explosion. Del shook his head at his son and Jay clasped his hands behind his back, his face reddening.

"Ms. Moon gave me her files," Helma said, motioning to the folder in her hand. She avoided blaming or taking credit as much as possible, so although she might not agree with Ms. Moon's methods or the impolitic speed of these negotiations, now she said, "We hope to continue building the new library."

"On top of Uncle Frank's bones?" Jay asked.

"I believe the remains have been removed," Helma told him.

"Only in the physical sense," Jay persisted.

Helma set the file folders on a small table and sat in a straight-back chair. "If we could go over the negotiations and confirm Franklin's intent—" she began.

Somewhere else in the house the first notes of the Westminster chimes sounded, and Del held up his hand. "Ah, here are the others. Let's wait until they join us. Jay, get the door, will you?"

Chapter 15

Family Ties

"Others?" Helma asked.

Del's smile carried a hint of indulgence. "I bet your Ms. Moon left out a few details about this meeting." He shook his head and absently manipulated his hands into the child's game of Here's the Church, Here's the Steeple.

"Did she mention I said I'd talk to anybody *but* her?" he asked Helma.

"No, she didn't," Helma told him. Ms. Moon had acted as if representing the library was a rare and precious opportunity.

"Ha. Didn't think so. I bet she tricked you into coming here *for* her, right?"

"She asked me to represent the library," Helma said.

"No doubt. This is the entire family's business, so I decided to save you—and me—having to repeat the whole story too many times. Remember that old game 'Gossip'?"

"I don't play games," Helma informed him.

"Well, then consider what I've done as keeping every Harrington in the loop."

"Your brother is here, then?" Helma asked.

"And Frances. The last surviving Harrington woman. You've already had the pleasure of meeting my son, Jay. And that accounts for all the remaining Harringtons."

"But Frances's father just died yesterday."

"This is of interest to her," Del said, and Helma saw the flash of will that he'd likely used to bring all the Harringtons together so soon after Franklin's death.

It occurred to Helma that Ms. Moon had known that she would be facing all the Harringtons, neglecting to mention that detail to her, as well as Del's refusal to speak to *her*.

In they came: Franklin's daughter Frances, then Roosevelt Harrington, shepherded by Jay, who closed the door, swiped his hand across his hair, and took a position near his father's left shoulder.

Roosevelt, who everyone called Rosy, had unnaturally blond hair for a man approaching eighty. He was excessively slender, wearing sleek belted pants and a tucked-in turtleneck sweater. He'd never married and still cut a debonair figure.

Frances was costumed for winter, in white from neck to boots. Helma supposed the color would officially be described as "winter white." White wool pants and sweater, with an easy, well-fitted elegance. A white silk scarf draped her neck as lightly as if she'd just unveiled her head following a walk in Bellehaven's winter wonderland. Perfectly tailored, perfectly expensive. "High fashion awareness," Ms. Moon had written in her notes. "Mental lightweight."

Frances struck a pose in the middle of the room, running a pinkie finger across her full lips. A diamond sparkled on her middle finger. She gazed above Helma's head.

"I have a massage in an hour," she announced in a voice that broke like a teenage boy's, at odds with her appearance. "What do we have to do?" she asked. "Do I have to sign anything? If I do, I want my lawyer to see it first. I'm not signing anything."

"Don't worry, darling," Rosy said. "If you're forced to sign on anybody's dotted line, I'll vouch you couldn't read it."

Frances shook her finger at him. "That wasn't nice. I don't think it was nice at all." She turned to Helma. "Did you think that was nice?"

Helma rose. "I'm Miss Helma Zukas and I represent the Bellehaven Public Library."

"Call her Miss Zukas," Jay inserted.

"Zukas?" Rosy mused, frowning. "Is that Greek?"

"Lithuanian," Helma said.

Frances shook her head. Half her face frowned; not a single muscle above her nose moved. "Are you sure? I've never heard of a Lithuanian."

"You wouldn't have, my dear," Rosy said, waving a hand toward her as if he held a cigarette. "It's a Baltic nation. Not very fashionable. They do make a nice cheese, though."

Helma remembered Aunt Em's sister, her aunt Ann, saying once, "No one dislikes a Lithuanian because they aren't really sure what a Lithuanian is."

"Let's store the banter for now, and sit down," Del suggested, holding out his hands to indicate the sofas and chairs which all faced him. "Don't mind them, Miss Zukas. They're always like this."

"Uncle Rosy's mean to everybody," Frances said as she sat at the edge of an Eames chair.

"Not at all," Rosy said. "I simply ... what would you say, Jay? What's that term those in arrested development used to say? I remember, I 'tell it like it is.'" He separated each word with a tiny pause and sat on the cushiest sofa in the room, smiling gently to himself as he crossed his legs. He looked up at Helma. "Now where were we?"

"I was saying that I represented the Bellehaven Public Library," Helma told him.

"A fine institution," Rosy commented. "Take a seat, why don't you?"

"I've never been there," Frances said.

"No doubt," from Rosy. Despite his acid words, the tone of Rosy's delivery was fond. His eyes softened every time he looked at Frances, as did hers when she looked at him.

"In light of the tragedy," Helma went on, sitting down on a stiffly cushioned armchair, "we want to assure Franklin's family that we treasure the building site, and plan—with your agreement, of course—to create a new library that Franklin—and you—will be proud of."

"Very diplomatically stated," Rosy said. The foot of his crossed leg bobbed up and down.

"You're assuming," Del said, swiveling so he directly faced Helma, "that we are all in accord with Frank's gift. Do you have the agreement with you?"

From his expression, Helma suspected Del knew the agreement hadn't been finalized, perhaps didn't exist in any written form. "The new library will be a landmark," she said, and added, "The citizens of Bellehaven will be grateful to the Harringtons for generations," while inwardly wincing. Though what she'd said was true, she wondered if this was what Ruth had meant by "sucking up."

"I didn't get any money," Frances said. She frowned that half expression again. "Did I?"

Rosy leaned forward to answer. "I believe that's what the word 'gift' means," he said, winking broadly at Frances. "No compensation. Hence, no money. Gratis."

"Originally," Jay broke in, "we'd discussed that land as a prime site for development. Condos."

Del nodded, and Helma had the feeling that he had scripted Jay's words, that he hadn't wanted to be the one to broach the controversial topic of Bellehaven condos.

"And now?" she asked.

All four Harringtons exchanged glances, avoiding Helma. A grandfather clock in the corner ticked loudly into the silence. Then the men turned to Frances, and as if she'd been prompted, she sniffed and touched the corner of her eye with a tissue. "Poor Daddy. He was so young."

"Did you speak to your father yesterday morning?" Helma asked her.

She shook her head. "I tried to call him but he didn't answer. I didn't know he was—" She stopped and real tears filled her eyes. Rosy reached out and gently touched her shoulder. Even Del appeared about to rise and comfort his niece. "We had lunch a couple of days ago," Frances finally continued. "We always had lunch together on Mondays. Mondays are my allowance day."

"Did he have a lot of friends?" Helma asked.

Frances stared at her. "Daddy? Everybody loved Daddy. Everybody."

Del clapped his hands together. "That settles it, then. Whoever did it was after Randall Rice. Can we get back on topic?" He pointed to Helma's file folder. "What's in there?"

Helma laid her hand on the manila folders. "The library director's notes of conversations and meetings with your brother. His plans to leave a legacy to the people of Bellehaven."

"But no signed agreement?" Jay asked.

"I'm not an expert on contract law, or any kind of law," Helma said carefully. "But in these papers his intent was clear."

The doorbell chimed and Del frowned. "I'm not expecting anyone. They'll go away. This discussion takes precedence."

But whoever was at the door didn't go away. The Westminster chimes rang again, then partway, and again, as if the bell's button was being repeatedly and impatiently stabbed. If Helma had been at home, she would have expected Ruth. Only Ruth could make her electric doorbell "jangle."

Jay got up. "Keep talking. I'll get rid of them."

Del nodded to him and looked back at Helma. "The members of this family, as I said, never unanimously agreed to give the land to the library."

Rosy laughed shortly. "We didn't agree on what else to do with it, either."

"The possibilities weren't fully discussed," Del said smoothly, "because Franklin had the final say, and *somebody* convinced him to hand the land over to the library. He didn't exactly share his convictions with his brothers."

"His intent was clear," Helma repeated, touching the folders.

Del rocked in his chair. "If that *were* true, he would have signed a legal agreement deeding the land to the city of Bellehaven, don't you think?"

Frances looked up from her plum-colored, squared-off nails. "You mean it's really *my* land? I'm Daddy's heir, aren't I?"

"With a few exceptions, you're right, my dear," Rosy advised her. "And this is one of those exceptions. Thanks to the foresight of our father, the family jewels go from brother to brother before they go from brother to procreation."

"Which of you was born second?" Helma asked. "Who's next in succession?"

Del and Rosy looked at each other warily, and Helma was afraid that she'd crossed the line of good taste and now neither of them would answer.

But Rosy grinned. "Now there's the rub, isn't it, my brother? There was no doubt at this astounding Harrington birth that Franklin was first. In the excitement of not just twins, but *three* new Harringtons—triplets, of all the curiosities to occur in our humble family—can you picture it, the rushing nurses, stunned doctors, our poor exhausted mother with squalling infants dropping everywhere ...?" He shook his head and rubbed his jaw. "In all that ruckus and clamor, just exactly who was born second and third got lost."

"So first we have Franklin," Del said, continuing the story and holding up one finger. "The number one son. But then, since the line was muddled, Rosy and I have to agree." He wiggled his second and third fingers.

"But you've never had to before now," Helma said, "because Franklin was alive."

Rosy snorted. "Oh no. If Franklin wasn't interested—or just wanted to stir up a little trouble for his entertainment—he'd pass a decision on to us."

"To watch the fireworks," Del said glumly.

"Brother, I'm surprised you'd say that." Rosy clicked his tongue. "I'm sure we've agreed on several issues in our excruciatingly long lives."

"Name two."

Rosy frowned, then shrugged.

"You all lived in this house," Frances offered helpfully. "You agreed on that."

Both men's heads turned toward Frances in unison, and for a brief instant Helma saw their identicalness. She hadn't known all three men lived in the Harrington house, and her surprise must have shown because Rosy explained.

"Quite the contrary. We live beneath the same roof because none of us could outwit the other to get the whole house."

"You should see Uncle Rosy's side," Frances told Helma. "It's all ... " Words failed her. "It's just like Uncle Rosy. Different. Uncle Rosy and Uncle Del don't even have doors that connect. It's all been bricked up, and you have to go around the outside of the house and knock on their front doors."

"Thank you, Frances, for that charming explanation." Rosy turned to Helma. "You must come visit me someday, Miss Zukas. 'My side,' as Frances puts it, is more colorful."

All heads turned as the door opened, held by Jay. Sweeping in past him, dressed in a jade green cape that fell to her ankles, wearing shoes so tall her hair actually brushed the top of the door, makeup that transformed her into all eyes and lips, came Ruth Winthrop.

Chapter 16

Intentional Disturbance

As frequently happened when Ruth made an entrance, the inhabitants of the room stared, stunned to silence, as if an alien being had dropped into their presence and they were uncertain of its intent.

Ruth always appeared oblivious, which Helma knew she wasn't. Her every gesture, likely her every breath, was calculated for affect.

Ruth smiled, towering, gazing by turns at each of them, even Frances. The men's eyes widened, Frances's narrowed. Ruth waggled her fingers. "Hi, all," she said brightly as she slid the cape from her shoulders and Jay stumbled over a hassock to catch it.

All three men knew Ruth, that was obvious, and Helma doubted from Frances's pressed lips that she wanted to. Ruth's dress—a black velvet

affair that looked like an evening gown—was cut
low, exposing enough cleavage to make Helma feel
a chill.

"Ruthie," Rosy said, grinning. "What are you doing
here?" Exactly what Helma was wondering, too.

"Oh, I came to help Helma Zukas," she said airily
and waved a hand toward Helma. "I was in the library
yesterday."

"You saw Daddy?" Frances asked. "You saw him … "

"I missed that," Ruth told her, "but I did help Helma
interpret the documents the director gave her. And
since I know you all, well, it makes perfect sense,
right? And … " Ruth paused, and though there was
seemingly no reason for it, dropped her voice and dramatically raised her eyebrows. " … I know the chief of
police."

"And your point is?" Rosy asked.

"I don't know you," Frances interrupted, her chin
tilted upward and exposing a thin pink line beneath
her jaw, "so how can you know me?"

"You don't remember?" Ruth said, and shook her
head sadly, as if Frances's lapse of memory were a regrettable declining condition.

Frances bit her lip, clearly confused. Helma heard
Ruth murmur, gazing at Frances from head to toe,
"Ferragamo, Rolex, Versace, Gucci," then sniff the air
and end with, "Armani's 'Code.'"

"What does the chief of police have to do with this
conversation?" Del asked. His cheeks had reddened.
He rose to his feet in what might have been a menacing
stance, but since the top of his head only reached Ruth's

chin and he had to raise his face to scowl into her face, which Ruth would only see if she were to incline her head, which she didn't, the effect was wasted.

"Tell him, Helma," Ruth said, and retreated to stand next to Jay, distracting him by waving her hand as if her bosom was on fire.

Helma rose as her heart fell. All her careful preparations, her notes on nonthreatening language, her avoidance of the merest hint or threat or accusation. The new library site might as well have slid into the bay.

"There's nothing to tell," Helma said, ignoring Ruth's emoted sigh. "Of course we all know Wayne Gallant. I know how diligently he and the Bellehaven police force are working to discover the circumstances of your brother's death. It's a mistake for me to be here now. We can discuss the library site later, after Franklin's funeral."

She doubted that she'd mollified any of the four Harringtons. Del was still red-faced, Frances still wary-eyed, Jay still mesmerized by Ruth, and Rosy glanced around the room like a man watching a good comedic play.

"You're forgetting *I* asked *you* to come here," Del said. "What will exist after the funeral that doesn't exist now?"

"Perhaps nothing," Helma said, "but this clearly isn't the time to discuss the disposition of property."

"Tell Ms. Moon that," Ruth said, but her voice was overshadowed by Frances, who gulped back a sob. Her shoulders sagged. In an instant Del was at her side, pulling her against him, his own eyes damp.

"We're leaving now," Helma said as she picked up her files. "I'm sorry for the intrusion."

Ruth shrugged as if she'd arrived at the house in good faith and been disappointed by undeserved rejection.

"Let me help," Rosy said as he assisted Ruth in re-encasing herself in her jade cape. He opened the oak door, and as Helma left the room, he said in a low voice, "Call me in an hour." His face went bland and he said in a louder and more solemn voice, "Take care, ladies."

As soon as Rosy closed the door, Ruth demanded, "What did he say to you?"

"I'll tell you when we're outside," Helma said.

"Uh-oh, I know that tone. You're mad at me, I can tell. I just stopped by to help. And maybe a little research for a new painting. I'm working. This is work."

Helma stopped on the landing of the grand staircase. "Ruth, I'd carefully planned what to say to the Harringtons. It's a very sensitive situation."

"So then, did one of them confess to blowing up Franklin?"

"Of course not. We were discussing the library site."

"It's all tied together, just wait." Ruth touched her finger to a gold-framed oil depicting cows grazing— but appearing to float—in a field at the foot of a stylized Mount Baker. "Gad, that's a horrible painting. And because I brought up the explosion, the guilty Harrington will be exposed, you wait and see. *Then* you'll thank me."

"Why believe Franklin was killed by his own family?"

"Why not? Like charity, it all begins at home. Besides, nobody in that little group seemed *that* twisted up by Franklin's death. At least not to me. Did they to you?"

"They're self-controlled," Helma said, continuing down the wide steps, admitting to herself that neither Rosy nor Del had exhibited the grief she'd expected. "And Frances is definitely grieving."

"I bet it's an act."

"That's cruel, Ruth. Franklin was her *father*." The memory of Helma's own father's death unexpectedly descended upon her: that dark disbelief. No, Frances's tears had been genuine.

"Meal ticket, too," Ruth said. "Do you know what Frances does for"—she made quotation marks in the air—"her career?"

"No, I don't. Do you? For a fact?" Helma reached the bottom step, where a worn piece of Turkish carpeting had been replaced by a patch that almost matched.

"Definitely. I'm shocked she didn't give you one of her little embossed cards. She's a professional closet organizer."

"Organization is a highly valuable skill," Helma told her.

"Maybe to you. How many people *pay* to have their closets organized, that's my point. Can't be very lucrative. I bet Daddy Franklin footed ninety-four percent of Fran's expenses."

"That doesn't mean she didn't love him," Helma asserted.

"Conceivably. So what did Rosy say?"

"He asked me to call him in an hour."

"See," Ruth said smugly as she pulled open the heavy front door. "I told you. He's going to spill who did in big brother. My arrival put the pressure on, set the scene for confessions."

Mist hovered above the melting snow, and the air was filled with the sounds of water. Eaves dripped, the gutters ran, storm drains swelled, tires splashed.

"Did you drive?" Helma asked outside the Harrington house.

"Taxi. Do you like my costume?"

"That's exactly what it is."

Ruth swirled her cape around her body. "Tut tut. I wanted to fit in with a family still weighted down by old money. You know, evening gown before brunch, tennis togs, ascots and smoking jackets. All that juicy rich stuff."

"I don't believe the Harringtons are *that* kind of rich," Helma said as she unlocked the doors of her Buick. "Where'd you find that dress?"

"Back of my closet. It's one of my better Goodwill discoveries."

After refusing to leave until Ruth buckled her seat belt—"If I permanently wrinkle this it'll be your fault," Ruth said—Helma pulled around the low silver BMW parked in front of her Buick. Frances's car, she guessed. The three brothers might have shared the Harrington house, but she doubted their offspring lived there.

"Hey, wait," Ruth cried, unbuckling her seat belt.

Helma braked, stopping the car. "What did you forget?"

"Nothing. Don't you see him? Rosy's waving to us."

And he was, standing outside the front door of the Harrington house. Ruth rolled down her window, and Rosy Harrington ambled—that was the most fitting word Helma could think of—toward them, as elegant as a 1930s movie star wearing a smoking jacket. He held a cigarette between two fingers raised to shoulder level.

"Come on around to my side," he said when he was close enough that he didn't need to raise his voice. He nodded toward a narrow graveled driveway that glistened wet where the snow had melted. "That leads around the house. I'll meet you there."

"You got it," Ruth told him. "Want a ride? My friend Helma's car may look like a doddering old relic but she keeps it as pristine as spanking new."

"I'll walk. Gives me time to finish this." He tapped his cigarette.

"Those things'll kill you," Ruth warned him.

"This is just a mental aid. It's not lit."

Helma drove the gravel path to the rear of the Harrington house. This side faced the alley, which had been renovated to appear as if it were the house's main entrance. It had a pillared approach, potted plants, a mailbox, and glass-paneled doors, even a landscaped lawn and a curb on the alley. Helma parked her car behind a vintage silver Mercedes.

They waited for Rosy beside the Mercedes. Ruth stroked the car's hood and sighed lovingly. "I bet he's going to tell us that Frances and Jay are involved in some sticky nasty first-cousin business and did away with Papa because he didn't want grandchildren with extra toes and fingers and the IQs of a field of stumps."

"Jay and Frances barely acknowledged one another," Helma said.

"That was just to draw suspicion away from themselves. Maybe they want to build a new Harrington mansion on your precious library site." Ruth looked toward the broad meadows of Cedar Falls Park, where children were building snowmen on the trampled wet snow and screaming over snow battles. "Wonder why they didn't build near the water in the first place."

"Waterfront property on a working bay like Washington Bay wasn't as desirable in the 1800s as it is now. I suppose then it was the equivalent of living next to a train switching yard," Helma had time to say before Rosy stepped around the corner of the house.

"Welcome to my humble abode," he said, ushering them up the sidewalk to the gleaming glass doors. He paused before unlocking his door to jab his cigarette into an urn of sand. The urn was littered with unsmoked cigarettes spiking from the dirt like a forest of tiny poles.

This was not at all like Del's portion of the house. The foyer had parquet floors, bright Persian rugs, white walls, and paintings from the Art Deco period. Ruth whistled appreciatively and Rosy bowed his head in gracious acknowledgment.

"Come into my parlor," he offered. "Lovely dress by the way," he told Ruth.

Chintz and gold, palms and wall hangings in hues that reminded Helma of Ruth's paintings.

"Tea?" Rosy asked. "Coffee or wine?"

Helma declined but Ruth said, "I haven't had my morning alcohol."

Rosy laughed and said, "Me, neither. I could use it. All that talk made me thirsty."

"Is this part of the original house?" Helma asked after Rosy brought a small glass of red wine to Ruth.

"Hard to believe, isn't it? Del calls it sacrilege. Pop would be spinning, true, but dear mama would be delighted. She hated that mausoleum."

"And there's actually no connection between your quarters and Del's?"

"Neither physical nor mental. And definitely not socially. We agreed to close it off when we divided it."

"Like two kids who draw a line through the center of their bedroom," Ruth offered.

"Exactly. Enter only on invitation. Franklin's entrance is off Cedar Street."

"Do his quarters resemble yours?" Helma asked.

"More like Del's, only less stodgy."

"But neither Jay nor Frances live here?" Helma asked.

"Not yet. They'll have that option when Del and I are carted off."

There were no firm chairs in the room. Every piece of furniture was overstuffed and deep. Helma thought more precisely when her body was in vertical alignment, but the closest was a wing chair with bolstered arms, and still she felt like the chair was wrapping itself around her. "You wanted to speak to us?" she asked Rosy.

He nodded and sat on the coffee table. "I can see you're floundering, so I wanted to give you some straight background."

"Why?" Helma asked, alert to this unexpected generosity.

"Don't choke gift horses," Ruth told her, and swallowed half her wine.

"You're mixing your metaphors, my dear, although it's good advice," Rosy said to her, and to Helma, continued, "Maybe I want to put the Harringtons in a more favorable light. We didn't exactly come off as the family from the little house in the big woods over there." He waved his hand deeper into the house, toward his brother Del's side. "Our great-greats had their shady quotients, even I admit that. A wayward bunch, a little swindle here, a little corner-cutting there. But we remainders are plumb ordinary. Just folks."

"Did you agree with Franklin's plan to give the site to the library?"

"To be honest, I didn't care. Unlike my brother, who *I* believe must be the youngest—he certainly has all the characteristics—I've accumulated enough resources in my lifetime to pander to my every desire until I'm stiff in my cold, cold grave. So if Franklin wanted to pass on a little slice of dirt for the greater good of the Harrington name, I was fine with it."

"Do you two fight over everything?" Ruth asked.

"Unimaginative, isn't it?" Rosy said. "Del and I have our moments, as if we're using a chain saw to surgically remove some invisible Siamese joint. You'll notice we haven't been able to tear ourselves too far apart from one another physically."

"And Franklin?" Helma asked. "Did the three of you disagree often?"

"Ah, Frankie." Rosy swirled the wine in his glass. "By being granted the title of eldest, he had the surety of kingship, don't you see? It gave him extra cachet, allowed him to be more generous. He tended to look beyond any scrappiness. Above it all. Now, that kind of person can *really* make you mad."

"Does me," Ruth agreed. "How about Frances and Jay? They must get along better. You know, being first cousins?"

"They barely notice each other. Different ... interests. At least they're not at each other's throats. Frances is a love, believe it or not. She can't read anything that goes beyond skin deep, but she's our own dear girl and we'd buy her the moon if it was for sale. And Jay is inspired by mathematics: how to turn one dollar into two. Or ten."

"Then you would support the library being built on the Harrington land, as Franklin planned?" Helma asked. From deeper in Rosy's portion of the house came the chirping of a parakeet.

"I would," Rosy said firmly. "It's somewhat of a stretch to believe Frank *didn't* deed the land over to the city before the excavation began." He frowned. "Can I have a peek at the agreement he *did* make?"

"I left my files in the car," Helma told him, grateful she had. It was a viable excuse to keep the papers private until Ms. Moon consulted a lawyer.

"I see. You may have a little work convincing my brother. At one time he and Jay hoped to build condos that would knock Bellehaven's eyes out, and be a blight upon the land, I'm sure."

"Will you help?" Helma asked bluntly.

Rosy grunted. "Nobody can convince Del of anything." A look crossed his eyes. "Except ... "

"Who?" Helma asked.

Rosy shook his head. "Nope. She's out of the equation. Sorry. I misspoke."

She. Helma recalled Aunt Em's claim about Del's "her," that "she" lived in Aunt Em's retirement apartments. No, that was gossip.

"You're being too, too coy," Ruth accused him.

"No, shockingly indiscreet is a better term. That's what getting old does to you. My sincerest apologies." And he actually bowed his head, first to Helma, then to Ruth, who looked torn between disbelief and guilty pleasure at his obeisance.

He jotted something on a piece of paper and gave it to Helma. "This is my private phone number. You'll probably want to ask me a few questions, maybe clarify what you hear."

"Are you offering to be a source of the truth in Harrington matters?" she asked.

"Something of the sort."

Rosy walked them to his front door. "It's been a delight," he said. "Be careful of the ice out there."

As the two women walked to Helma's car, Ruth asked, "So tell me, what did we—or he—gain here?"

"He wanted to leave us with a better impression of the Harringtons," Helma said.

"When in actuality he gave us a *worse* impression: infighting, scandal. Him and his Oscar Wilde complex. And that 'she' nonsense he was implying about his brother? Shockingly indiscreet, my ass. He *wanted* to give you a little naughty news to throw us off track."

"I don't know. Aunt Em mentioned—" She stopped. Aunt Em never lied, but she *did* jump to conclusions, and the account of "her" had yet to be substantiated. She was already around the hood of her car when Ruth screeched.

Helma froze. Aunt Em's tale slipped from her mind because she looked past Ruth and saw that the passenger's side window of her Buick had been smashed from its frame.

Chapter 17

Vandals on the Loose

"I knew they shouldn't have given those kids another day off school," Ruth said.

Chunks of safety glass lay on the gravel alleyway, more of it scattered across the Buick's front seat. One long cracked strip of window glass still clung to the door frame.

"Don't touch anything," Helma ordered Ruth. "Back away from the car."

Ruth remained by the car, "on guard," while Helma returned to Rosy's front door and asked him to phone the police.

"Kids should be in school today," he said, echoing Ruth. "Guaranteed pandemonium when they're let loose on the city."

The response from the police was far more than was warranted by Helma's single broken window. Three patrol cars screeched into the alleyway, sirens screaming, doors slamming.

"What on earth did you report?" Ruth asked Rosy, who stood waiting with them.

"I told the 911 girl there was criminal activity at the home of the brother of Franklin Harrington, Belle-haven's recent murder victim," he told them with a twinkle. "I thought that might encourage haste on their part."

"This is excessive force for a broken window," Helma said. Not only was Detective Carter Houston stepping from the passenger side of a patrol car, but Wayne Gallant emerged from a plain blue car.

The policemen immediately fanned across the driveway, heads turning, eyes darting, as they searched for the perpetrators. Carter stepped back to let Wayne take the lead as they approached the two women and Rosy. Although Carter's face remained perfectly bland, Helma had the distinct impression that when he recognized her and Ruth, he rolled his eyes

"Is anyone injured?" Wayne asked, his eyes examining all three of them with piercing swift glances.

He stood "loose," his right hand relaxed at his side, yet Helma sensed that if there was a flash of danger, that hand would dart into his clothing for a weapon. She didn't see a bulge but had no doubt he wore a gun, perhaps in his waistband, or in a holster beneath his arm. Or maybe—

Ruth elbowed her.

"No," Helma told him, jumping a little. "No one's injured. A vandal broke the passenger's side window of my car. I suspect it was unsupervised children."

"Did you see anyone loitering around your vehicle?" Carter asked.

"No, although we did observe a group of preteens throwing snowballs in the park approximately forty-five minutes ago."

"You got rid of your woolly bear hat, Carter," Ruth said, nodding to Carter's head, bare of yesterday's black Russian-style hat.

He raised his hand as if he were about to feel for his hat, then dropped it to his side and stiffly asked Ruth, "Did you just get in, Miss Winthrop?"

"Get into what?"

"Your evening clothes," he said, motioning to Ruth's cape, which had opened to reveal her elaborate gown.

"Oh, this," she said, twirling one edge of her cape over her shoulder like the Phantom of the Opera. "Very astute, Carter. Have you ever been to a costume ball?" And before he could respond, she went on, "Who would you impersonate? Sherlock Holmes? Dick Tracy?"

Wayne Gallant spoke to two policemen, then told Helma, "We'll check for prints and look around but there's probably not much here to go on."

"Could it have been a snowball?" Helma asked. A couple walking three identical Corgis stood on the other side of the driveway, watching. More people were heading their way from the park, approaching with curiosity and caution.

Wayne peered through the broken window. "I don't see any snow inside your car. The window was struck with considerable force. Was anything taken?"

"I never leave tempting items in my car," she told the chief. "Maybe Ruth—" She stopped and leaned closer to her gaping window.

The Harrington files. She'd left the Harrington files on the front seat when she and Ruth had gone inside Rosy's. Now the front seat was bare. "My files," she said. "There was a file containing four manila folders sitting on the front seat."

"What kind of files?" Wayne asked.

"Pertaining to the library site. And the Harringtons."

"Coincidence?" Ruth said. She waved her hand toward the Harrington house. "My my. And here we sit, eyeball deep in Harrington Land."

"Did you lose anything?" Wayne asked Ruth, while behind him Carter scribbled in a small notebook with an expensive looking pen.

"I didn't leave anything in the car except my earrings; they were pinching my ears. A little discomfort for beauty is one thing, but I have no interest in out-and-out pain."

"Where are they?" Wayne asked.

"In the ashtray, which I knew was as clean as the moment this car was released from the factory."

Wayne opened the driver's door and, using a cloth, pulled open the ashtray on the dashboard. "There aren't any earrings here now."

"What?" Ruth leaned in beside him. "That is so rotten. Somebody strip-searched your car, Helma."

"Could you check beneath the seats?" Helma

asked the chief. "In case I accidentally tucked my files underneath." Even though she knew that was unlikely.

The files were nowhere in her car; they'd been taken by whoever broke her window.

"The thief either took Ruth's earrings and my files when they broke the window ... " Helma began.

"A smash and dash," Ruth supplied.

"... or they wanted one of the two missing objects and hoped to make it appear a car prowl," Helma finished.

"Well, my earrings were worth about seventy-nine cents, so *they* weren't the pièce de résistance."

"Do you have copies of your files?" Wayne asked Helma.

She was about to admit she didn't when she realized how close Rosy Harrington stood, coolly watching the goings-on. He could hear every word they said.

"Ms. Moon has another set, I believe," Helma said hopefully.

Surely Ms. Moon would have copied them before thrusting them on her. Certainly she would have.

"As soon as we're finished I'll call a tow truck to pick up your car," Wayne said. "You'll probably have to leave it in the shop for a day or so to get that window replaced."

"I can drive you wherever you want to go," Ruth offered. "This is getting good. I'll paint at night. Besides, I can help."

Carter Houston raised his pen from his notebook, looked from Ruth to Helma, then bent back over his notes without comment.

"Is your car here now?" Wayne asked Ruth.

"You expect me to drive in this getup? I made my entrance in one of Bellehaven's three yellow cabs."

"I can give you a ride home," Rosy Harrington offered.

"Good idea," Wayne said. "We'll finish going over the scene and clear this out of here for you."

"Call me immediately if you find my files, please," Helma said. "They're vitally important."

"Will do," he told her, and walked her to Rosy's Mercedes, lagging behind until Ruth and Rosy were deep in conversation and couldn't hear.

"It's been a while since we've had a chance to talk." Wayne cleared his throat. "Would you accompany me to dinner tomorrow night?"

Helma was startled to see pinched uncertainty on the face of the Bellehaven chief of police. It *had* been a while, and not without reason, but perhaps now …

"Yes," she said, "I'd like that," and he smiled down at her, all uncertainty gone.

"Thanks." He touched her arm, and Helma accidentally leaned into his hand. "One other thing, Helma, before you hear it somewhere else."

She froze. "Yes?"

"Randall Rice died a half hour ago."

And when she didn't say anything, thinking of the solitary figure lying amidst machines in the room at the end of the hall, he said, "It was expected."

"Was he alone?" she asked.

"Relatives flew in from California last night, a sister,

I think," he told her, and somehow that made it easier to hear.

"I'll be talking to you later, then." And off he went on his police duties while she climbed into the leather backseat of Rosy Harrington's Mercedes.

"Wagons ho," Rosy said.

As they pulled away, Helma peered back at her Buick with its gaping window, vulnerable to the elements, broken glass scattered around it, while Rosy hummed a cheerful ditty and tapped the steering wheel with a new unlit cigarette.

Chapter 18

Taking a Ride

"Can you drop me off at the library, please?" Helma asked Rosy.

"Your wish is my greatest desire," Rosy told her as they passed a house where a woman dressed in coveralls was scraping snow from her garden with a rake.

"You sure?" Ruth asked. "Rosy and I are stopping by Joker's. You could join us." She made drinking motions with an invisible beer stein.

"No thank you," Helma said, deciding that since Rosy and Ruth had already begun drinking wine at Rosy's house, she wouldn't mention it wasn't even noon yet. There was no legitimate reason why it should, but Rosy's presence stopped her from telling Ruth about Randall's death.

A hand-printed sign was taped off-center on

the front door of the library: CLOSED—NO HEAT. Helma read it with approval. She tried the door anyway, and it opened into the library foyer. Unlocked.

The lights were off and the public area deserted. No one staffed the circulation desk and the computer screens were dark. She was surprised that the library public had believed the sign. The world was so cluttered with signs, she thought, that people had grown numb to them.

After she untaped and realigned the sign in the center of the door, she walked through the public area to the workroom, stopping to push in a chair and pick up a wrapper from a Coffee Nip caramel: Ms. Moon's favorite candy.

The heat was still off and the air felt colder than outside. Helma could see her own breath as she made her way through the book- and box-crowded aisles of the quiet workroom to Ms. Moon's office.

As if someone had shouted a warning that she was on her way, Ms. Moon sat at her desk, hands folded, facing the doorway and no surprise on her face at the sight of Helma stepping into her office. The electric heater hummed and glowed in the corner.

"Ah, Helma," Ms. Moon said. "You've heard about Randall, I presume?"

"Yes," Helma told her. "I have."

Ms. Moon gazed deep into the middle distance, then brought her eyes back to Helma. "Since we still don't have heat, I thought it was best to close for the day. I trust your meeting with Del Harrington was successful. Did you agree on a date for new negotiations, or," she beamed, "when an agreement could be finalized and signed?"

"I might have been better prepared if you'd informed me I'd be meeting with the entire Harrington family."

Ms. Moon waved her hand as if Helma were mentioning trivialities. "It was the same issue whether you only spoke to Del or the whole clan."

"Or," Helma added, "that Del had refused to speak to *you* on the subject."

"There are seasons when energy outflows don't align. Del recognized that—I admire him for his awareness." She raised her eyebrows. "Both the children were present?"

"Frances and Jay," Helma supplied.

Ms. Moon nodded. "Currently single, I presume?"

"Both were alone," Helma told her, and Ms. Moon sighed and nodded as if that fact made one less complication. "And the family's amenable to the library being built on the site?"

"There are reservations," Helma told her. "Del and his son talked of developing that area for condos."

Ms. Moon shuddered. "Certainly not *now*, not right on top of the scene of their brother's death. It would be like *Poltergeist*, don't you agree?" A heavy vehicle rumbled past the library, but since Ms. Moon kept her drapes closed, it was impossible to identify it.

"I've not seen the movie *Poltergeist*," Helma told her. "The explosion was actually beside the excavation, not in it."

"Still too close for condos," Ms. Moon said.

"But if you're superstitious about condos occupying the site, don't you feel apprehensive about a *library* being built on the same spot?" Helma asked. "It does now have an association with death."

Ms. Moon laughed. "Oh no, a library's *different*. No one would be actually *living* above death. That's what upsets spirits, I believe, when people *live* on top of them: cooking and showering and snoring, all those daily things. It's insulting. Whereas a library denotes respect for the past, the written word. It ... " She trailed off, gazing at Helma, who didn't have a clue what she was talking about, but believed the director was making some sort of case for the new library building.

"Do you have copies of the files you gave me?" Helma asked.

Ms. Moon stiffened; her nose twitched and eyes narrowed. "Why?" she asked.

"Did you give me the originals?" Helma said.

"Why?" Ms. Moon demanded again.

"I'd like to be sure I've seen all the pertinent files," Helma told her, which was definitely the truth.

"You have every single note and sheet of paper existing that alludes to the library site, or the Harringtons. Naturally, I gave you the originals, since I knew they'd be completely safe with you, safer than in my own file cabinet."

Helma's heart sank, but she bravely carried on. "You're certain his intent was to give the site to the library?"

"Definitely. Didn't you read my notes? We'd even discussed the presentation ceremony." The heater in the corner turned itself off and its glow faded. "With

a big red ribbon and champagne," she whispered. "In
real champagne flutes, not those plastic ones with the
bottoms that fall off."

"I doubt if the city would approve of champagne,"
Helma pointed out.

"Sparkling cider, then, but I still want *real* glasses."

Helma heard a soft thump from the workroom side
of Ms. Moon's closed door. She glanced toward it expectantly but the sound wasn't repeated. "How did
Randall Rice feel about the new library site?" she asked
Ms. Moon.

"Since this first phase wasn't costing the city a red
cent, he was totally thrilled. Randall was such a penny
pincher," Ms. Moon added, as if recalling a fond ec-
centricity instead of an attribute that had sent her into
sputtering frustration.

"Was Randall involved in any of the negotiations
with you and Franklin?"

Ms. Moon shook her head. "Not at all."

"But they knew each other," Helma persisted.

"Certainly. Randall was much younger, but they
departed this world together—almost together—that
must mean something." She brought her fingertips together. "Freed into eternity, yet bound forever."

Helma thought of money-conscious, stiff Randall
Rice and the gentlemanly Franklin. Not exactly what
she'd consider a happy pairing for eternity.

"The police were here this morning," Ms. Moon
said, "asking about Randall and Franklin, too. I told
them to come back when the entire staff was present.
Just Dutch and Glory and myself were here."

"But they've left now?" Helma asked.

"Glory has, but Dutch is still here."

"I didn't see him," Helma said. "And the front door is unlocked."

"Could you ask him to lock it, please?" Ms. Moon said. She waved her hands in shoo-shoo motions. "You may as well leave, too. Tomorrow will be more harmonious, I just know it."

But first Helma returned to her cubicle and telephoned Hunky's Auto Repair where Wayne said her Buick would be towed.

"Unless we install a recycled window, it'll take at least a week," the mechanic who'd answered the phone by saying, "Hunky speaking," told her.

"I prefer a new window," Helma told him, "fresh from the factory."

There was a pause on the telephone and Helma heard hammering, then the racing of an engine. "I can get the recycled window tomorrow. Your car's twenty-five years old. A new one will take a week or more."

"Do you have loaner cars?" she asked.

"No. Sorry."

Helma considered Ruth's offer to drive her everywhere. Ruth, who regarded schedules as mere suggestions, who drove her own speed and only obeyed driving laws she believed were pertinent to her particular circumstance. And who, if she followed past habits, would suddenly take her looming deadline to heart and disappear into her painting, forgetting all other existence, leaving Helma stranded.

"Can you make my car drivable?"

Another pause. "I guess we could tape a sheet of plastic over the window, but it'll look pretty sorry."

"If you'll order a new window and tape up my old window, I'll pick up my car at five this afternoon."

"It'll look like ... Are you sure that's what you want?"

"It is."

"You got it, then. Don't say I didn't warn you and don't leave anything valuable inside."

After she hung up, Helma rose in her cubicle and was startled by movement behind a stack of newly arrived books waiting to be processed.

"Dutch?" she said.

He jumped and whirled around, facing her over the boxes, his eyes tensed. Perspiration dotted his forehead.

Helma fought the urge to step back, and instead said in the same imperative tone of voice she'd once used to distract a two-year-old from the electrical outlet he was aiming his mother's car keys toward, "The library's front door is unlocked, Dutch. Could you lock it, please?"

Dutch nodded. His lips twitched.

"After that, go home," she added.

Dutch nodded again and fell into step behind her to the shadowy and still public area. He was so silent she couldn't hear his footfalls, only feel his presence and smell the odor of cigarettes behind her. She hadn't known Dutch smoked.

"Hello, Helma."

Both Dutch and Helma jumped. At a table near the

circulation counter sat Boyd Bishop, his face partially in shadow. Helma had forgotten his phone call the morning before, when he'd invited her to see something Franklin Harrington had shown him.

Boyd rose. He was long and lanky, a man who might have stepped out of the westerns he was so dedicated to writing and so unsuccessful at publishing. He grinned at Helma. "The door was unlocked so it looked like an invitation to me. Got your boots and mittens?"

"I do," Helma said, touching her bag, "but I didn't realize we'd settled on a time."

"We didn't," he said easily, buttoning his faded denim jacket. "I couldn't reach you by phone so I took the direct route. My car's out front."

There was no reason for her *not* to go. In fact, she still wore her coat and her pull-on leather boots. The library was closed; her car was in the shop. It was just ... sudden.

But it also indirectly involved Franklin Harrington.

"It'll only be a three-hour tour," he said, and she frowned at the familiarity of the words. She'd heard them somewhere else.

"All right," she decided. "I'm ready."

His bright teeth flashed. "Great."

"You may lock the door behind us," Helma reminded Dutch, who nodded but didn't respond. He stood beside the circulation desk, arms folded, and watched them leave the library.

Boyd's car was a small wagon. A profusion of yellow sticky notes were adhered to the dashboard, a pencil tethered to a radio knob, and on the backseat she noted a stack of spiral notebooks. When he turned on the engine, the narration of a talking book filled the car—a western.

"I've got chains in the back," he told her as he switched off the audiobook. "So don't worry; we can make it through any of this glop that's left."

"Exactly where are we going that we might need chains?" Helma asked as they turned the corner at James and Sunset. "The streets are mostly bare now." In fact, just then they passed a digital sign on a bank marquee that read: 41°.

"Out in the county," Boyd told her.

"Out in the county" was how Bellehavenites referred to property outside the city limits, a term that took in vast areas of land and terrain: mountains, lakes, forests, farmlands, and small picturesque villages. All holding only one thing in common: it was not Bellehaven.

"How far out in the county?" Helma asked. "The area outside the city limits covers approximately 2,100 square miles."

"Approximately, huh?" he said, chuckling. "Well, I don't think I'll tell you. It'll be a surprise." Boyd was long of body, and he drove leaning forward as if he might rest both arms on top of the steering wheel.

"I don't like surprises," Helma informed him.

"Hard to live without a few," he said, turning onto Merritt, one of the main roads that led out of Bellehaven.

They drove north, and the farther they drove, the more snow they encountered. It lay in compacting drifts across fields, in the shade of lawns, on roofs and fence posts.

"How did you meet Franklin Harrington?" Helma asked.

"Everybody said he was the go-to man for local historical information, so I did. He was pretty generous with his knowledge. Loved to tell stories about this area."

"What was your subject?" They passed three horses in a field, all roan, all wearing heavy coats that buckled beneath their necks and chests.

He laughed. "We're getting to it."

Boyd turned onto a secondary, snowier, road that led across farmlands toward low mountains. Helma knew Bellehaven, she'd lived there twenty years, but rarely, she admitted, did she venture off the county's main roads. She was accompanying Boyd into unknown territory.

He slowed the car, not because of the slippery road, as she expected, but because he was looking past her out the window. He braked. "Now there's a pretty sight," he said.

At first she thought he meant a rolling field where stubbles of cut corn stuck up through the snow, but then she recognized the snowy white movements.

"Swans," she exclaimed. At least a hundred of the majestic white birds had settled in the field. They pecked at the corn stalks, stretched their gigantic wings and graceful necks, and moved in stately grace around one another. "I'd heard they wintered here."

Boyd nodded. "Trumpeters. They fly down from

Alaska for the winter. See the gray ones with the pinkish bills? Those are the kids."

They watched for a few more minutes, as two of the gray juveniles circled each other, necks thrusting, beaks meeting. "Looks like fowl play," Boyd said, and Helma had to groan.

Before he restarted his car, Boyd asked, "Now that was an okay surprise, right?"

"Is that what Franklin showed you? The swans?"

"Nope. Consider that a bonus." He turned right, onto yet another, even narrower road with only one set of tire tracks marring the snowy surface. They'd risen higher, to the edge of the foothills, away from the farms into a bordered forest of evergreen and deciduous trees. They didn't pass any more driveways or houses, only an abandoned and collapsed building, overrun by vines and blackberry bushes.

"Right here," Boyd said. He pulled onto a rutted turnout and shut off the engine. "Bundle up. There's a wind up here."

Helma did, and followed him through a fringe of fir trees. He stomped the snow flat for her, seeming to recognize a trail she couldn't discern. From somewhere nearby she heard water splashing and tumbling over rocks.

The trees ended and the land dropped away in front of them. A straight drop. Helma held her breath and stepped back, her hand out to touch a tree trunk and banish the elevator feeling. Winds blew upward, rising from beneath them as the view opened up to the west, across farms and fields and streams. The Canadian mountains loomed to the north, their peaks touched by sun.

"This is beautiful," Helma said, looking out over the land as she held firmly to the tree. "Why did Franklin show you this?"

"Keep looking. I'm setting my new book here."

"Then this book isn't a western?"

"It's a *north*western. There were similar elements in the Wild West and the Northwest a hundred years ago. Bad guys, good guys, horses and beautiful women. Greed." He shrugged. "Maybe a new angle will catch a publisher's attention."

"What am I looking for?" Helma asked, still gazing over the scene, spotting a bird flying *beneath* them. "You said it was more visible in the snow?"

"That's right." He pointed beneath them to a small forest. "I'll give you a hint. This book has a train in it."

"I don't see any trains."

"Think of the past," he urged her. "A hundred years or more."

"But there's nothing in ... oh."

"See it?" Boyd asked, his voice rising.

And she did. There, across the land beneath her, beside a stream and through a woods that had grown along its path, now defined by the snow, cut the smooth raised bank of a railroad grade, interrupted now and then by a road or pasture. "The snow," she said. "It emphasizes it. The tracks are gone."

"Pulled out in the early 1900s," Boyd said. "You can't really see the grade when you're on a level with it, but from up here it's obvious. The gravel bed discourages any big trees and keeps it level, too, so that's why the snow fixes it like that. You'll find it on old maps but otherwise it's long forgotten. A lot of old history wasn't documented like it is now."

"Where did the tracks lead?"

"From the Canadian border into Bellehaven. There were spurs up to a few old towns and mines. Gone now." He pointed below them to a collapsed building. "Franklin said that from there up to one of the mines seventeen miles away, tracks were built in seven weeks, including hauling in the gravel, building up the grades, and putting in a couple of bridges, too."

Helma felt the rough bark of the tree through her mittens. "Seven weeks? How could that be possible?"

"Ah, that was a different era. Don't forget, the rest of the country was way ahead of us. The railroads brought in laborers to do the work, laborers who didn't complain. Chinese, Irish. I've seen old photos of newly arrived Chinese laborers waiting to be picked up at the depot in Bellehaven, big groups. All bound for grueling work: railroads, mines, building. No unions to fight for conditions and wages." He gazed out at the view. "People came and went and hardly left a mark. Brutal times."

"Then your new book will include laborers?" Helma asked him.

"Hard to write about the Northwest and that time period without including them."

"I'm sure I can find some material in the library for you to—"

Boyd held up his hand. "No work talk today. Besides, I like the research part of writing. See that square down there? Right beside the grade? I bet it's the foundation of an old station. Maybe a water tower for the steam engines."

From their height, the square, made visible by the melting snow, appeared impossibly tiny.

"Did the Harringtons own this railroad?"

"One area they didn't get their fingers into, railroads. I wish now I'd written down every story Franklin told me. He's a real loss to the history buffs of this area."

"I heard Randall Rice had an interest in history, too," Helma said, following the ghostly line beneath them with her eyes. A dog or coyote ran between trees and disappeared. "Did you talk to him, too?"

"Once." Boyd shrugged. "Randall claimed he was a history expert. I'm surprised he didn't have calluses from patting himself on the back. But he wasn't so eager to share his knowledge. One of those 'I know it so I own it' types."

"Did you ever see Franklin and Randall together?"

"Nope. You turning into a detective?"

"I was just curious."

"Careful, curiosity can get you all tied up in knots."

"Their deaths are very confusing."

"Yeah, I heard it was a mess." He touched Helma's arm. She wore mittens; his hands were bare, his long fingers reddening from the cold. "At the risk of sounding like one of my own books, I'll say that even the biggest balls of twine eventually unravel."

They made their way back to Boyd's station wagon and climbed inside. "Thank you," Helma told him sincerely as she buckled her seat belt. "For this. And the swans."

"You bet." Boyd started the engine and began turning around, looking over his shoulder as he backed up. "Will you go out to dinner with me this weekend?"

Before she could answer, Boyd's car slid on the slick snow and Helma felt the sickening sensation of the earth falling out from under her.

Chapter 19

Rescue

"I don't think I can drive out of this one," Boyd said.

He and Helma stood outside his car, viewing the situation. The car's passenger side wheels had slid off the edge of the turnout and the car sat at a precarious angle in deep snow, only a few feet from sliding downward into the trunk of a giant old cedar tree. Boyd had helped Helma out the driver's side, then returned to retrieve her scarf and mittens.

"Hope there's service up here," he said as he pulled a cell phone from his pocket and began pressing numbers on the tiny device.

"I'm glad you carry a cell phone," Helma told him.

"Doesn't everybody?" he asked. "I heard a cell phone was involved in Franklin's—" His attention shifted as his call went through.

"No," Helma heard him say. "I have a passenger. Helma Zukas." He tipped his head and looked at her. "That right?" he said into the phone. "I'll tell her."

Boyd closed his phone and tucked it into his rear pants pocket. "Talk about coincidence. The tow truck is run by Hunky's Auto Repair. They have your car. Hunky said you can pick it up any time."

It was a half hour before they heard the tow truck grinding its way up the road to them, and by then Helma's feet were as cold as her nose. She'd rejected Boyd's offer to tuck her hands into his pockets but accepted the red plaid blanket he kept in his trunk, and now stood with it draped around her shoulders.

"There's gotta be a way I can use this in a scene in one of my books," Boyd said. "Trade that car for a horse and buggy, add a marauding grizzly and a couple of train robbers."

"Don't forget the marshal," Helma said.

He laughed. "And I just might add a woman who keeps a cowboy so off balance it's like walking on one leg."

The truck was still a long way off, gears shifting, engine straining.

When it finally arrived, a large man in his fifties dressed in a green jumpsuit stepped from the truck, the orange and red lights gyrating unnecessarily since there was no traffic within miles. "It's usually a couple of kids I end up pulling out of here," he said, eyebrow raising as he looked from Boyd to Helma.

In a laconic voice, Boyd asked, "You wouldn't be saying anything the lady here might find offensive, would you?" Lazily spoken, holding himself quiet.

"No, sir," the driver said. "Not at all."

They followed the tow truck back to Bellehaven, while Boyd told Helma about his favorite game as a child, called Tinky Pinky.

"I don't play games," she told him.

He grinned. "And you don't like surprises. No playing, okay, but a good librarian should know how it works. So here goes: I think of two words that rhyme. And then I say 'tink pink' if they're one syllable words, 'tinky pinky' if they're two syllable words, and so on. Are you listening?"

Helma nodded, looking out the window for landmarks she recognized.

"So," Boyd continued, "if I were to say 'chubby feline' and 'tink pink,' your answer would be?"

Helma looked at him blankly.

"Fat cat," he said. "Get it? And if I said, 'warmer liquid' and 'tinky pinky,' your answer would be?"

He held out his hand and flexed his fingers as if he were coaxing an answer from her. "If I were playing," Helma told him, "which I'm not, I would probably offer, 'hotter water,'"

"And you said you couldn't play games."

"I said didn't, not couldn't."

They descended from the wilder snowy heights to the temperate and civilized waterfront where only shaded piles of snow remained. Boyd stopped his car beside the wide doors of Hunky's Auto Repair. "Sure you don't want me to stay until you get your car?" he asked Helma.

"No. I'll take over from here, thank you."

"Then how about changing your mind about dinner tomorrow night?"

"I already have a commitment."

"That won't stop me, you know," he said, grinning so easily Helma couldn't be offended.

"That's been my experience so far," she said, "but I *do* have a commitment."

As she stepped out, he said, "Try this one: Stubborn library employee. Tinkity-tink pinkity-pink."

Helma closed the door and waved, seeing the words but not saying them: *contrarian librarian.*

The plastic sheet the Hunky's people had used to cover the passenger window of Helma's Buick was, surprisingly, opaque.

"Don't you have clear plastic?" she asked the mechanic, who had not been the driver of the tow truck.

"Not here," he told her, unperturbed by her dismay. He twirled a grimy wrench like a pistol.

"It's too dangerous to drive with plastic I can barely see daylight through."

"Most people would think driving with a plastic window of *any* kind was too dangerous," he said, looking at her from the bottoms of his eyes.

So finally, after Helma gave the receptionist her automobile insurance information, she climbed into her car and drove to the nearest strip mall that had a hardware store, choosing one that took a route requiring only right turns.

And then she was forced to buy a fifty-foot roll of

clear plastic and a 250-foot roll of tape wide enough and strong enough to hold the plastic to her door frame.

She had no choice but to install the plastic on her car in the strip mall's parking lot since the drive home required several unsupported left turns.

In Helma's trunk between her first aid kit and a mat for unexpected forays into parks or beaches, was a tool-box in which she kept a clever multiple-use tool sent to her one Christmas by her brother. She opened the tool-box on the pavement beside her car and concentrated on creating as smooth a transparent surrogate window as possible—a tedious and time-consuming task.

Working intently, she was oblivious to her surroundings until a man said, "*Miss* Zukas, is that you?"

Stepping up beside her Buick was Del Harrington's son, Jay, and behind him, Franklin's daughter, Frances.

"It is I," Helma said.

He looked at the roll of tape in her hand and the half-covered window. "You should let an auto repair shop fix that."

"I am correcting deficient repair work," she told him, "until my replacement window arrives."

Frances stood five feet away, gazing beyond Helma and her cousin as if she weren't in any way related to either of them. She'd changed clothes and now wore a knit rust-colored coat that nearly reached the ankles of brown leather boots with tall narrow heels.

"Dad and I own this strip mall," Jay said. "I could find somebody to finish this for you. They'd do it for *me*."

"No thank you. I'm quite capable." On the far side of the lot a car alarm bleated repeatedly and tediously.

"I believe you."

"I assume the police spoke to you after my car was vandalized," Helma said.

"They did. We didn't see or hear a sound, did we, Fran? Anything stolen?"

She was surprised the police hadn't told them about the missing files.

"Hurry up, Jay," Frances interrupted. "We have appointments."

"Franny's helping me choose funeral-appropriate clothes," Jay explained. "She doesn't want me to look like some second-rate developer."

Frances inserted her pinky nail between two front teeth that were so white they were nearly blue. "I'll wait for you near Anton's perfume counter," she said.

"Be there in a sec," he said, and Frances nodded to both and neither of them before she left.

"A pair of earrings was stolen," Helma told Jay.

"Must have been good ones." Jay pointed to the upper corner of the window. "It's a little loose right there." He picked up the roll of tape from the roof of Helma's car. "I don't know how much we'll be seeing you regarding this library business, but Dad was mighty irritated you left him and snuck off to Uncle Rosy's."

"There was no sneaking involved," Helma corrected. He was right. The upper corner *was* loose. She used her Christmas tool to peel back the tape.

"Looked that way," he said as he spun the roll of tape around his finger. "And appearances count."

"Perceptions are not my concern."

He brushed off his hands. "They should be. Playing both sides is a bad move. You know the Middle East?"

"Not personally," Helma told him.

"But being a librarian, you're probably up on all its ins and outs. The Harrington triplets are like Middle Eastern countries. They fight all the time, can't stand each other, but you make one of them mad and they're liable to *all* land heavy on you."

"And you know this from experience?"

"From day one." Jay laughed shortly and set the roll of tape back on her roof with a thump. "You take care now," and he headed off toward the shops.

Helma finished taping the plastic, a far inferior material to glass, its only advantage that she'd be able to at least see through it. She folded the end of the tape over on itself so the leading edge could be found again and turned to her open toolbox on the ground.

There, in the open lid, as if they'd been tossed there, were three silver coins and two one-dollar bills. Helma turned in every direction, but aside from the sympathetic glance of a passing mother struggling to keep three children in tow, she didn't see who might have left the cash.

Back at the Bayside Arms, Helma searched her car again. The police *might* have missed the files. She found nothing but a half a peanut under the front passenger seat, likely from Ruth's pockets. Ruth tended to live in waves of indulgence: for a while listening only to jazz, then wearing only purple, or drinking only pulp-filled orange juice. Her latest addiction had been an absolute certainty that peanuts were rife with youth-preserving oils. She tucked peanuts in every available pocket or depression, and the smell of peanut butter often overpowered her usual musky perfume. This obsession couldn't end soon enough.

The plastic window had been transparent, all right, but even after her care in taping it as tightly as possible, the window had flapped like a loose sail, filling her car with flutter and rude sucking noises no matter how slowly she drove.

Helma ate her dinner at her dining room table with her back to her kitchen: one small baked potato, half a baked chicken breast, and a sliced cucumber, all arranged on a plain white plate. All her dinnerware was plain white; patterns and colors mixed too unappetizingly with food for her tastes.

If the library files had been stolen from her car and destroyed, the library didn't possess a shred of evidence supporting Franklin's intent for the library site.

She thought of the gaping hole in the earth, the yellow police tape. The site would be forever shadowed by Franklin's and Randall's deaths, deterrents from the excitement of fine literature and the thrill of pure research. Always there would be the knowledge, spoken or not: somebody died here.

But still, her files—the files that were her responsibility—had disappeared while in her possession.

Helma pushed away her plate, her appetite lost. She

gazed out at the darkness of Washington Bay. There had to be other written proof of Franklin's plans. If only she hadn't been so thorough in organizing the papers. If she'd left out just one.

It was a fruitless exercise but she did it, anyway: checking beneath the table, behind the sofa, even in the trash. Nothing.

She was rinsing her hands when her telephone rang.

"Wilhelmina," Aunt Em said when Helma answered her telephone. "I thought you would come here to meet *her*."

"Oh, Aunt Em, I'm sorry." She'd forgotten about Aunt Em's plan to point out the woman involved with Del Harrington. Aunt Em and Helma's mother thrived on intrigue. And although Helma was not a supporter of gossip, she couldn't deny Aunt Em whatever she asked.

"Tomorrow, I promise."

"Good," Aunt Em said, "because your mother and I are watching her for you."

"You need to come down to Joker's."

"Ruth, it's eleven-fifteen. At night. I'm getting ready for bed."

"Why? It's only eleven-fifteen."

"That's what I said." Helma took the sauce pan of milk she was heating for a bedtime drink off the stove. Music blared from behind Ruth, nearly drowning out her voice.

"It's about you-know-what."

"I don't know what."

"The ka-boom," Ruth said in not-so-subtle code, her voice gleeful. "Frances, the offspring, is here. She's been irrigating her sorrows and now she's sodden so you can pump her for every detail you want."

"Ruth, did you have peanuts with you this morning?"

"Very relevant, Helma. I have some now, so I guess so. I'll be waiting right here. Better hurry. Bye."

Helma had no intention of dressing in the middle of the night to visit a bar on one of Ruth's misguided adventures. She poured her warm milk into a cup and carried it to her bedroom, ignoring Boy Cat Zukas's irritated hiss as she passed his basket.

Five minutes later her phone rang again and she wasn't surprised to hear Ruth's voice. This time it held no glee. "Helm, I think we need to do a good deed. Can you come down here? Please?"

"Is it Frances?"

"No. It's worse. I'll wait out front for you."

Helma hung up, considering. She knew Ruth's voice. She'd sounded not only serious, but sad. But it wasn't Frances. "It's worse," Ruth had said.

It only took Helma a few minutes to rinse her cup, dress in plain slacks and a dark sweater, then remove the curler from the stubborn strand of hair on the left side of her head.

As she'd promised, Ruth stood hunched in the raw night outside Joker's, her hands in her coat pockets and her collar up to her ears. Her hair was blown into a wild tangle that would require a goodly amount of effort to smooth out. She wore spattered coveralls she usually painted in.

"What is the good deed?" Helma asked her.

"You'll see." She led Helma into Joker's, which was warm and bright and smelled of alcohol and fried food. Joker's had finally made its transition from fishermen's bar to Bellehaven hot spot by exorbitantly raising its prices, and now it was packed nightly with the mon-eyed and in crowd the owners had coveted for years.

"Back here," Ruth said.

Helma spotted Frances at the bar sipping from a drink that had froth and a straw. An empty glass sat beside her. She was dressed as Helma had seen her in the strip mall parking lot, but she slouched on her bar stool, tapping her fingers against her glass. Her lipstick had worn off her lower lip.

"Just a minute," Helma told Ruth, and walked over to Frances, who looked up, her gaze distant.

"Frances," she said, standing directly in her line of vision. In Helma's experience, subtleties were lost on people who'd been imbibing alcohol. "Did one of the Harringtons break my car window and steal my files?"

"Ruth said you're going to figure out who killed them," Frances said, ignoring Helma's question. She raised her drink but the straw missed her mouth.

Ruth stood at the end of the bar, impatiently tapping her foot and blowing air upward.

"Who do *you* believe killed your father?" Helma asked Frances.

"Not one of us. Not a Harrington." But she didn't sound as positive as her words. "They fight all the time, but they love each other like ... " She waved a hand.

"Like brothers?" Helma supplied.

Frances nodded. "Like brothers. They wouldn't kill Daddy, and Daddy wouldn't kill them." The straw found her mouth and Frances sipped so deeply her cheeks dimpled.

"Hurry it up, Helma," Ruth said. "We don't have all night."

Helma left Frances, who'd gone all slumpish again, and made her way to Ruth. "Back here," Ruth said. "We have to get him home. You drive. I've imbibed." And she pointed to a corner table at the rear of Joker's.

Dutch leaned against the wall, an empty shot glass in front of him. Helma had never seen Dutch without perfect posture nor in any state except total personal control. Even his buzz cut appeared lax.

"He's been drinking straights. Let's get him out of here. You drive around to the back door. I'll meet you there with Dutch slung over my shoulder."

Helma stood for a moment, staring at this apparition of Dutch who was actually slack-mouthed, and Ruth said, "That last part was a joke. Come on, I'm trying to save him—and your precious library—a little egg on the face."

"That's very considerate of you, Ruth. Do you know where he lives?"

"Not where Carter dropped him off yesterday, I bet. I'll ask. Go."

Helma drove her Buick around the back of Joker's

and parked beside the Dumpster. A man in an apron sat on the back step smoking a cigarette.

"Could you assist us in removing a fellow smoker from the bar?" she asked him.

"The guy in the corner?"

"Yes, do you know where he lives?"

He narrowed his eyes. "Where are you taking him if you don't know where he lives?"

"That's what I'm attempting to find out."

"No idea, but I'll help you pour him into your car. Do it all the time."

Ruth had Dutch, who was mumbling incoherently, on his feet and aimed toward the back door. "Good. Reinforcements," she said when she saw the man with Helma. "Thanks, Bill."

Dutch was docile, and once they got him into Helma's car, he sank into a heap, half lying on the backseat.

"Did you find out where he lives?" Helma asked Ruth.

"Over there somewhere," she said, pointing toward the lower end of Washington Bay.

"Ruth, I am not driving aimlessly around Bellehaven with an unconscious and inebriated man in the backseat of my car."

"It's kind of sweet, really, don't you think? Big gruff Dutch as helpless as a baby?"

"Ruth."

"Okay, okay. I'll go back and ferret out a real honest-to-God address."

"Thank You."

While Ruth went inside, Helma sat at the wheel,

gazing straight ahead. Dutch's presence filled her car with the grainy odor of whiskey.

"I'm fine, ma'am," Dutch's voice slurred from the backseat.

"I don't believe you are, Dutch. We're taking you home."

"I knew," he said in a voice filled with despair.

It was a statement too intriguing to let pass, even from an alcoholically unreliable man. She turned to look at him. Dutch's head leaned against the seat back like a man contemplating the stars through her rear window. "What did you know?"

"Two times the fool," he said, his voice ending in a groan. "All the little body parts come raining down like cats and dogs. Dancing in their bones, they were. Too late."

It was a gruesome but poetic ramble. It was curious that alcohol-induced ramblings were often delivered in a poetic fashion. The loosened tongue, Helma thought. It was a state rife with dangerous and ill-advised disclosures.

"Why were you a fool, Dutch?" A car drove slowly past, and she recognized it as an unmarked police car. It continued toward the bay.

"I knew it and I let it. Like cats and dogs." His sigh ended in a hiccup. "It's not very far."

"Your house?"

"No. Hell isn't very far," Dutch said in the clarity of his normal voice. "Not if you've already got a good run at it."

The passenger door opened and Ruth climbed in.

She held up a slip of paper. "Here it is. Let's go."

Helma looked at the address and turned her car toward the north. Dutch fell silent.

"What did Frances say?" Ruth asked.

"That you told her I'd solve her father's death."

"I said that to soften her up for you. Did you find out any of Daddy's secrets?"

"She insisted the Harrington brothers are filled with nothing but brotherly love."

Ruth snorted. "Like Cain and Abel?"

By the time they reached Dutch's house, he was snoring as vigorously as Helma would have expected from a military man.

"Are you sure this is the correct address?" she asked Ruth.

"How would I know? All I know is that number on that little sign matches the number on this little paper."

Helma had expected an apartment, but it was a small, tidy house with winter remnants of elaborate gardens and landscaping. Only a porch light shone from the property. The rest of the house was dark.

"It doesn't look like there's a Mrs. Dutch," Ruth said. "I expected maybe a rifle range, not the Secret Garden. Let's see if one of these works." She held up a set of keys on a brass ring. "I took it off him at Joker's so he wouldn't try to drive."

The third key turned with a satisfying click. Ruth opened the front door and flicked on the interior lights. They stood in a meticulously tidy living room. Bookcases lined green walls. As every book lover did,

Helma made a quick scan of Dutch's titles—political thrillers, military history. Above and between them paintings of scenery and flowers. All of it serene and stable. Restful.

"A haven," Ruth commented, and Helma agreed. Looking around his home, she felt as if she were seeing Dutch unprotected, in his underwear.

They went back to retrieve Dutch, walked him into the house and settled him on his sofa, a tapestry pillow tucked beneath his head. Helma turned on the lamp on the end table. Light glowed down on the shiny cover of a book titled: *Weapons of the World*. A Village Books bookmark protruded from the pages. She slid her fingers beneath the bookmark and opened the book to a page on explosions and explosive devices.

"I did it," Dutch mumbled.

"What's he talking about?" Ruth whispered.

"I don't know," Helma said as they left, jiggling the door handle once to be sure it was locked. But she was afraid for Dutch, very afraid.

Chapter 20

The Heat Is On

As Helma drove to work Friday morning, glancing through her luffing passenger window she spotted two teenage boys in shorts jumping across a pile of dirty snow, even while the temperature on the Bailey Bank blinked forty-two degrees.

Wayne Gallant stood on the loading dock by the library's back door, and when she spotted him as she locked her car, Helma unaccountably dropped her car keys. He walked toward her, smiling.

"They told me you'd be here at 7:58." He tapped his watch. "And here you are, to the minute. Do you set your clocks by the library's clock?"

"Actually," Helma told him, "all my clocks are set to the U. S. Naval Observatory's atomic clock." She had made it her habit to recoordinate her clocks' times on Tuesdays, the same evening she emptied all the wastepaper baskets in her apartment.

His grin widened and he nodded toward the plastic taped to her window. "They couldn't replace it yesterday, eh?"

"I ordered a new window rather than allow a recycled window."

He whistled. "Must be a special order for a car this … old. Soon you'll be able to drive it in the Snow to Surf parade with the Model Ts and Edsels."

She could tell he was teasing so she politely laughed but couldn't help pointing out, "Those cars are usually restored; mine is completely original, even the seat covers. Except for the passenger's side window, of course. You were waiting for me?"

He nodded and unconsciously reached toward the notebook he carried in his jacket pocket, then pulled his hand away. So this was police business, then.

"Is it about Franklin's death?" she asked.

"Mostly. And Randall Rice's," he added.

"I've been told the explosion was intentional and of an amateur nature," Helma said.

"And who told you that?"

"I'm not at liberty to say, but you must have an idea how it was detonated. Was it a trip wire of some kind?" She paused and gazed into the chief's face as he calmly looked into hers. There was no response to her question, no raised eyebrows, no twitch at the corner of his mouth.

"A timer?" she asked, and he slightly shook his head, not in denial but at her questioning. There might even have been a trace of amusement in his eyes.

"Let's go inside," he said, touching her elbow.

Helma thought furiously, then took a wild stab, "Was it detonated by remote control?" She recalled recent news stories, then Boyd Bishop's unfinished sentence. "A cell phone?"

Just a twinge, a very slight single tremble of his left eye. Anyone without Helma's sharp skills of observation, or who hadn't spent attentive time with Wayne Gallant, wouldn't have noticed.

"We're going to hold off on an official announcement that the deaths are homicides until after Franklin's funeral tomorrow."

"When is Randall's funeral?"

"Monday."

"Then Franklin was the target?" she asked.

"Don't know that yet. I'd like to line up a few more ducks before we throw it open for public speculation. Two prominent men like this." He continued holding her elbow as they crossed the parking lot to the workroom door. His hands were bare and Helma felt the pressure of his fingers through her coat. "Your director said your meeting with the Harringtons yesterday was strictly library business." Wayne Gallant gazed at her with as rapt attention as she'd given him.

"Yes," Helma said, "she was instrumental in my being there."

"It's a can of worms that Franklin didn't transfer the land to the library before he died. Hang onto the originals of those files you lost."

"The files weren't *lost*," Helma reminded him as he dropped his hand from her elbow and she passed him through the open door. Around her the air hummed.

Warm currents overtook the cold drafts that accompanied them inside. The heat was on. "The files were *stolen*. I still hope they'll be recovered."

"We're keeping an eye out but I'm not optimistic. They might have been thrown into a garbage can once the thief realized they were worthless to him."

"Or her," Helma modified.

"Or her," he agreed. "I'll see you tonight, then, for dinner. Six o'clock?"

Helma agreed, and watched him leave the workroom, heading toward the library's public area, pulling his notebook from his pocket by the time he reached the door.

From her blue bag, Helma pulled out a library book she'd been reading at home: *A Guide to Workable Agreements*. She wasn't finished but she decided she might as well return it to the circulation desk now, right then, at that very moment.

Wayne Gallant stood at the circulation desk talking to Curt, one of Dutch's staff members, and naturally, Helma approached them quietly, remaining out of sight so as not to disturb their conversation.

"He called in sick," Curt was saying. "He's at home, though."

"Thanks," the chief said. He jotted something in his notebook and left through the front doors.

Movement caught Helma's eye and she turned to see Glory Shandy spin around and duck into the magazine area, in the opposite direction from her.

"Dutch isn't here today?" Helma asked Curt, who was shoving bar-coded books beneath the scanner.

He shook his head. "He called in sick." He looked toward the front door where the chief had exited. "Talking to those guys always makes me nervous."

"It's a common reaction," Helma told him. "We all have deeds in our past that we feel we could be apprehended for, even years later."

"*You*, too?" Curt asked.

"I'm sure I must," Helma assured him.

"I had to buy more red paint so I stopped by to be sure Dutch was among the living. He's not here. Do you think he's okay?"

Helma looked up from her completed Internet search. She hadn't found a single hit on Douglas Kipling Vanderhoof.

"He requested a sick day," she told Ruth, who leaned on the upper rim of her cubicle wall. Ruth's hair was pulled into a rough knot, highlighted with a blue smear of paint.

"Last night was too, too weird. Maybe I'll drop by his house, now that I know where it is." She glanced at Helma's computer screen. "Who's Douglas Kipling Vanderhoof?"

"That's Dutch's given name."

"You *think* it's his given name. After last night, I'm not so sure."

Ruth's voice carried across the workroom. Helma stood and saw only George at his desk in his cataloging corner. He looked up and grinned at Ruth. She threw him a kiss. Ms. Moon was in her office, on the telephone.

"Do me a favor, would you?" Ruth asked Helma in a quieter voice. "Look up Shiny Waters."

"What?"

"Not what, *who*. You know, the supposed artist I'm being forced to share my show with."

"With whom you're being forced to share your show," Helma corrected.

"Just tap the little keys, please," Ruth said crankily. Ruth didn't own a computer, and Helma doubted she'd ever used one. Whenever the subject of computers was raised, Ruth would say blithely, "I can't be bothered."

The responses to a search on Shiny Waters had nothing to do with art.

"I knew it," Ruth said. "An absolute unknown." She precariously rocked the makeshift walls of Helma's cubicle. "The owner's letting her cousin ride *my* coattails. Shiny Waters probably makes baked clay mobiles. Or collages."

Helma knew better than to discuss the mediums of other artists with Ruth. "Why don't you just ask the gallery owner?" she suggested.

"And admit I don't know?" Ruth asked.

Helma turned off her computer. "I'd like to check one last place for my missing files."

"Forget 'em. The files don't count anymore. People are dead, Helma."

"I'm aware of that, but I still intend to find them. They were my responsibility. Did you drive here?"

Ruth nodded. "I left my motor running."

"That's ill advised. It's an invitation to car thieves."

Ruth shrugged. "Then I'd collect the insurance and

buy a car that comes in my size. Can you just waltz out of here?"

"Ms. Moon expects me to be gone," Helma said.

"Ah yes. She expects you to dash out into the big bad world and fight for the library, justice, and her somewhat tarnished image."

Ruth had left the bright blue VW Beetle running, parked in the library's lot, behind Helma's Buick. "Where to?" she asked.

"I'll drive," Helma said. "You can park in my place while we're gone."

Ruth gave an exaggerated theatrical gasp. "Ooh. Me in the sacred library parking lot. Be still, oh beating heart."

When they'd switched cars, Ruth opened the passenger door. "How long will you have this plastic?" she asked, poking it with her finger and leaving a small indentation like the plastic bubbles of packing material. "And where are we going?"

"A few days. And we're going to Cedar Falls Park, by the Harringtons' house."

"We're going to spy on them."

Helma told her about Wayne saying a thief might have thrown out her files once he realized they were worthless.

"When did you talk to him?" Ruth asked. She turned on her seat, eyes eager as they always were in all matters related to men.

"This morning," Helma told her, slowing for a woman pushing a stroller. "He was in the library."

"Did he come to see you? To make nice?"

Helma frowned. "He spoke to me briefly, but he really came to talk to Dutch."

"Oh geez. You don't think he heard about last night, do you?"

"Dutch didn't do anything illegal last night," Helma reminded her.

"Maybe not, but something screwy's going on there. Dutch was not his own normal beloved broomstick up his ... self" Ruth's eyes narrowed in suspicion. "And exactly what is it you want *me* to do in Cedar Falls Park?"

"*We* can check the trash bins at the park. There's a flashlight beneath your seat and an umbrella in the back we can use to push the trash aside."

Ruth looked down at her coveralls, the same ones she'd worn the night before. Orange and red blots stained the legs. "I see. And I look like a likely candidate for digging in garbage, right?"

"You're taller," Helma said reasonably. "You can reach farther."

"Swell."

Helma parked beside the park's restroom, and Ruth felt beneath the seat for the flashlight. "What's this?" she asked, pulling out a paperback book in a Ziploc plastic bag. She held it up. "It's a dictionary, Helma. You carry a *dictionary* in your car?"

"It's my car dictionary," Helma told her. "We all frequently need to look up a word or phrase."

"Why didn't I think of that? Okay, I'm ready. You're locking your car? There's no window. Why are you locking it?"

"Sometimes the illusion of invulnerability is sufficient to forestall an assault," Helma explained.

"I'm all for that."

They walked through the park, checking each trash can—none of which had been emptied since before the snow. After Helma had pushed aside trash in the first metal container with the umbrella tip, Ruth said, "What the heck," and leaned into the next can and then the next, shoving aside debris.

Two women bundled for a brisk walk paused, and one of them said, "That is so pathetic," to which Ruth responded from her garbage can, "But don't worry, if you keep exercising, you can lose most of it."

A man with a black plastic garbage bag slung over his shoulder stopped in front of Helma, "This is *my* trash can, and I'll take that." He pointed to the aluminum can in her hand, which she'd actually picked up from the park grounds and had intended to put *in* the trash.

"It's yours," she said, giving it to him and noting his damp jacket. "It would be healthier if you spent the night at the mission instead of in the park."

"I did that already, remember?" he asked as he dropped the can into his black bag, where it clattered against what sounded like other cans.

Helma peered into his face and recognized the homeless man who'd taken refuge in the library the morning Franklin died.

"Hey," Ruth said. "It's our Homeless Citizen. You living at the mission?"

"I eat there," he said warily, taking a step back. He

set his plastic bag on the ground and began digging in his pocket. "I know what you're looking for."

"You do?" Ruth asked. "You took it?"

He dug into his pocket. "Here," he said, and held out a yellow pencil to Helma.

"No thank you," she told him.

"You've got to. It's yours."

Helma took it with two gloved fingers. On the side was printed, BELLEHAVEN PUBLIC LIBRARY.

"I fix what I mess up," he said.

"Spread your message," Ruth told him. "Hey, did you see anybody break the window on a car parked over there?" She pointed toward the Harrington house.

"That wasn't one of mine," he said, picking up his bag. "Not mine."

"Whose was it?" Helma asked.

"Don't know, don't know, don't know," he sing-songed. "Gotta go, don't know, no show," and he headed off toward the denser trees.

"Do you think he really knows who broke into your car?" Ruth asked, watching him duck behind a cedar tree as if he were under pursuit.

Helma shook her head. "I don't. There's one more place to look. I'll take the women's restroom and then I'll stand outside the men's while you look inside."

"Chicken," Ruth said, but she went inside the men's restroom while Helma stood guard, turning away one man walking his dog. Finally, the restroom door opened and Ruth appeared, chatting amiably with a young red-faced man. "Sorry, Helm," she said. "Nothing there."

The Harrington house was visible from her car. Helma stood beside the driver's door, gazing at it. Her car had been parked outside Rosy's entrance, and they'd sat in Rosy's living room, where no windows looked out toward the cars.

"That's where the file is," Ruth said, waving a hand toward the house. "Not out here. One of them has it."

"If they do, they committed a crime to get it."

"And your point is?" Ruth asked. "Breaking your window and stealing a file is nothing compared to blowing up a couple of people."

"But not their own brother. I can't believe that." Helma unlocked her car door. "Franklin was so thorough doing research for his book, I expect that he kept his own records about the library site negotiations, too. Notes, maybe even the rough draft of a contract. They're probably in his house."

"Well, if one of the Harringtons is responsible for his death, you can bet all trace of Franklin's notes is long gone, too."

Chapter 21

Aunt Em Leads the Way

"So you want to burgle Franklin's house and thumb through his files?" Ruth asked. "Is that what you're saying?" She raised her voice above the flapping window plastic. "Hard to pull off that one without being seen."

"I don't participate in illegal activity."

"Right. Maybe you could become Frances's new best friend, hang out and paint each other's toenails. Where are we going, anyway? Drop me off so I can get back to painting."

"Aunt Em wanted to see me." Helma slowed her car. "I'll take you home."

"That old dolly. Okay, on second thought, count me in. I want to be her when I get old—minus the accent, natch. Have you noticed how the older she gets, the more Lithuanian she gets?"

Helma nodded. "There's a theory that as we

age we become more condensed, more exactly what we are."

"Withering down to our cores," Ruth said. She put her hand flat against the plastic window. "This plastic is driving me crazy. We should have taken my car."

"I prefer to drive rather than ride."

"Yeah, with me, all your driving would have to be from the backseat," and she laughed at her own questionable humor.

Three young men were clearing away the last of the snow in front of the Silver Gables, watched by four female residents who sat on sofas in the lobby.

"The tall one reminds me of my grandson," one of the women was saying as Ruth and Helma entered.

"Not *me*," said another woman, licking her lips.

Helma's mother, Lillian, opened the door of the apartment she shared with Aunt Em. She'd recently decided to let her dyed blond hair "go natural," which Helma had expected to mean fade to gray. But instead, her mother had taken a thirty-year-old color photo of herself to her stylist and now sported hair color similar to old photos of Lucille Ball, multiple shades brighter and redder than Helma remembered Lillian's original hair. "Helma dear," she said, squeezing Helma's arm. "Ruth," a little cooler. "What are you doing here?"

"Aunt Em wanted to talk to me."

Lillian frowned. "Now what's she up to? You know how she gets those crazy ideas. Always thinking she knows more than everybody else. 'Inside information.' Hah. And you're crazy if you listen to her."

"What are *you* up to, Mother?" Helma asked, motioning to the jumbled papers and maps on the dining room table, unwittingly opening the floodgates to her mother's current pique with Aunt Em. After lifelong warfare, their current peaceable kingdom had only been in existence for three years.

"Oh, that. We're planning our trip back to Michigan in May. Emily *knows* we always go to the Waters County graves first because I like to get flowers from the Bell girls' nursery. You remember them, don't you? The youngest, Stella, had the cutest lisp. But no, *this* year Em wants to buy flowers in Grand Rapids when we get off the plane, *then* head north. I told her the flowers will be withered to sticks by the time we get there, but you know Em."

Through Helma's childhood it had been an annual event: "visiting the graves" before Memorial Day. Delivering earthy smelling geraniums, scraping lichen off tombstones, clipping grass that grew too close. After she left Michigan, "visiting the graves" became a compulsory tourist event whenever she returned. Since her mother and Aunt Em had moved to Bellehaven, it was the destination of each trip "home," no matter what time of year. The more the family died, the farther afield Aunt Em and Lillian had to roam to cover them all.

"Where *is* Aunt Em?" Helma asked. Behind her mother, the television was tuned to a talk show where a woman shook her first at a bald man. The sound was turned off.

"She's in the Fitness Room."

"Exercising?" Helma asked in surprise. Aunt Em was tottery and shaky and unable to stand more than a few minutes. She liked to say she was "pulling it all inside" to save her brain, which Helma supposed was a bit like Ruth's statement of "withering down to our cores."

"Hah. That's a good one. No, she goes down during the men's weight-lifting class, not that any of them lift that much, but she just *has* to watch. I wouldn't do that; it makes a woman look too easy. It's cheap."

"Maybe she just likes the view," Ruth said.

"You sound like her," Lillian huffed.

"I'll go find her," Helma said. "Do you want to wait here?" she asked Ruth.

"Oh dear," Lillian said hurriedly. "It'll be much more interesting to go with Helma."

"That's just what I was thinking," Ruth said sweetly.

The sounds of clanging metal and men's voices wafted from the door of the Fitness Room on the building's second floor. Helma entered first. Old rock music with too much bass sounded from speakers hanging in all four corners of the room.

"Not bad," Ruth commented, gazing around at fifteen to twenty men working on various shiny metal machines. Helma thought she recognized a machine similar to one that filled the living room of her next door neighbor, TNT.

"Yes," she agreed. "It's quite a nice facility."

Ruth gave a short laugh, then pointed to the sidelines where Aunt Em, in a deep purple pants suit, sat on a plastic chair, resting her arthritic hands on her cane, a smile on her face as she watched the men. She was alone.

"Yoo hoo, Wilhelmina, Ruthie," she called, lifting her cane and waving it at them.

"Do you have a favorite?" Ruth asked Aunt Em after they'd greeted her, nodding toward the exercising men.

"I'm too old for favorites." Aunt Em's sagging eyes sparkled. "But that one is looking better every time." She raised a hand toward a pewter-haired man on a rowing machine, the youngest man in the room. Ruth nodded and shook her hand as if it were hot.

"You wanted me to meet someone," Helma reminded her.

Aunt Em looked puzzled.

"A woman," Helma prompted.

Aunt Em nodded. "That's right. Her."

"Who-her?" Ruth asked.

Aunt Em made hushing motions and said in a whisper nearly as loud, "Cornelia. The secret lover. Del's."

"Del *Harrington*?" Ruth asked.

Again the hushing motions. "That's right. For years and years. Marie Armitage said so and she's lived in Bellehaven since she was born so she knows all the juicy stories. She said it was a scandal long ago." Aunt Em shrugged and looked sorrowful. "But scandals aren't so scandalous now. We'll go meet her." She leaned toward Helma and whispered, "And him *married* the whole time."

"I really don't have anything to say to her, Aunt Em," Helma said.

"Think, think. You'll find the words," Aunt Em said as they helped her up from the chair. A faint odor of musky perfume like Ruth wore wafted from Aunt Em's clothes. "For your investigation."

"Just because two men have died, that doesn't mean I'm investigating," Helma told her.

Aunt Em paused and patted her arm. "Of course you are. Or your chief is. You should know the … players."

Ruth winked at Helma over Aunt Em's head as she asked, "Where to, Agatha Christie?"

"What is the time?" Aunt Em asked. She held up her wrist to them, which was circled by a watch, but Aunt Em no longer saw well enough to read the numbers.

"Twelve-seventeen," Helma told her.

"She's in the café." She pronounced the word as "kaffee." Her voice dropped. "Holding a court, to be seen."

The bottom floor of the Silver Gables held shops, including a florist, a hair salon, and a small café, which was designed with walls of blond wood and operated by a pink-cheeked crew of young women. Most of the tables were filled with diners from the apartment building.

"That's her," Aunt Em said. "The one with the blue scarf and red hair." Then she said in a lower voice, "Your mother's red is too brassy."

The woman sat alone at a table along the wall. She was gazing down at her plate and holding a knife and fork. Helma's first impression was one of loneliness: a small and thin woman with bowed shoulders. Her red hair was perfectly coiffed and tinted.

And then she raised her head and was transformed.

Helma now beheld a woman who probably never betrayed any emotion except pleasant, an elegant woman who'd spent a lifetime soothing, smoothing, and organizing, a woman likely admired and respected, even sought out, but not known intimately as close friends and lovers knew each other.

She smiled at the three approaching women and set her fork and knife on the rim of her plate, beside a chicken breast she'd cut into pieces the size of postage stamps.

"Cornelia, this is my niece, Wilhelmina. She's investigating the bomb." Aunt Em made explosion motions with her hands, like Jay had. "I told her how you knew the Harringtons."

Behind Helma, Ruth muttered, "I couldn't have said it better myself."

"So meet now," Aunt Em continued, mixing up her words in her excitement. "And this is Ruth. I'm showing you Cornelia Seattle."

"Actually, it's Settle," Cornelia said, nodding to Ruth and Helma, then asking Helma, "Are you with the police force?"

"I'm a librarian."

"But she has a master's degree," Ruth added helpfully.

"I represent the library in the negotiations with the Harrington family regarding the new library site."

A tremor of ice passed through Cornelia's eyes. She inclined her head. "And you would like me to ...?" she asked, her voice gracious, but Helma felt like a cold wind had suddenly blown through the café.

'I'm sorry," Helma told her. "I'm not implying anything at all. There's nothing I wish from you."

Cornelia's lips pressed together and she gazed coolly at them, her face devoid of all emotion. Helma, Ruth, and Aunt Em stood silently, awkwardly.

"It's me," Aunt Em broke in. "I'm a nosy old woman and you each know Harringtons so I … I made you meet."

Cornelia picked up her knife and fork again. "It was a pleasure," she said, and began cutting her postage stamp chicken into even tinier pieces.

She had terminated the interview, and there was nothing for them to do but retreat in a timely and orderly fashion. Which they did, Ruth and Helma on either side of Aunt Em.

When they reached the café entrance, Aunt Em said, "I didn't do so well."

"You're right," Ruth cheerfully agreed. "She'll run a mile next time she sees you."

"You didn't do any harm," Helma said, at the same time wondering if Cornelia would report the awkward meeting to Del.

"No. Ruthie said it right," Aunt Em said sadly, giving a deep sigh. "I think all crooked sometimes."

"It'll be okay," Ruth reassured her. "I do that kind of stuff all the time."

"If Cornelia Coldfish tells Del we bushwhacked her during her lunch like that, you may as well kiss off your new library," Ruth said as they drove away, a plate of oatmeal cookies pressed on them by Aunt Em on the backseat. "Or ever speak to another Harrington as long as they all shall live."

Helma drove thoughtfully. She should have known Aunt Em would take the direct route, and stopped her before they'd ever reached the café.

"Why would Cornelia and Del keep a liaison a secret?" she asked. "Assuming Aunt Em's correct, of course. Del's a widower."

"Yeah, but only a recent widower," Ruth said. "Mrs. Del died a year or two ago. Maybe they kept it hush-hush in concession to the grand old family name? Years ago—and I'm aware it could have been a tactic to soften me up—but Del implied in a cozy moment that he was a misunderstood husband." She peered over at Helma. "Trite tale, isn't it?"

"Perhaps," Helma conceded. "I haven't wanted to believe the theft of my files and Franklin's death were connected."

Ruth stretched, turning her hands inside out. "Isn't that what I've been saying all along? Franklin and Randall get blown up, your files that prove Franklin wanted to give land to the library disappear, and voilà, the site's open for development. Who gains, I ask you—only Harringtons."

"That points to a Harrington committing both crimes," Helma said.

"Exactly. The question is, which one?"

Helma shook her head. "It's too obvious."

"Who said murder had to be tough to figure out? Sometimes the obvious answer is the right answer."

"Then why Randall Rice?"

"Because he was there?"

"*Why* was Randall there?"

Ruth flicked the plastic window. "Hell, I don't know. Maybe he saw Franklin and stopped for a nice chitchat about the nasty weather, is it ever going to clear up, my bones ache, et cetera and so on, and zap, the Big Bang."

"I need to talk to someone who knew Randall."

"He didn't exactly hang out with people *I* know," Ruth said. "And he wasn't married. One of our loyal city government employees must know him. Somebody who works ... worked, for him." Ruth tapped the dashboard. "I know. Drop me off by city hall."

"Who, Ruth?"

"Never mind. I'm just going to do a little subtle checking. Don't worry about a thing."

"What about your painting?" Helma asked in a last attempt to dissuade her. "You said you had to get back to painting. Your show ..."

"It's all schlock," Ruth said, slumping in her seat, her voice dark. "Why else would I be stuck in a show with some joker nobody's ever heard of? Who the hell ever convinced me I could paint, anyway? All that stuff I do is crap, pure and simple crap, with a capital C."

When Helma wisely didn't respond, Ruth shrugged and said, "I know, I know, I'm my own worst critic."

"That's probably best," Helma told her.

Chapter 22

Hidden in the Stacks

In her cubicle, Helma phoned Frances Harrington. She moistened her lips with a single-use disposable lip balm and dropped the packaging in her trash as the phone rang. She didn't know where Frances lived but she imagined her in a condo—with bamboo floors, slate counters, and pale rose walls. And definitely an uninterrupted view of the bay.

There was no answer, only a chirpy answering machine message, and Helma hung up without leaving a message.

She opened the ceramic box on her desk, chose a plain yellow M&M, and placed it on the center of her tongue.

Pulling herself closer to her desk, she did what she should have done earlier: she checked the online catalog for Franklin's self-published histories of Bellehaven. The Bellehaven Public Library had what Ms. Moon called an "evolving collection development policy" regarding self-published books. They weren't as easily identifiable as they once were, and their quality ran the gamut of literary aspirations. Many of the local histories were self-published but had been included because little other information existed.

The library owned two books by Franklin Harrington: one covering the history of the scenic highway that edged the bay, and the other the draining of a north county lake in the 1920s to create farmland.

When Helma examined the books, she wasn't surprised that they contained little mention of the Harringtons, despite the family having been prominent from Bellehaven's inception. Franklin had been jealously saving all the Harrington history for his newest book. "All Harrington all the time," he'd once said jokingly.

As Helma stood in the 979.7s of the History section perusing Franklin's books, she heard a squeak, very like a cartoon "Eek!" She didn't watch cartoons, but had occasionally been trapped in their presence.

She turned toward the sound. Glory was backing into the C-F aisle of the Biography section, her lips pursed and her eyes wide on Helma.

This was absurd. Seeing Helma looking at her, Glory stopped and raised her hands in front of her in a "surrender" attitude, palms up.

Helma avoided pursuing people unnecessarily, so she waited. Glory came forward as if drawn by a string, her cheeks flushed.

"I was only doing my duty," she said, grimacing. "Just like you do."

Helma had no idea what she was talking about. "I beg your pardon?"

"I thought if—" Glory stopped. Her eyes narrowed as she peered intently at Helma. Her shoulders relaxed and her flushed cheeks faded away.

"Oh," she said breathlessly. "Oh. The heat. Isn't it great to have heat again? I love it. Bye."

"Gloria," Helma said in a quiet voice that stopped her in her tracks.

"What?"

"Have you spoken to the police?"

"About what?" Glory asked in melodious tones, actually batting her eyes.

Helma took a step toward her, and Glory backed up two steps, her back against the shelf end. CASTRO TO FERBER, the sign above her head read. "Did you use Dutch as an *excuse* so you could talk to the chief of police?"

Glory straightened herself to her full but minimal height. "I don't have the slightest idea what you're talking about," she said, actually raising her nose into the air.

"I believe you do."

"Do not. Besides, Dutch *wasn't* here when the bomb went off. *I'm* not the person who's hiding *that* fact." And Glory turned and walked through the stacks, her stride punctuated with angry stomps.

Helma reshelved Franklin's books and returned to the workroom, seeing Ms. Moon standing beside her cubicle too late to avoid her.

"Helma," Ms. Moon said. "Do you have any news to report about the site?"

"The Harringtons have not informed me of any decision regarding the library site," Helma told her. "We did discuss meeting again after Franklin's funeral."

"That long?" Ms. Moon said, clearly disappointed. "Oh, I nearly forgot. Feel free to take the rest of the day off in compensation for tomorrow."

"I'm not scheduled to work tomorrow," Helma told her. "I believe Harley's working this Saturday."

Ms. Moon smiled. "I didn't mean working in the library. I meant Franklin's funeral. It's at one o'clock."

"I wasn't planning to attend."

Ms. Moon pulled another sad face. "As the library representative in this matter, naturally you'll be attending. I would, too, but I've had reservations for a play in Seattle for *months*. I nearly canceled when the snowstorm hit, but you know how they always say it's safest to fly right after a plane crash."

"Yes?" Helma asked, struggling to see the analogy.

"Nature's the same. Once the storm ended, what were the chances of another one?"

"I doubt Nature is as dependable as airplane inspection crews."

"It's all about balance," Ms. Moon went on. "Yin and yang, day and night, tit for tat. I'm routing a sympathy card around the library for you to take to the funeral, and I've already ordered flowers."

"From which budget?" Helma, who was responsible for the nonfiction budget, asked.

"Now don't you worry about *that*. Your plate is full already. Oh," Ms. Moon added, "I hope you won't invite your artist friend to accompany you to the funeral."

"Ruth Winthrop?" Helma asked. "I hadn't even considered it."

"Good," Ms. Moon said cheerily.

Frances Harrington didn't answer the second time Helma dialed her number, so she phoned Ruth.

"What?" Ruth answered.

"Can you take two hours from your painting to attend Franklin Harrington's funeral with me tomorrow?"

"Sure. It's a date. What time?"

"It's at one o'clock."

"This oughta be good," Ruth said.

"I thought you'd feel that way."

"Oh. Wait. Do you want to hear what I learned about Randall?"

"As long as it can be substantiated."

"There isn't much, anyway. Nose to the grindstone. He loved to save a penny for our little piece of Belleheaven. Liked his history best if he got the credit for it. You know: set up a memorial for Fido who rescued some sailor a hundred years ago, a marker where *he* thinks the first whorehouse stood. Never married, never attends office parties. As big a jerk as I always believed he was."

"Who were your sources?" Helma asked.

"Ah, ah, ah," Ruth said in a reproachful voice. "Just call them 'anonymous.'"

The third time Helma telephoned Frances Harrington, she answered.

"This is Miss Helma Zukas."

"Who?" Music played in the background. Helma was not a musical woman, except in a cursory way through answering reference questions, but the music behind Frances was the kind that reminded her of the time a rubber band got caught in her vacuum cleaner.

"From the Bellehaven Public Library. We spoke yesterday." She didn't mention their encounter at Joker's the night before.

"Oh. The librarian."

"Yes. As your father's heir, would you be interested in bequeathing his new historical account to the library?"

"Do you mean Daddy's new book?"

"Yes. I know he was nearly finished with it."

"Daddy was always working on his histories. I wouldn't know which one you're talking about."

Exactly as Helma had hoped. "I understand. He had many interests. I helped him often with his research. Perhaps his brothers would recognize it."

"I doubt it."

"If it would help you, I'd be glad to look at his manuscripts and choose the most recent version. Someone here could finish any details he left uncompleted, and we could add it to the library's collection."

"I'm not hauling all that stuff to the library."

"Then what if I were to quickly peruse his work and tell you which was the correct version?"

Frances hesitated. "Is this a trick?"

"We would be honored to have his book in the library," Helma told her honestly.

"Would there be any money for it?"

"Perhaps if we indexed the book, if your father hadn't, you could then look for a publisher to purchase it. Money would be involved, yes." She closed her eyes, thinking the only way money would be involved would be if Frances *paid* someone to publish it.

"Okay. I guess, but we'd have to meet at Daddy's and I don't feel right about it, not yet."

"Another member of your family could join us," Helma offered.

Frances sighed. "Okay, let's get it over with. I'll meet you at Daddy's door in twenty minutes."

"Which is your father's door?"

"On the Adams Street side. The doors aren't visible to each other. You know how they were."

"I'll be there. Thank you." Helma hung up, shocked by how easy that had been. Ms. Moon had called Frances a "mental lightweight." But from what Helma had observed, Frances was also far too trusting.

Franklin's entrance to the Harrington house was the shabbiest of the three brothers. Cracked steps, a faded oak door. As Helma raised the iron knocker cast in the shape of a woman's fist, she realized the windows of the door were leaded, the knocker original. Franklin hadn't refurbished or modernized, which was in accordance with his interest in history.

Frances opened the door. She wore a blue ski sweater

and wool pants. Light shadows beneath her eyes were the only evidence of her evening at Joker's. She gazed at Helma without expression.

"Thank you for letting the library have your father's papers," Helma finally said.

"Well, you haven't found them yet," Frances countered

The interior of Franklin's quarters was professorial. Bookcases lined the walls. A hint of pipe smoke mixed with Frances's perfume. Old black and white photos of Bellehaven hung on the walls: logging scenes, miners standing before a black hole in the earth, and graceful sailing ships docked at wharves along a section of Washington Bay that was now lined with parks.

Frances led Helma to her father's study, where a huge oak desk dominated the room. An electric typewriter sat on a low long table to the side of the desk.

"Your father didn't use a computer?" Helma asked.

"Not Daddy. You're lucky he didn't write it all out in longhand." She pointed to a neat stack of papers and folders. "But there's most of it. He was very organized."

"May I look through his papers?"

Frances said, "That's why you're here, isn't it?" then added in a tone that made her statement, if not true, at least a warning, "Jay will be here in a few minutes."

Helma began sorting through the folders, conscious of Frances's eyes on her. Her palms were damp. All that really registered about the first few sets of papers was that they had nothing to do with the library or the library site.

She worked deliberately and slowly, viewing each page, hoping her estimation of Frances's attention span was correct.

It was. After five minutes Frances asked, "How long will this take?"

"I hope not too long, but I do want to proceed carefully." Helma returned to lifting page after page. Printouts of microfilmed newspaper articles and photocopies of old histories, covering a multitude of local subjects: flora and fauna, coal mining, weather and farming, logging, the rise and fall of the county's small towns.

"About last night," Frances said hesitantly. "At Joker's ... "

"You asked me if I'd help discover who killed your father," Helma reminded her.

Frances nodded and flicked her father's electric typewriter on and off. The machine lurched and spun its print ball in a most irritating manner. "But I didn't mean that, not really."

"You also said the perpetrator wasn't a Harrington."

"It wasn't. They love each other."

"You claimed that last night, too." Helma handed Frances a stack of papers she'd already studied, just to remove Frances's hands from the typewriter. "Did you grow up in this house?"

"My grandmother lived in this portion of the house," Frances said, idly fanning the pages. "She died when I was eight, and the very *next* year, when I was nine, my mother died. That's when Daddy and I moved in.

Uncle Del and Uncle Rosy were already here. The three of them raised me." Then she said softly, rolling the papers into a tube, "I owe everything to them. It was like having three fathers."

"What about Jay?" Helma asked. "Did he grow up here, too?"

"Partially. Uncle Del had another house, too. On the water. Aunt Dorothy preferred that house."

Helma began sorting through another stack of Franklin's papers that centered on Bellehaven's architecture: Gothic, "painted ladies," craftsman. "Your aunt died?"

"A couple of years ago." Frances looked away.

There was no easy way to ask about Cornelia, so Helma didn't.

"Do you mind if I go in the other room?" Frances asked.

"Of course not," Helma told her, holding a sheaf of paper in her hands. "I'll be as fast as I can."

As soon as Frances left the room, Helma abandoned the pile of history and searched the papers on Franklin's desk.

Nothing but more history. Washington State, Bellehaven, ships and shipping. A low file cabinet stood next to the desk and Helma opened it, holding in the catch and coughing to cover any sound.

Helma Zukas was not a thief. Frances *had* given her permission to peruse her father's papers. Helma wouldn't remove a single paper without permission, not even if she discovered a note written in Franklin's own hand giving the library site to the city. She would take action, yes, but she would not ... steal. Definitely not.

More history. The second drawer held financial records that Helma carefully avoided scrutinizing, then a gap and more financial records. She slipped her hand in the gap, as if files had been removed.

She flipped the pages of Franklin's desk calendar. The sound of a glass clinking came from the living room.

There were several dates on the calendar marked with Ms. Moon's name, or "library," but nothing concrete.

"Find what you're looking for?"

Long ago, subjected to the practical jokes and severe teasing of her cousin Ricky, Helma had discovered it was in her best interests to never portray shock when she was surprised, and now she raised her head and smiled. "Hello, Roosevelt. Frances is allowing the library to add her father's Harrington history to the local history collection."

"And you're looking for it in his calendar?"

"No, I'm not," she said. Never complain or explain, her father had always advised.

"Well," Rosy said. "If you'd asked me about it, I could have given my copy to you."

"I hadn't realized there *were* copies."

"They were what he called his last drafts," Rosy said as he spun a small globe on Franklin's desk with his index finger. "Before he sent them off to be printed. He gave one to each of us Harringtons, that's all I know."

"Then Frances has a copy, too?"

"Yes, but I doubt she ever cracked the cover. Probably didn't even know what it was." He nodded to the bookshelf behind Helma. "That's Franklin's copy, in the green three-ring binder. Take it."

Helma removed the plastic binder from the shelf and opened to the first page: *A History of the Bellehaven Harringtons.* Ten or twelve loose sheets slipped from the binder. She picked them up, evened their edges, and tucked them into the binder's inside pocket.

"It appears complete to me," she said, turning the pages. "There's already an index."

"No surprise," Rosy told her, looking down at the typed sheets. "But he said he had a few last minute details to check. He was the fussiest of the renowned Harrington triplets."

"He was meticulous," she said, seeing Franklin wrestling with and trying to verify hundred-year-old dates. "I didn't hear you come in."

Rosy laughed. "There may not be a door between mine and Del's quarters, but there are doors from Franklin's to both of ours. Big Brother in the literal sense, you see." And he laughed again, but without much mirth.

Helma held Franklin's history to her, thinking that if one of the Harringtons had removed her library files from her car, and Franklin's library files from his file cabinet, then certainly no others existed. Ms. Moon's information was lost.

Chapter 23

Keeping Company

"Wear this," Ruth said, holding up a red sweater. "Only don't button it beyond the third button. Don't you have an eye-zinging necklace that can strategically dangle?"

"Ruth, I'm wearing what I have on. I feel more comfortable in my own clothes." Not only that, but Helma had seen the shine of cat hair on the sweater's sleeve. She didn't touch cats and she certainly didn't *wear* them.

Ruth dropped the red sweater in a heap on Helma's sofa. "Suit yourself. I was just trying to help move things forward. You two are the proverbial molasses couple."

"I need to feel more certain about him again," Helma told her.

"Any woman who waits for *that* might as well embrace her single bed for all eternity," Ruth said.

"So what does he think of Cowboy Boyd? Like maybe you're playing games with *him*?"

"Boyd is just a friend," Helma said.

Ruth slapped her forehead and dropped into the rocker. "Those are the deadliest words on earth, how many times have I told you? 'Don't worry, dear. We're just friends.' Geesh."

"Perhaps to other people, but in this case, it's the truth: Boyd *is* my friend."

Boy Cat Zukas eyed the red sweater as if it were some kind of prey, then tentatively and slowly set one paw outside his basket. Helma picked up the sweater, folded it into thirds, and handed it to Ruth. "He'll be here in six minutes."

"I guess that's my cue." Ruth hefted the folded sweater. "I wish I could do this. It hasn't looked this good since I bought it. "

"All it takes is attention to detail," Helma said. She'd seen Ruth's closet: whites hanging among blacks; unbuttoned shirts sliding off hangers, shoes in a jumble; sweaters mixed with socks and underwear.

"That right? Not different genes? Seeya tomorrow for the funeral. Sure you don't want me to drive?"

"I'm sure."

Wayne and Helma had dinner at Shaker's, a moderately priced but dependably well-maintained restaurant near the bay. After they were seated by a hostess who *didn't* tell them their server's name, Wayne said, "I understand you had an automobile mishap yesterday afternoon."

"How did you know that?" Helma asked.

"Talked to the mechanic this morning. He told me."

"Does he share all his business with the police?" Helma asked, remembering the tow truck driver who'd been dispatched from Hunky's Auto Repair shop where her window would be replaced.

"I usually follow up on my cases," he said. "It came up."

He regarded her thoughtfully until the atmosphere grew uncomfortable and Helma asked, "And there's no further information about the broken window on my car?"

"None," he said, and opened his menu. "Are you attending Franklin's funeral tomorrow?"

"Ms. Moon has asked me to," she said, and he nodded. Piano music flowed over from the bar area of Shaker's. Helma recognized "Strangers in the Night."

After they ordered, he leaned back and asked, "Would you mind if we took a few minutes to discuss police business?"

"Police business is always of interest to me." Helma folded her hands in front of her plate. "Do you wish to discuss Franklin and Randall's deaths, my broken window, my missing files, the explosion, or any rumors you may have been told?"

He gazed at her solemnly for a moment, and she watched as his eyes shifted and warmed. It was perplexing how expressive they could be. Helma swallowed but couldn't look away from Wayne's gaze, not even when he laughed and reached across the table to cover her folded hands with one of his own big warm hands.

"Not very subtle, am I?" he said, grinning. "At least not to you. Del Harrington stopped by to see me today." He paused as if waiting for her to speak, and when she didn't, he continued, and she could tell he was trying to keep the policeman's tone from edging his voice. "He said you came to the Harrington house this afternoon under pretense, that you convinced Frances to let you in so you could search her father's papers."

"All I removed was Franklin's history, which he'd been working on for years, and I did that with both Frances and Roosevelt Harrington's permission. In fact, Rosy found it and gave it to me. It'll be a welcome addition to our collection."

"But you didn't find Franklin's files about the library site, did you?" He leaned forward, his Baltic blue eyes penetrating into hers. She was helpless.

"No," she admitted. "They'd been removed from his file cabinet."

He pushed back his graying hair, revealing his widow's peak. "You really *did* go through his papers?"

Helma realized her mistake. Rosy *hadn't* seen her with her hands in Franklin's file cabinets, and surprisingly, Wayne had guessed that was what she'd done. "If the files had been there, I wouldn't have removed them, I would have notified the police at once."

"Del wonders if ... " He paused as the waiter set a basket of rolls on the table. Helma touched the cloth napkin over them to be sure they were warm. They were.

Then he said what she was expecting. "Del wonders if an agreement ever existed."

"I do believe it was a verbal agreement," Helma told him. "And the notes in the files would prove that. Although now, a library on that site ... "

Wayne nodded and shifted in his chair. "But still, you'd like to prove Franklin's intent, right?"

"If my car hadn't been broken into and my files stolen, it might not feel so important. And Franklin's death. I ..." She paused to square her fork on her place setting.

"Helma," Wayne said, waiting until she looked up before he continued. "I talked to George in the library. He told me that the two of you debated whether to follow Franklin that morning."

Helma nodded. "I discouraged George. I thought Franklin would be insulted, that he'd believe we were checking up on him."

"He probably would have. Whatever happened out there, it didn't have anything to do with you. You're not responsible." Wayne lightly touched her hand again. "You don't *owe* Franklin."

"Like every responsible citizen in Bellehaven, I'd like to see Franklin's homicide solved, that's all. And," she added, "to discover who took the files."

"The Harringtons are a powerful family."

"They also may have committed one or more crimes. You're not saying powerful families are immune from acting as, or being prosecuted as, criminals?"

"That's not at all what I'm saying, but calling them criminals is a rash statement for *you* to make." He looked up as the hostess led an elderly couple past them to a window table.

Helma dropped her voice. "Certainly you've considered who gains the most from those files going missing."

"Such an agreement might not stand in a court, anyway," he said. "All I'm saying is that the Harringtons are suspicious of you and your motives. Be careful."

Their dinners were served. Wayne's consisted of a complicated seafood pasta mixture decorated with unnaturally curled strips of red and green peppers. Helma's plate held a fillet of grilled salmon without seasoning, and a small salad with vinegar and oil on the side. Her tastes were for the discrete and definable, not food that had been mixed into oblivion.

Wayne took a sip of his red wine and asked, "How well do you know your circulation manager?"

"Dutch?" Helma asked.

"Douglas Kipling Vanderhoof, called Dutch," the chief said. "Yes."

"I don't know him well personally, but in my estimation he is an excellent library employee. Courteous, thorough, professional."

"Does he carry a cell phone?"

"I've never seen him with one."

"Did you see Dutch just prior to the explosion on Wednesday?" he asked as he twirled pasta expertly against his spoon.

Helma set her fork beside her plate. "A curious question," she said. "Did someone tell you Dutch *wasn't* in the library just prior to the explosion? Someone you could trust to always be truthful?"

She was rewarded by his linguini slipping off the bowl of his spoon. "Just covering all the bases, that's all," he said, and didn't meet her eyes.

"But since you've raised the subject," Helma told him as he repositioned his pasta, "I'd like to discuss cell phones and explosives. Rhetorically, of course."

"Rhetorically?" he asked, abandoning his linguini and setting his silverware on the edge of his plate.

She nodded. "I've done a little research at the library, and it's my understanding that should an explosive be detonated by a cell phone, a component of the cell phone is wired to the explosive and then triggered by dialing the number of that cell phone. Isn't that correct?"

"That's a viable method, yes," he agreed.

"That cell phone number could be called from *any* telephone," she said. "Anyone dialing that number would detonate the explosive, even a misdialed number."

"Theoretically," he agreed again.

Helma felt his policeman's eyes examining her, and she gazed steadily back at him. "I also understand that if the cell phone detonator is recovered, its designated number and all the phone calls made to it can also be recovered."

"If the SIM card, as it's called, hasn't been obliterated," he told her, and she couldn't discern from his calm steady gaze whether he was still speaking rhetorically or not.

So she asked. "Was it?"

Chief of Police Wayne Gallant actually reared his head back and grinned at her. A hot prickle sizzled at the back of Helma's neck. He raised his hand. "Don't be offended. I was admiring the extent of your research skills, not to mention ... well, your ability to expand on a very limited amount of information."

"It's nothing any well-trained and observant librarian can't do," she said, thinking he was trying to distract her, even if he *was* correct. "In that case," she continued, "why are you asking questions about Dutch? Or his cell phone?"

His grin didn't fade; it froze. "Helma," he finally said, his voice sounding almost regretful. "You know I can't answer that."

But still there was more he *could* have said. Rhetorically, of course.

Helma excused herself to use the restroom, which she had to walk through the restaurant's bar to reach.

But in accordance with the rest of Shaker's, the bar was a well-mannered establishment. A television quietly played a golf match from somewhere warm, drinkers sat at tables speaking in low voices. It wasn't at all unpleasant.

As she passed through the bar on her return, her mind on Wayne's questions about Dutch, someone said, "It's the librarian."

In the low light it took her a few seconds to recognize Jimmy Dodd, the driver of the casino bus. He sat at the bar alone, a glass in front of him filled with what looked like milk.

"I am a librarian," Helma agreed. "Was your drive to the casino successful?"

"You bet. We pulled in at twenty minutes before five." He laughed. "I had a busload of white-faced women, though. Those roads were about as nasty as I've ever seen them."

"The police advised you against driving."

"Yeah, well, remember Bonita Wu? If I'd been a horse, she'd have whipped me bloody to get to the casino come hell or high water."

Helma nodded, picturing the ancient iron-willed woman.

"Can I ask you something?" Jimmy asked.

"You may," Helma said. The bartender, a young woman, looked at her inquiringly, and Helma shook her head.

"You know the old guy who blew up?" Jimmy asked.

"Mr. Harrington? Yes."

"Bonita had a bug up her ... a bee in her bonnet about him. Do you think they knew each other?"

"What did she say?" She moved closer to Jimmy, dropping her voice. Through the arch into the dining room she could see Wayne Gallant, his head turned her way. He might have been looking at her—or at the golf game playing out on the television above her head.

Jimmy shrugged. "She asked me if I knew what he did, where he grew up, stuff like that. Now, I don't know the woman; it just seemed a little out of character for her."

"Did they speak in the library?" Helma asked, trying

to remember. There'd been so much going on, with the snow and the stranded passengers.

Jimmy nodded. "Yeah, but I didn't hear what they said. It didn't look like anything but nice-weather talk."

"Where did you pick up Bonita in Vancouver?" Helma asked. Wayne was definitely leaning forward, watching her and Jimmy.

"Chinatown. We have a pickup site near the Sun Yat-sen Garden." He raised his glass of white liquid toward her. "Milk," he affirmed. "Haven't touched a drop in nine years. But about Bonita. She shouldn't be hard to find, say if somebody wanted to, even in a town that big."

When Helma returned to the table, Wayne said, "You saw somebody you knew?"

"His name is Jimmy Dodd. He drove the casino bus of women that sheltered in the library during the storm."

"That's where I've seen him, in the library. You appeared to be having an animated conversation." He looked at her intently.

She could have told him about Franklin speaking to Bonita and Bonita's curiosity about the dead man. She could have said, "This may not mean anything, but … " She could have, but she didn't. "He was telling me the harrowing tale of his drive through the snow to the casino," is what she *did* say.

Chapter 24

Final Rites

On Saturday, after Helma washed Boy Cat Zukas's dishes in soapy water, she glanced at the clock above her sink. Five minutes to twelve. There was plenty of time.

She dried her hands and phoned Ruth, who didn't answer until she had dialed her number four times without leaving a message.

"This could only be you," Ruth's gruff voice came on the line. "I'm working."

"It's noon, Ruth," Helma said. A man's voice, which may or may not have belonged to Paul, muttered in the background.

"So it's noon. Like I said, I'm also working."

"I'll pick you up in thirty minutes. Bring your passport."

"Why?"

"Thirty minutes. Goodbye." And Helma hung up.

* * *

Helma chose a tasteful navy blue skirt and her favorite red and blue sweater, beneath her dressiest blue wool coat, complemented by a black scarf and black leather gloves. She shouldn't have been surprised by Ruth's attire when Ruth slammed her front door without bothering to lock it and joined her in the Buick.

Black. From head to toe. Including a black hat with a brim as wide as her shoulders. The only touch of color was Ruth's scarlet lipstick. Even her eyes appeared to have extra black mascara and eyeliner.

"I thought I'd blend in better wearing this," Ruth commented as she tipped her head to keep her hat from bumping the plastic window or the car roof.

"We'll sit in the back," Helma said, putting her car in gear and glancing at Ruth's gigantic hat. "I'd like to see who else attends."

"Oh. Do you mean the bomber? I thought the murderer always returns to the scene of the crime, not the funeral of the victim. Why the passport? Are we fleeing the country?"

"Just a quick trip to Canada. I'd like to speak with Bonita Wu."

"We don't need passports to go to Canada. 'Children of a Common Mother,' hadn't you heard?"

"Not yet, but it does make crossing the border more efficient."

"Yeah, I'm all for efficiency. But what's up with Bonita?"

Helma described her conversation with Jimmy Dodd, how he'd seen Franklin and Bonita talking.

"Sorry I missed it. *I* would have given you a better description than Jimmy. I'm a genius at catching nuances. Do you know where she lives?"

"Only in Vancouver's Chinatown. Wu's a common name, but a few well-placed questions should give us her address."

"Prob'ly. Ancient old ladies with wills like General Patton tend to get a rep far and wide. It's the only way to maintain your viability at her age, I guess. Turn into a force of steel. Okay, I'm game."

Helma parked in front of a faded bungalow, far enough from the funeral parlor so they wouldn't be caught in any funeral procession. They sat in the final pew, early enough to view the attendees.

And of course, despite the tragic focus of the service, most of the attendees turned to view Ruth, who, Helma noted, kept turning her "good side" for maximum exposure.

A closed casket stood in the front of the room. Ruth frowned. "Is that thing big enough?" she whispered. "Did they get all of him?"

City employees, business people, several contemporaries of Franklin. A contingent arrived from the Silver Gables. Helma spotted Cornelia, Del's rumored lover, on the arm of a woman who might have been an attendant from the retirement apartments.

"Look who's here," Ruth said, nudging her.

Helma was about to nod, thinking she meant Cornelia, when she saw the direction Ruth was gazing.

Passing their pew in the central aisle, leaning a little into one another as if they were holding each other up, came her mother and Aunt Em, both of them wearing identical blue coats. A few feet past them, as if she had antennae or as if Helma produced a fragrance only discernible to someone who'd birthed her, her mother turned and looked squarely into Helma's face, her lips widening in a smile of pleasure.

Lillian gripped Aunt Em's arm and pivoted her around, squeezing past the couple already in Ruth and Helma's pew, murmuring, "Excuse me, excuse me. It's my daughter," to flounce and settle next to Helma.

"Such a tragedy," she said to Helma, patting her arm.

"It was quick," Aunt Em said, leaning past Lillian to see Helma. Aunt Em wore a black hat Helma remembered seeing in a photograph taken during World War II. "That is good, when it's quick."

Helma sat squeezed between Ruth, her mother, and Aunt Em. Lillian clucked her tongue and whispered, "The chief couldn't come with you?"

She shook her head, and on the other side, Ruth elbowed her and snorted.

"Who brought you?" Helma asked her mother.

"We came in the van," Lillian said. "We all knew Franklin. It took *two* vans to bring us all. But I still haven't figured out what our program will be instead of Franklin's book reception. There's that woman with the singing dogs but we've had her before."

"Twice," Aunt Em hissed.

At last, when the room was packed, organ music softly played and the family entered: Roosevelt and Delano first, Delano the more bent of the two but both with formal, impassive faces. Jay wore a black suit with a touch of mafioso, or maybe FBI, in the cut. Helma wondered if Frances had helped him choose it. Frances wore black as well: a two-piece wool suit with a maroon blouse and high-heeled black slouchy boots.

As Frances passed, the tears sliding unheeded down her cheeks were plainly visible. Helma's mother dabbed at her eyes. "Poor thing," she whispered.

Helma gazed down at her hands and inhaled for the count of four, held her breath for a count of four, and exhaled to the count of eight, keeping at bay the funerals of her life. All those who'd gone too soon, too violent, or too loved.

Neither Del nor Rosy gave tributes to their brother; the minister recalled Franklin's love of his daughter and Bellehaven and all things green, and said his passing was a tragic loss to the community. "Franklin always dreamed of writing a book about Bellehaven," he claimed, and Helma resolved to write a note after the funeral reminding him that Franklin *had* written books about Bellehaven.

Once the excitement of viewing and being viewed wore off, Ruth's head began to nod, and Helma risked nudging her when a snore emitted from beneath her black hat. Ruth yelped and the mourners around them shifted and turned.

Finally, an instrumental but still recognizable version of "I Did It My Way" poured from the speakers, signaling the end of the service, and the mourners stood and filed out.

"There's a reception in the lobby." Lillian told Helma at the door. "The Swiss Bakery catered it."

"I have an appointment. You go ahead."

"Well ... " She hesitated. "If you're sure you don't want to. They might have those apple pastries you like"

Aunt Em briefly hugged Helma and whispered, "Did you see the way Cornelia and Del kept looking at each other?"

"I couldn't see that well," Helma told her.

Aunt Em nodded in dreamy satisfaction. "Love," she said. "Star-crossed love."

A man hurried away, weaving through the crowd, catching Helma's attention by his quick movement among the milling and conversing. He wore a hat, his bearing upright.

She craned to catch a better view of him but the crowd closed in and she couldn't have said for sure whether she'd actually seen Dutch or not.

Helma turned her Buick onto the freeway ramp. The plastic window flapped and the air pressure inside her car rose and fell until her ears ached.

Ruth removed her hat and tossed it in the backseat, then bushed out her hair. "This is a time waster. Bonita can't tell you anything. She's not even *from* here."

"I want to know what she *can* tell us," Helma said.

It was too loud in her car to hold a conversation, so they drove the twenty miles to the border in silence, the plastic flapping the entire way.

"Uh-oh, look at that line," Ruth said as Helma

braked. "Is there a hockey game tonight? It'll take us hours to get across, and by then Bonita Wu will be tucked into bed like a good old lady. Let's go back. My paintbrushes are going to dry out."

Helma pulled into line behind a van a quarter mile from the border and shifted her car into neutral. "It'll move fast."

"Yeah, right." Ruth slouched down in her seat. "Wake me up when we get there."

In fact, the line did creep forward inordinately slow. Helma turned off her engine at each car length forward. Car fumes seeped through leaks in the seal of her plastic window and her car smelled of exhaust. "There are masks in the glove compartment," she told Ruth.

"No," Ruth said in disbelief, and punched the button of the glove compartment so it dropped open. "Oh my gosh, there *are*. What are these for?"

"The exhaust. I bought them in the paint department when I put new plastic on my window. They won't remove all the exhaust, but they'll help." She took one from Ruth's hand and slipped it over her mouth and nose. At first the mask was uncomfortable and she had the sensation of not enough air to breathe, but then she forgot it. Ruth held hers in her hand, snapping the rubber band.

The car in the line to their left crept forward, and Ruth said, "Look at that. If I did that, I'd have to tuck my knees under my chin."

All Helma could see through the car's tinted windows were the passenger's two black-booted feet rudely displayed on the dashboard. She thought of summertime when she'd spotted bare feet protruding from car windows like dogs catching the wind.

They kept pace with the car with tinted windows, and the third time it pulled ahead, the black boots were tapping against the windshield, keeping time to a bass beat even Helma could hear through the closed windows, when she suddenly remembered.

"The boots," Helma said. "The black boots at the hospital belonged to Frances Harrington."

"What are you talking about?" Ruth asked.

"When I went to see Randall—not to visit, just to observe—a pair of black boots was lying beneath a chair in his room. The same black boots that Frances wore to the funeral today."

Ruth nodded. "You sure? I saw Frances's boots. Silver buckles. Slouchy. They were Dolce & Gabbanas, not exactly footwear you buy at dear old JCPenney."

"I don't know that. I only know they were the same."

"So let's scrap Canada and confront Frances," Ruth squealed. "Oh. My. God. Do you think little Frances had a thing with Randall?" She stuck her finger in her throat. "If you can feature that. They plotted to kill Daddy, run off together and spend his zillions, only Randy screwed up and got himself blown up, too."

"We're already in line," Helma pointed out. "It's too late. We'll talk to Bonita first. If it's warranted, I'll tell the police about Frances and Randall."

Ruth sniffed. "What do you mean, *if*?"

And then, only five cars from the border agent's kiosk, Helma's attention was caught by a bus entering the United States in the southbound lanes. Sleek and black and shiny with bright graphics proclaiming it: THE NETTLE CASINO EXPRESS — WIN BIG!

She watched it slowly pull away from the crossing and gazing up at its tinted windows, spotted the unmistakable grizzled face of Bonita Wu sitting directly behind the bus driver, her mouth moving as she spoke to him in what appeared a directorial fashion.

Chapter 25

Backing Up

"Hey, you can't get through there! What are you doing?"

Helma backed up her Buick bumper-to-bumper with the car behind her, at the same time motioning for the vehicles in the other three rows at the border crossing to let her through. "I just saw Bonita Wu in a casino bus."

Ruth swiveled her head, looking at the traffic around them. "Where?"

"Coming *into* the States, heading south."

"Well, then we'll go through the border and come right back. She's not going to get away from you. Remember what you said five minutes ago about it being too late to turn around? I don't think you're supposed to turn around when you're this close to an international border. It looks a teensy bit suspicious."

"There's no sense going through the border now," Helma said reasonably.

"In this car ..." Ruth flicked the plastic window.

" ...they might wonder."

"Define 'this car,'" Helma said as she motioned for a driver to back up, ignoring his rude gesture.

"It's old, it has a broken window." Ruth slid farther down in her seat, forcing her knees onto the dashboard. "I cannot believe we are crosswise blocking three lanes of traffic fifty feet from men with guns. There is no road, Helma."

"If I stay on the shoulder we won't have any problems."

"You are still going the wrong way. Everybody's looking at us. Those MiG jet things are probably going to fly in and blow us off the face of the earth."

"MiGs are Russian-made jets, which neither the United States nor Canada deploys," Helma explained. "Both the Canadian and American air forces use Boeing-manufactured fighter jets: the F-series and the Hornets."

"I am so reassured that I'm about to be blown up by American-made weapons. Will you please let me out."

"You're becoming hysterical, Ruth." Helma finally maneuvered to the wide shoulder and turned against the waiting traffic. "At least we know where Bonita's going. We don't have to chase the bus."

"I only want to live."

"There," Helma said in satisfaction as she reached the last freeway exit before the border and turned up the ramp. "We're going with the traffic now, perfectly legal and orderly. We'll proceed directly to the casino."

But blocking their way off the ramp was a green and white United States border patrol car, its lights gyrating. A tall and lean young officer stood beside the car, motioning for Helma to stop.

"Oh, Faulkner," she said as she braked, stopping precisely where he pointed and waiting as he approached the car.

"Our first international incident," Ruth said glumly.

"Good afternoon, ma'am," the officer said politely, one hand resting above the holster on his shiny black belt. "Please remove your mask."

Helma had forgotten the white mask. She pulled it off her face, snapping the band painfully against her cheek as she did so.

The officer nodded. "Now, care to tell me what you're doing?"

"I changed my mind about traveling to Canada, that's all."

"May I see some identification?"

Helma gave him both their passports and her driver's license. "Wait here, please," he said, and took the documents with him to his car. At the top of the exit, another border patrol vehicle approached, this one an SUV with its lights gyrating. It stopped crosswise, forming another level of blockage.

"Don't make any sudden moves," Ruth warned as the second officer, just as young but Hispanic, stepped out of the SUV. He spoke to the agent holding the passports, then approached their car. He nodded to them and leaned down to look in through Helma's window, placing his forearm on the frame.

"How'd you break your window, ma'am?"

"I didn't," Helma explained. "It was done by a vandal who then rifled my car."

"It's dangerous to be driving with only plastic as your passenger's protection."

"I'm waiting for the replacement window," Helma explained. "It's a special order."

"I bet."

"Have we done anything wrong, officer?"

"An inadvisable and dangerous traffic maneuver. You caught our attention." He peered closer at Ruth. "Going to a funeral?"

"Just been," Ruth said. "How'd you know?"

Unaccountably, he grinned. "Only a hunch."

Helma suddenly realized that he was keeping them occupied and under surveillance while the other officer verified their identification. In case she and Ruth might decide to do something illegal. As if they were dangerous women who might try to ... make a break for it.

The first officer returned and handed their passports through the window. "You appear to be clean, ladies. Except you." He scowled at Ruth. "You owe eighty-six dollars in library fines."

"Oh, that," Ruth said in what was a misguided tone of dismissal. The library had just begun submitting overdue fines to a collection agency, and all those fines were now appearing on financial credit reports and lien checks. Surprisingly, it had been Ms. Moon's idea.

"You're free to go, but next time, if you change your mind, try to do it before you pass the final exit."

"Final exit?" Ruth said, guffawing. "Is that a joke?"

"Ma'am?" he asked.

"Never mind."

They reached the Nettle Indian Casino forty-five minutes after Helma had seen Bonita Wu on the bus entering the United States. The casino was built like a long house, with thirty-foot-high totem poles towering on either side of the front door. Four casino buses were lined up side by side in the lot behind the building. The parking lot was filled with cars.

"I'll let you out while I park," Helma told Ruth. "You can start looking for Bonita."

"And if I find her?"

"Stand by her. I'll see you."

"Just like sticking a bookmark in a book, right? Look for the tall one."

"It *will* be easier to spot you than Bonita," Helma told her.

"Yeah, yeah."

Helma found an oversized space far enough away from the building that it was unlikely anyone would choose to park next to her. She checked all four doors to be sure they were locked, even though a child could poke its hand through the clear plastic. Then she entered a casino for the first time in her life, standing at the door to get her bearings.

There were no windows, too many lights, yet still a sense of darkness and neon and the confusion of the electronic ding and ring and clatter of machines. People sat as if under enchantment at rows of computerized machines, backlit by flashing colorful screens. She didn't see Ruth anywhere.

She followed a corridor of red carpeting that seemed to spiral back on itself into more banks of slot machines that promised big winnings and true happiness. Helma, who'd been born with a keen sense of direction that had once helped her lead her father and uncles out of a misadventure in the Michigan woods, was suddenly uncertain which direction was north, or south. It was all excessively disorienting.

"Excuse me," she said to a man in a security guard uniform. "I'm looking for a tall woman dressed in black who entered five minutes ago."

He didn't answer but turned and raised his arm toward a section of the casino that held card tables.

"Thank you. Do you think you could turn down the volume of these machines?"

He merely gazed at her, and Helma reminded him, "Loud and continuous noise contributes to early hearing loss. You might bring that up at your next staff meeting."

She found Ruth seated on a tall chair at a green gaming table. Ruth barely looked up when she asked, "Did you find Bonita?"

"Not yet, but I'm ahead by twenty-five dollars. One more," she said to the dealer.

"You talking about Bonita Wu?" the burly man sitting beside Ruth asked.

Helma nodded.

"Everybody knows that one. She's at the high stakes table, where she usually is. Over there. She's some lady."

In the riotous lights, it took Helma a few moments to make out the tiny woman playing at a table set apart from the others. Again she wore a sleeveless shirt on this winter evening.

"I'm going to talk to her," Helma told Ruth, who nodded without looking up and said, "I'll be there just as soon as I double my money. Then I'm quitting. Honest."

The casino sounds were diminished at Bonita's table, as if their game required more concentration. Helma stood behind Bonita, waiting for a pause in the play. She didn't understand the game but Bonita had the most chips in front of her. The dealer was solemn-faced, mechanically precise. Three other players also sat at the table, two of them Helma recognized as women who'd been stranded in the library with Bonita.

When the dealer grabbed a fresh deck of cards to start another round, Bonita turned her tiny body and removed her glasses. She squinted at Helma. "You're waiting for me," she said in her unaccented English, not as a question.

Helma nodded. "I'd like to ask you a question about that day in the library."

Using both hands, Bonita rose awkwardly from her chair. Helma reached out to help but pulled her hand back at the scowl on Bonita's face. Bonita led her along another stretch of red carpeting toward a black leather sofa in a quieter corner. When they sat down, Bonita said, "It's about Mr. Harrington?"

"Yes. I was curious what he said to you in the library."

"Before he died," Bonita finished. "Why?"

"I'm not connected to the police," Helma told her. From the other side of the casino came sudden yelps of pleasure, then scattered applause.

"I know. You're a librarian." Bonita gave a small shrug. "He asked me about my family."

"Did he know your family?"

"No."

"But he was curious about you," Helma said, encouraging the reticent woman. "Did he ask where you were from?"

Bonita nodded. "And my parents. He wanted to know if my parents had lived in Canada and what they did. Long ago. I told him my grandfather came from China to mine and work on the railroad. My parents were born in Canada. I'm a second generation Canadian."

A man in black picked up empty glasses from the table nearby and placed them on a tray, nodded to Helma but didn't appear to see Bonita, and left, glasses clinking.

"Did your father work in the United States?" Helma asked.

"Not him. He was an accountant in Vancouver. But his father, my grandfather, died in this country. He rode a train south from Canada to find work in California. And my grandmother never heard of him again. Her heart was broken."

"And you told Franklin that?"

"I did." Bonita licked her lips as if they were dry, and Helma paused to retrieve a paper cup of water from a nearby fountain.

"What did Franklin say?" Helma asked after Bonita emptied the cup.

"He told me that some family stories are better left unknown, that the past belongs in the past."

Helma pondered Franklin's words; curious sentiment for someone who'd made the past his avocation.

Ruth joined them, a dejected look on her face.

"You didn't double your money," Helma guessed.

"I might as well have dropped it in a collection plate when I walked through the doors and got it over with."

Chapter 26

Late Night Disclosures

"So okay, we've been enlightened by Bonita," Ruth said in a loud voice, holding her hand against the plastic that was loosening in its window socket. Helma planned to replace it as soon as she got home, which might give her a few miles of semisilence before she was forced to replace it again. "She and Franklin shared a little chitchat about her roots. So what does that mean, that Franklin is somehow entangled in Bonita's history? I don't buy it. Franklin was interested in *everybody's* roots. He once asked me if I knew how tall my grandparents had been."

"When did he ask you that?" Helma turned her car up Howe Road, taking two lane roads back to Bellehaven instead of the freeway.

Ruth shrugged. "Remember when I volunteered to drive old people to doctors' appointments?"

Helma did. One brief week when Ruth had been struck by an altruistic urge that had stuttered and died after she garnered three tickets and four complaints on only five trips.

"Well, I took Franklin to an eye appointment. He had the vision of a kid, by the way, and when he wasn't jawing about Bellehaven's golden olden days he was asking about my family's evolution from the mud flats to my own elevated level."

"You didn't tell me that," Helma said, slowing for a yellow bulldozer that had backed close to the road.

"It was no big deal. Look at that." Ruth pointed to the fresh colonial-style sign beside the road. "'Opening soon: Deer Meadows. Fine Living,'" she read aloud. "How come they always name these places for whatever they chase out: Deer Meadows, Eagle Ridge, Wolf Valley."

"Nostalgia?" Helma guessed.

"I'm for truth in advertising," Ruth said. She pulled down the visor and checked her makeup, running a finger under one eye and coming away with a black smudge on the tip.

Helma turned up Alm Street, toward Ruth's house, which was at the edge of the more genteel side of Bellehaven—the modest edge.

"C'mon in," Ruth said as Helma stopped in front of her small bungalow. "Let's call Frances about her Dolce & Gabbana boots and Randall."

Helma hesitated. Ruth's house left her uneasy, impatient to go home and clean her own apartment.

"Close your eyes if it helps," Ruth said. "We'll go in the back way and no further than my kitchen."

Inside her kitchen door, Ruth kicked off her boots, where they landed in a haphazard pile of footwear. Helma focused on the kitchen table, avoiding the counter where dirty dishes were stacked among piles of old mail and candy bar wrappers. Ruth's house smelled of oil paints and paint thinner, and if she raised her eyes, Helma knew she'd see paintings in every stage of completion or abandonment. Ruth's abodes served only one purpose: as studios with a place to sleep. She was disdainful of dusting, scrubbing, and sorting, claiming to be "searching for a higher order."

"Four more to go and I'll have enough paintings for the show," Ruth said as she looked through her kitchen window and across the alley to where Paul lived. She frowned. "He's not home. Again. Whaddaya think about that?" She drummed her fingers on the counter, still gazing at Paul's dark house.

"Are you and Paul ..." Helma began.

"What's that saying about getting what you ask for?" Ruth said, overly bright. She stepped away from the window and asked, "Want to see my newest? It's so good it'll leave Shiny Waters weeping in a corner."

"I'll wait for the opening," Helma said as Ruth handed her cordless phone to her.

"Oh so politic," Ruth said. "You're scared to see them, aren't you? Do you need a phone book?"

"No, I remember the number." Helma rarely forgot telephone numbers or addresses, and in fact remembered them more easily than names. She dialed Frances's number and heard a message to call back later.

"Try the Harrington uncles," Ruth urged. "I bet they were trying to keep the Frances-Randall connection a big secret from you. Daughter in the clutches of a clandestine affair with Daddy's enemy, and they both go up in smoke. It looks bad."

"I'll talk to Frances first," Helma told her. "Randall's sister flew in from California after he was injured. The boots may have belonged to her."

"Not if she counted pennies like her brother did." Ruth held out her hand. "I'll call Joker's and just see if she's there. Now that Joker's has graduated to the new hot spot, it's one of Fran's favorite hangouts."

Helma gave her the phone, and Ruth punched two numbers, having the bar's number on her automatic dialer. She spoke into the phone, listened, and clicked off. "She hasn't been there. Where else?"

"I'll call her later, from home," Helma said, eager to return to her own apartment, where she knew which was the most recent mail and that all the food in her refrigerator was edible.

Ruth absently pushed telephone buttons. "You know how you can program your phone with names using the letters of the alphabet assigned to the numbers?"

"Not really." Helma was convinced it better served the memory to memorize telephone numbers, the same as a pencil and paper preserved mathematical skills.

"Probably not. But if you programmed your phone with M-O-M, to call your mother, the numbers are 666, did you ever think of that?"

"No, Ruth, I haven't."

* * *

Replacing the plastic on her window was easier than her first installation. She was smoothing out the final wrinkles when Walter David's motorcycle pulled into the car port beside her. Moggy, his white Persian cat, sat in the special basket the building manager had constructed on the passenger seat.

"Nice job," he said as he climbed off his bike. "That's nasty stuff to work with."

"Thank you," Helma said, and pressed down the tape edges with the external bowl of a soup spoon. Helma believed in availing oneself of opportunities that presented themselves, so she asked, "You said you knew Frances Harrington?"

"Fran? Sure. Wonder how she's doing with her dad gone." His motorcycle pinged as the engine cooled.

"Did you know either of her husbands?"

Walter unbuckled Moggy from his improvised seat belt, and the cat compliantly lay in his arms, its eyes half closed. "The first one, Ted, was in high school with us. That lasted about six months—kids' stuff. He died a couple of years ago in a car wreck. The second one was from Seattle. Don't know much about him. But any man would have stiff competition with the triplets hovering around like the mafia. Not that Fran was a bad kid; she wasn't. In school, she was like this princess. New car when she hit sixteen, new clothes, her own phone. They gave her anything she wanted. They totally doted on her."

Helma heard Walter's hesitancy. "But?" she prompted.

"Heck, I don't know, there was just something kind of … lost, I guess it was, about her. I can't explain it, like she couldn't figure out how to do things on her own. She was good at hiding it, I think, but it was like she was waiting for directions."

"Did you ever date her?" Helma asked him.

He laughed, and Moggy opened her round eyes. "No way. Not me. She was way out of my league."

Boy Cat Zukas lay curled in his basket, partially buried beneath his cushion, while Helma sat at her table skimming through Franklin Harrington's history. Franklin had been proud of the earliest Harringtons, that was obvious, referring to those who'd engaged in unethical business deals as "rogues and scalawags," as if they'd been clever boys outwitting a Keystone Kops legal force, not actual criminals who would have spent time behind bars in today's world.

Until the 1940s the new library site had served myriad purposes, all of them related to the Harringtons: a mining office, then the shipping office for goods coming into the harbor, later as the central office for the Harringtons' many financial enterprises. In 1947 it had burned in a fire and the land lay empty, unused for decades, as the city of Bellehaven grew to encompass the site and property values soared.

She'd tried to reach Frances Harrington, phoning her number every thirty minutes. There was still no answer.

Franklin's book grew wearying. No family detail escaped his self-congratulatory Harrington-centered retelling. Frankly, after all his research, she was surprised. A more cynical person would have believed that the Harringtons felt their sailing into Washington Bay in the 1800s was as momentous as Columbus's voyage across the ocean.

When her doorbell rang, Helma wasn't disappointed to close the covers on the Harringtons. The clock over her stove read 9:22, late for any visitor except Ruth.

When she peered through the viewer in her door, it wasn't Ruth at all, but a man. It took another few moments to recognize the magnified and distorted face. When she did, she opened the door in surprise.

"Dutch!"

He stood ramrod straight on her doormat, his arm out as if he were about to salute. A muscle in his cheek jumped. He was bareheaded, his eyes red. "May I come in?"

Helma didn't move. Dutch emitted a strong odor of alcohol.

"I'll only take a minute of your time," he said, and she heard the pleading note beneath his brusqueness.

This was Dutch, not some stranger. But still she hesitated, remembering the scene in Joker's, the trip to Dutch's house, his absence from the library. "Did you drive here?" she asked, stalling for time.

"I walked." He waited, tensely watching her.

Finally, she said, "Come in," and stepped aside to let him in, glancing into the parking lot and along her deck for signs of any witnesses. She saw no one.

"Sit down," she said, pointing to her sofa.

"I'd rather stand, ma'am."

So they stood facing one another in the middle of the kitchen, Helma next to the sink, Dutch beside the stove. She waited.

Dutch rubbed his jaw and opened his mouth as if loosening a tense muscle. "Thank you for the other night—at Joker's—and for bringing me home."

"You're welcome."

"The police have questioned me," he blurted out. "The chief of police. And that detective, too."

"About Franklin Harrington?" Helma asked, not at all surprised.

He gave a single abrupt nod. "And other things, too. My past."

Helma glanced at Boy Cat Zukas. Ruth claimed that animals *knew*, that they were able to smell deceit and criminal intent a mile away. Boy Cat Zukas unconcernedly licked his paw. "Is that a problem?"

"I have certain knowledge," he said.

"About the Harringtons?" she asked. Dutch couldn't possibly have stood any straighter.

"About ... ordinances."

"Laws exist to—" Helma began. "Oh. You don't mean ordinances like legal rulings, you mean 'ordnances' like ammunition."

He nodded sharply. "And explosives."

"From your military career?"

"Yes, ma'am."

"The police would *expect* you to possess that knowledge," Helma said. "They wouldn't suspect you for possessing knowledge you were trained to use." She refolded the dish towel that hung on her refrigerator door and told Dutch, "I saw a book on an end table at your house, when we brought you home. A chapter on explosives was marked."

"I know. I was trying to remember." His words came out in a rush. Misery was plain on his face, aging him. "There's more. The police questioned me about my cell phone. It's gone. I can't find it."

"You lost it?" The cell phone. Wayne had asked if Dutch had a cell phone.

"I don't know. I can't find it." Dutch's voice descended to a whisper. "They searched my house—with a warrant."

"Did they remove anything?"

He met Helma's eyes, then looked away. "Only the book you saw. That's all."

"Where were you when the explosion took place?" she asked. "You weren't at the library."

He shook his head, swinging it back and forth like a bear. "I went after Franklin. The snow … He was old. I followed him." He heaved a deep breath. "I can't remember it all. When I was in the military, there was an … incident. I couldn't help anyone then, either. I was worried about him. In the snow … He looked like my grandfather … "

"Dutch," Helma said firmly, unconsciously standing straighter herself. "It's important to sort this out in a logical order. Once the incidents are chronologically coherent, the implications make more sense. First and most importantly, did you have anything to do with the explosion?"

"No," Dutch said. "I don't remember it all, but I know I didn't."

"Good. Now, you followed Franklin. What did you see?"

Dutch closed his eyes, and Helma thought it was not to *help* him remember, but *against* his memories. "He was walking in the snow. He was fine, a little hunched against the weather, but he wasn't having any trouble. He didn't slip or stumble. I didn't want to scare him or embarrass him by letting him see me, so I stayed back."

"And did you see anyone else in the snow?" Helma asked.

"I think so. I don't recall exactly. If I did, they weren't clear."

"Randall Rice?"

"I couldn't say, ma'am. There was an explosion. I knew what it was and I froze." He lapsed into silence, standing at attention as if awaiting the passage of a court-martial sentence.

"But you didn't tell the police any of this?" Helma asked.

Dutch shook his head, looking down at his feet. "Only that I didn't know what happened to my cell phone."

"You need to speak to the police, Dutch," she said quietly. "You have to give them this information."

"Do you believe me, ma'am?"

"Yes," Helma said. "I do."

"Are you going to report me?"

"No. This is *your* responsibility. I won't mention it

unless you choose not to tell them. This is vital to the police investigation, Dutch, and it needs to come from you."

He nodded, but still stood soldierlike in her kitchen, and finally Helma said, "You may go now."

Dutch nodded tersely and left her apartment, marching down the steps of the Bayside Arms, across the parking lot and into the night.

Chapter 27

Family Secrets

It wasn't until late Sunday morning that Helma dialed Frances Harrington's home phone number and heard a message directing the caller to dial her cell phone number.

The morning had dawned in a silvery mist. No rain, just wisps of mist and clouds that seemed to catch on every vertical surface and gather in long fingers ten feet above the waters of Washington Bay. The snow was gone, the air damp and heavy.

Helma dialed the cell phone number and Frances answered on the second ring.

"You tricked me," Frances said coldly when Helma gave her name. "You weren't looking for Daddy's book; you were trying to find his library files. Uncle Rosy told me."

"Your father's book *will* be added to our library collection. Your uncle Rosy found it for me,"

Helma corrected. "It was on your father's bookshelves. He also said your father presented each Harrington with a copy, but you didn't mention to me that you had a copy."

Frances was silent for a moment, as if thinking that one over. "I don't remember. He was always giving me stuff he thought I should read."

"But you didn't?"

"I'm not that interested in history."

"I'd like to speak with you for a few minutes." A seagull hovered above Helma's balcony, its black eyes casting across her deck.

"Go ahead."

"In person," Helma told her. She opened her balcony door and the seagull squawked and flew off.

"Definitely not. Uncle Del said not to trust you. I'm not getting taken in again."

"You can keep your eyes on me every second," Helma offered. "This is about Randall Rice."

She heard an intake of breath, then silence, and finally, "You can come over, if you come right now."

"Where are you?"

"At Daddy's."

"I'll be there in fifteen minutes. Will your uncles be present?"

"Not for this," Frances said.

Even if it was made in animosity, Helma was grateful for the brothers' decision to divide the Harrington house so the doors were invisible to one another. She didn't care to confront either Rosy or Del.

Frances might have been waiting on the other side

of the door, so quickly did she open it when Helma lifted the hand-shaped knocker. Her hair was undone and tangled, her eyes red and puffy. She wore faded jeans and a pale green cashmere sweater. "What about Randy?" she demanded, standing in the open door-way, as if to bar Helma's entrance.

"May I come in?"

Frances threw open the door. "Don't touch any-thing."

"You're cleaning out your father's house already?" Helma asked, peering around at the cardboard boxes stacked near the front door.

"Jay's moving in here. And he's welcome to it. Free doesn't mean it's worth it. Living here now would be like living in a tomb."

Helma imagined Jay growing old in the Harrington house, carrying on the tradition of his father and un-cles as they faded into the past. She supposed that at some point the house would prove too much for one man, and in the current spirit of preservation, it would be given to the city and become a public landmark. The final crowning event to Franklin's Harrington history.

"Now," Frances said, crossing her arms. "What about Randy?"

"You were having an affair."

"That's ridiculous," Frances said, and her voice broke the way it had the first time Helma met her.

"You were at the hospital with him the morning he died, or was it all night?"

"Why do you think that?" Frances challenged.

"I was there. You sat in the chair by his bed. You'd

removed your ..." It was too much to give the designer's name. "... boots."

"I was not there," Frances said, but her voice was no longer adamant. "Besides, I never saw you." She clapped her hands over her mouth, realizing she'd given herself away.

"Did your father know about the two of you?"

"No." She shook her head vigorously.

"Are you certain?"

If Frances could have scowled at her, Helma knew she would have. "Yes, I'm 'certain,'" she mimicked. "He didn't know. If he had, he would have ki—" She stopped. "Don't get any ideas. No one knew. Daddy and Randy hated each other, so he and I only met out of town."

Helma refrained from mentioning the thousands of stories about people coincidentally bumping into each other in the remotest corners on earth. "Why didn't they like each other?"

"People just don't sometimes. They both were into old things." Frances shrugged. "They hated each other a long time before Randy and I got together—we met a year ago when I redesigned his closets. That's what I do, you know: closets. Daddy believed Randy sabotaged one of his history projects."

"Did he?"

"What?"

"Did Randall sabotage your father's project?"

"How should I know? That was years ago. Daddy wanted the city to preserve some old building but they said it was too expensive. And then later Randall talked the city into preserving it, and Daddy was furious because Randall got all the credit for it. Randy was writing a history of Bellehaven, too."

"Did you read Randy's history?"

"No. He didn't really have much written down that I know of." She thought for a few moments, picking at the nail polish on her thumb. "He did say he could prove his history easier than Daddy could. To be honest, I didn't want to know about either one of their stupid books."

"They weren't friends," Helma said. "So who would want to kill them *both*?"

"I don't know." Frances's voice was plaintive, nearly a wail of grief and frustration.

"The only subjects they had in common were local history—and you. Was there someone else who they might have shared as an enemy?"

She shook her head.

"Did your uncles know about you and Randy?"

"No."

As if on cue, there was a knock on an interior door and Frances looked over her shoulder. "That's Uncle Del's side. Come with me."

Helma would have followed her, no matter what, to see this entrance into Franklin's quarters. It was like boys' secret passageways. Her own nephews would have loved it.

The door wasn't a revolving bookcase, but it *was* beside an oak bookcase. Frances hadn't removed the books in here, and they lined the shelves: history of all kinds, American, European, Asian. Military history and natural history. Although they weren't in Dewey decimal system order, Helma quickly noted with approval that they were grouped by geographic area, and within those, by historical period.

Both Del and Rosy entered when Frances opened the door, and Helma perceived from their set faces that the two men had reached a mutual decision of some kind.

"Miss Zukas," Del said. "You're here again. I'm surprised."

"I think not," Helma told him, "or you wouldn't be appearing through the walls."

"Are you upsetting poor Frances?" Rosy asked. His tone was light but Helma heard his mistrust, even veiled anger. He searched Frances's face.

Helma caught the look of entreaty in Frances's eyes aimed at her. "We were discussing her father's history. She hasn't read it. Have you?"

"Tedious work, I'm afraid. Kept him out of trouble, though."

"What kind of trouble?" Helma asked.

Rosy looked at Del. "I'd say the librarian has a suspicious nature."

"When someone suffers a violent death, it only makes good sense to be suspicious," Helma told him.

"But aren't you departing from your original concern for the library site?"

"It's connected," Helma told him.

Frances had stepped to the side, letting her uncles take over the conversation.

Del gave a deep sigh. "Sit down, Miss Zukas. We have a bit of information to share with you."

Helma removed two books on Middle East military history from a leather chair, then returned the books to the chair seat. "I'd rather stand."

"Then *I'll* sit," Rosy said. "I'm aged and decrepit."

"We regret to inform you," Del began as he lowered himself into a leather chair, "that the files taken from your car have been destroyed."

Rosy nodded toward Franklin's den, where Helma had searched the file cabinet. "As have been Franklin's files." He snapped his fingers. "All gone."

"Who destroyed them?" Helma asked.

"Oh, I couldn't tell you that. I can assure you, though, that they're forever gone."

"Along with any record of Franklin wanting the site to go to the new library," Helma said.

"So sorry."

Helma turned to Rosy. "You lured Ruth and me into your side of the house so your brother or Jay could steal the files from my car."

"You could have brought them in with you, my dear," Rosy said calmly. "That's what *I* would have done. You left them all vulnerable on your car seat in a vehicle made before car alarms even existed. Frankly, I'm surprised it had safety glass."

Of course, she realized, he was right. "That was still thievery and destruction of property," she said.

Both Rosy and Del shrugged with identical lifts of their shoulders and rise of their eyebrows. "So, my dear," Rosy said, "you can return to the library business Bellehaven relies on you for. No more thoughts of murder and library sites."

"Some things just weren't meant to be," Del added. He smoothed both hands along the sides of his head as if sleeking back youthful hair. "Being born a few minutes earlier doesn't confer *all* rights. The disposition of that land should have been a joint decision. It was vital in the Harrington's past and it was never intended to leave the family."

"And far more lucrative," Helma said. "You keep secrets well."

"As every family should," Del said easily.

"And Cornelia?" Helma asked, taking a wild stab.

The response was not as she expected. Del leaned forward, his fists tight. Both he and Rosy shot protective looks at Frances, who was suddenly paying attention and asked in a puzzled voice, "Who's Cornelia?"

"Corneli*us*," Rosy told Frances smoothly. "One of my ... friends."

"Everybody knows about Uncle Rosy," Frances told Helma, her cheeks pinkly indignant. "You can't threaten him with anything like *that*."

Helma saw the relieved expression on Del's face as he leaned back into the leather chair. Whatever Del and Rosy thought she knew, they were desperate to protect Frances from that knowledge.

Chapter 28

What Can Never Be Proved

"I'll accompany Miss Zukas to her car," Rosy told Frances and Del, sweeping his hand in a grand beckoning gesture from Helma to the door.

Frances considered her and then said, "Thank you, Helma." Helma heard a multitude of things in those words: gratitude for not mentioning Randall Rice in front of her uncles and a disguised plea that she continue to be discreet.

"You're welcome," Helma said. "I appreciate our conversation." Unless a crime was involved that in some way touched on Randall and Frances's secret liaison, she *would* remain discreet.

Rosy hummed annoyingly until the door closed behind them and they'd stepped into the cool weather. A breeze stirred the evergreens, and the air above them was filled with a sound like breathing.

"You're getting to be a regular here, aren't you?" he asked. "Maybe we should make you an honorary Harrington."

"You're not a family I'm interested in being associated with," Helma told him. "You all take crime very lightly."

"Self-preservation, my dear. Who knows? Once the dust has settled, your library may still end up with its site."

"You mean once the numbers are ... crunched, if the site doesn't prove to be lucrative enough for you."

Rosy laughed. "See, you *would* make a good Harrington." He opened Helma's car door. "And don't worry about the burden of keeping any secrets from us. We've known about Franny and Randy for some time."

"Did Franklin?"

Rosy shook his head and rolled his eyes. "God, no. If he'd known, he *would* have blown up Rice. Not himself, though. If there's one thing Franklin wanted it was to live forever. Funny, isn't it, to want to live so you can spend your time looking backward?"

"Why didn't Randall and Franklin get along?" Helma asked.

"Old men's petty rivalries." He held up his hand, which now held a fresh cigarette. "I know, I know, Randall wasn't old, but he had the mental age of an eighty-year-old crank. Those two coots could have come to blows over, I don't know, whether or not it rained on Tuesday, April tenth, 1888, at two-fifteen in the afternoon. Of course, I would have sided with the guy who said it had."

"And Cornelia?" Helma asked.

Rosy stiffened. "Forget about her. It doesn't matter now."

"Frances doesn't know?"

"And she never will, either, understand?"

Helma looked at him, considering. The jolly, sharp-tongued man was gone. He sounded thoroughly threatening. What damage could knowing about Cornelia and her uncle Del do to Frances?

"That died with Franklin," he said, and suddenly it began to make sense.

"Goodbye, Rosy," Helma said, already preoccupied as she turned on her engine and Rosy closed her door, nodding curtly.

Helma glanced around the lobby of the Silver Gables, looking for either Aunt Em or her mother. Fortunately, neither was in sight. She stopped at the wall directory with its push-pin letters and found C. SETTLE listed in alphabetical order. Apartment 402. The fourth floor. Her mother and Aunt Em shared an apartment on the third.

Since she avoided elevators whenever possible, Helma took the stairs, climbing all four flights without pausing.

Apartment 402 was on the west end of the building, the side with the view toward the water. C. SETTLE, was printed on a three-by-five-inch placard beside the door.

Helma pushed the doorbell button and heard murmured voices inside and then footsteps approaching the door.

The woman Helma had seen with Cornelia at the funeral opened the door. She had a pleasant wide-eyed face without makeup, her hair pulled straight back into a low ponytail.

"Yes?" she inquired.

"I'd like to see Mrs. Settle, please. My name is Helma Zukas. It's regarding the Harringtons," she added at the woman's hesitation.

"She's resting," the woman told her.

"I'll only take a few minutes of her time," Helma said, inwardly wincing as she used the same words that Dutch had used on her doorstep the night before. "Would you inquire if she'd see me?"

The woman wavered, then agreed, closing the door, leaving Helma standing in the hall. She was plainly visible to anyone in the elevator, and when she heard its *ding!* as it stopped on the fourth floor, she kept her back turned, hoping that neither her mother nor Aunt Em were aboard.

"She'll see you," the woman said, opening the door to Helma. "But please, don't be long. She's very tired."

"The past few days have been very draining," Helma said, but the woman didn't respond.

Cornelia Settle sat upright on a white brocade sofa, her hands folded over a crocheted afghan that was neatly spread across her lap, although she wore a creamy wool dress with long sleeves and a high neck. She appeared exhausted, fragile, but still determined, someone living on resolve that rarely failed her.

"Mother," the younger woman said. "This is Helma Zukas."

Cornelia nodded. "I believe we've met."

"It was an awkward encounter," Helma said. Cornelia's apartment was furnished tastefully—and expensively, Helma noted. Potted plants stood in front of the windows, a newer flat-screen television near the entrance to the kitchen. But there were no bookcases and only a *TV Guide* on the coffee table. Cornelia was not a reader.

"Catherine, dear," Cornelia said to her daughter. "You can leave now. I'll be fine."

"Are you sure?" she asked doubtfully, casting a quick glance at Helma.

"Positive. Call me in an hour. We'll chat."

Helma closely watched the younger woman as she kissed her mother and said goodbye. "And don't forget the dish in the refrigerator. Just warm it up in the microwave for two minutes and—"

"Yes, dear. Now stop fussing."

When Catherine was gone, Cornelia smiled wearily at Helma. "Rosy phoned to warn me about you. He thought you were on your way here."

"He was right. I came directly from the Harrington house." Cornelia beckoned to the Regency style chair opposite her, and Helma sat down.

"He called you 'most curious and most persistent.'"

"That's fair," Helma told her, and Cornelia smiled faintly again. She picked up a silver dish from the coffee table. "Mint?"

"No thank you." A framed photograph sat on the coffee table: a woman and a young girl about five, wearing 1950s clothing. Cornelia had been lovely, her full mouth even then holding determination and willpower.

"The rumors are that you've had a longtime affair with Del," Helma said. "For years."

"And?"

"The affair was with Franklin, not Del."

Cornelia didn't deny it. She merely continued to gaze at Helma as if she'd said it might rain tomorrow.

"Yet you encouraged the rumor, or at least never denied it. From the beginning? Why?"

Cornelia dabbed at her mouth with a tissue. It came away red with lipstick. "Haven't you ever begun a deception and become so caught up in its entanglements that it was impossible to unravel?"

"No," Helma told her honestly. "Entanglements can be avoided with proper planning and unraveled with steadfast resolve."

"You're very fortunate, my dear. I'm not so clever. I've ended up spending my entire life caught in my own web."

"Does Catherine know the truth?" Helma asked.

Cornelia showed no surprise at the question. "Not even DNA could divulge the truth," she said with a touch of defiance in her tired voice.

"That was very bold, to attend Franklin's funeral with Catherine."

"People already believe they have the answer to that one; it actually makes us safer from unwanted conjecture."

"But why?" Helma asked. "Why the subterfuge? Franklin had been a widower for years."

"Thirty-one," Cornelia supplied. Her bosom fluttered with a caught breath. "Before he was married, he and I were ... close. It was so trite, really. We quarreled, I went to Europe and discovered I was pregnant. I couldn't give up Catherine and didn't return for seven years. By then, of course, Franklin was married and had a daughter. You've met Frances?"

Helma nodded.

"She's very possessive of her father, very doted on by her uncles. And her father adored her."

"That's why the doors between the brothers' quarters in the Harrington house—so you'd never be seen entering or leaving Franklin's house."

Cornelia nodded and picked a mint out of the silver dish. She didn't place it in her mouth, only rolled it between her hands. "It was complicated. Catherine is the oldest of the two, you see. The firstborn."

"And if Franklin were to acknowledge her ... "

"I couldn't bear to see Catherine involved in a public struggle for acceptance or repudiation. Frances could inflict real pain on my daughter. Franklin is ... was, very conscious of the lasting effects of scandal." A shadow crossed her face and she added, "Very aware of his family's place in history, also. His family's good name was paramount in all he did."

"Isn't Catherine curious?"

"She believes her father was a French businessman who died when she was a baby."

"I see. You must have loved Franklin very much."

"I did," she said simply. "He was the only man in my life."

"And I'm sure you'll always remember the last time you spoke to him."

Cornelia glanced at her sharply, then her eyes shifted away. She replaced the mint in the candy dish, and Helma was sure she was witnessing abnormal behavior for Cornelia. "I don't remember exactly."

Helma had had experience with truth that wasn't quite the whole truth. "On the morning of the snow storm?" she asked. "The morning he died?"

"Possibly." She examined her hands, which Helma noted were beautifully manicured.

"When he called you from the library?"

Cornelia didn't answer.

"I was standing near him when he made the call," Helma said. "He was asking you to—"

Cornelia slowly shook her head. Tears slipped from her eyes and down her lined cheeks. "I can't tell the police," she said. "You have to realize I will do anything to keep that part of my life from being disclosed, anything to protect my daughter."

"Can you tell me?"

"Will you tell the police?"

"Only if it has bearing on their deaths," Helma assured her, just as she had Frances. "I promise."

"He asked me to call Randall Rice at his office," Cornelia whispered.

"But Randall's office is only across the street from the library," Helma said.

Cornelia nodded. She picked up another mint from the dish and rolled it between her palms.

"Why didn't Franklin phone Randall himself?"

"He didn't wish to conduct business in a public place," Cornelia said, as if Helma should have of course known that.

"What was his message?"

Helma leaned forward to hear Cornelia's low voice. "For Randall to meet him, that Franklin could prove he—Franklin—was right. I asked him what he meant, right about what? But he told me Randall would know."

"Franklin wanted Randall to meet him at the library site? In the midst of a snowstorm?"

"He didn't say where." She bit her lip. "But I think so. He was completely engrossed in that site. The construction crew gave him his own hard hat, you know."

"And that's the message you passed on? To Randall himself?"

She shook her head. "No one answered at Randall's office. Because of the snow, the staff wasn't there. I couldn't give Franklin's message to Randall."

"So then what did you do?" Helma asked.

"There was nothing I *could* do. The next thing I heard, like everyone in town, was the explosion." A tremor shook her lips.

"Yet Randall met him, because they died together, or at least close to one another."

"I didn't talk to Randall," Cornelia repeated. "I don't know why he was with Franklin."

"Did Franklin ever tell you anything significant about the site itself? It's sentimental significance? Historically?"

She shook her head. "It was the first piece of property the Harringtons owned in Bellehaven, so there was a sentimental value, aside from its development value." She frowned. "Franklin had very strong feelings about it. He obsessed over every detail."

"Do you have any idea why?"

Cornelia shook her head. "He didn't tell me."

Helma looked around at the apartment's furnishings again. "Franklin took care of you and Catherine? You'll be all right?"

"I'll be financially secure until I die," Cornelia said. "And so will Catherine. But I'll never be all right."

Chapter 29

Calling for Time

When she heard Ruth's usual jangling ring of her doorbell, Helma was sitting on her sofa. She'd returned to reading Franklin Harrington's recounting of the Harrington family's involvement in every phase of Bellehaven history. Could the Harringtons possibly have been so ubiquitous?

Then she chastised herself for two reasons: first, because she doubted the dead man's veracity—she'd helped him with much of the research herself, hadn't she? And second, for her use, even mentally, of a word she considered overused to the point of meaninglessness: ubiquitous.

As for the library site, the Harringtons had been the property's first legal owners in history, and its current owners, and, she now believed, its final owners as well.

She marked her page with a bookmark that

read, "Do You Know Where Your Library Books Are?" and answered the door.

"I've got some juicy info for you," Ruth said, stepping inside and shrugging out of her coat at the same time she pulled a bottle of red wine from a voluminous pocket.

"Oh, Ruth," Helma said, remembering her unspoken promise to Frances when she'd left the Harrington house, and the veiled warnings of the Harrington brothers. "What did you do?"

"Nothing blatant, honest," Ruth said, grabbing a glass from Helma's cupboard, then opening drawers until she found a corkscrew. "I was so discreet my own mother—if she was still alive—wouldn't have known what I was doing."

"Who did you talk to?" Helma asked as she closed the cupboard door behind Ruth.

Ruth dropped onto the sofa and tried to insert the corkscrew into the wine bottle. "Look at this. It's a screw top. Do you want to hear this or not?"

"I'm not sure." She sat on the rocker opposite Ruth and held the rocker upright with her feet flat on the floor.

"Remember Jimmy Dodd?"

"The casino bus driver, yes."

"I ran into him out at the casino." Ruth shrugged. "I only went there to win back the money I lost, honest. Anyway, there was Jimmy, and you know what he was drinking?"

"Milk," Helma said.

Ruth frowned. "Did I already tell you this story?

But yeah, milk. So we're chatting away and he told me about this little guy in a plaid jacket who bopped into the library for a couple seconds before the explosion. Picture it. This guy looks around the room, doesn't talk to anybody, stops at the circulation desk, and nobody's there. And then he runs out the door. He doesn't talk to anybody."

"Did Jimmy know who the man was?" Helma asked. A plaid jacket. The police had found Randall Rice in the snow because of his plaid jacket.

"Not a clue, but I'd bet my last aborigine paint that it was Randall Rice. The description fit."

"Why didn't Jimmy come forward earlier? That sounds suspicious, Ruth."

"Nah, it's an Indian thing. He didn't want to get mixed up in a police mess, that's all. And don't think I'm ignoring my p's and c's by saying that; the majority of the population wouldn't: statistics prove it, and the omnipotent 'they' confirm it. So what do you think?"

"Randall and Frances *were* having an affair," Helma told Ruth. "Frances told me that today."

"See, I was right."

"I'm phoning Wayne Gallant," Helma said. "It's time he knew these facts."

"Want to give him an even bigger present?" Ruth asked, pointing the wine bottle at her.

"Providing the police with information doesn't count as a present, Ruth. It's our civic duty." She rose from the rocker, leaving it swaying behind her, and stepped to her telephone.

"Yeah, well, on my way here, I saw Frances trip-trapping into the Cocoon Day Spa. What say we just chat with her a few minutes and *then* call the chief of your dreams?"

Helma hesitated. She did have a few questions for Frances that would complete the information she wanted to give Wayne. "The Cocoon Day Spa is open on Sundays?"

"If they wanted to, they could go 24/7. C'mon. I'll take you."

But Helma was thinking about Jimmy Dodd's sighting of Randall Rice. If Cornelia hadn't reached him, why would Randall have walked across the street from city hall to the library during a snowstorm, not spoken to a single person in the library, and then simply left?

"He could have been just checking on the women," Helma said aloud.

"Who?" Ruth asked.

"Randall. Maybe he was the one who suggested their bus be sent to the library."

"Yeah, weird, isn't it? Let's go see Franny."

"What time is it?" Helma asked, even as she glanced at her own watch and saw it was 5:40, perfect timing.

"Don't worry. She's there."

"No. I'd like to drive by the mission first."

"Well, she won't be *there*."

The Promise Mission for Homeless Men sat on prime property near the bay. Following an unfortunate and unfair incident a few years earlier, Helma had been sentenced to fifty hours of community service at the mission, which despite one major incident, she'd dispatched with her usual efficiency and attention to detail.

Ruth made a U-turn in front of the mission and parked against the curb with a scrape and a jolt, flinging open her door. Helma got out, too, first unsticking a chocolate wrapper from the bottom of her shoe.

"You left your keys in the ignition," she told Ruth.

Ruth turned on the sidewalk and shrugged. "It'll be okay," she said, looking at three men lounging and watching them from the mission steps. "Right, guys?"

"It's cruel to unnecessarily leave temptation in another person's path," Helma said as she opened the driver's door and removed the keys.

Brother Danny, the director, was talking to the receptionist in the foyer when they entered, and Helma held out her hand to be shaken when it appeared he was about to hug her. His smile was wide and his southern drawl deep. "Helma, Ruth! Seeing you two is the best thing that's happened to me all week."

"It's Sunday," Ruth, who *did* hug Brother Danny, reminded him. "The *first* day of the week."

He laughed. "Then sure as shootin', it's *going* to be the best thing to happen to me all week. Care to join us for dinner?"

"Thank you, but not today," Helma told him. "We're looking for someone."

"What's his name?" he asked, handing the man at the desk a five dollar bill from his pocket. The face of the receptionist, a balding man in his sixties, didn't show any acknowledgment but he tucked the bill in his breast pocket and patted it with the flat of his palm.

"We don't know that, unfortunately," Helma told him. "He's about thirty-five, a little shorter than Ruth."

"That's me," Ruth said, "Measuring stick of humanity."

"He may be sleeping in Cedar Falls Park," Helma continued, "but he eats his meals here."

Brother Danny looked doubtful. "That covers a lot of territory. I could name about twenty men who'd fit that description. Anything unusual about him? Or at least unusual by these guys' standards?"

"His clothes are colorless," Helma said, and the director shrugged, shaking his head.

"Well," Ruth added, "I heard him call himself the Homeless Citizen of Bellehaven, like a title. You know, King of the Road or something."

"Ah, yes," Brother Danny said, grinning. "The Homeless Citizen. The man going around fixing what he messes up."

"That's him," Helma said.

"He's here all right, or at least he was twenty minutes ago. Down in the dining room."

Helma knew that everyone who ate in the mission's dining room had to sign in, although Brother Danny accepted whatever name a diner chose to use. He'd once told her that at least twice a week Elvis Presley, Marilyn Monroe, and even God dined at the mission. "Is that what he calls himself?" she asked. "The Homeless Citizen?"

"Usually. Sometimes the Fixer."

"Maybe he read Malamud," Ruth mused.

The dining room was on the mission's basement level, a windowless drab room where long ago someone had hung travel posters that had faded to uninspiring pastel. Helma would never have said she'd made actual *friends* during her time at the mission, but she did glance into the kitchen at the staff. Not a single face looked familiar and she silently hoped those she'd known had left the mission for better places.

"Boy, this brings back memories," Ruth said. She had been erroneously convinced that Helma would benefit from "chaperoning" during her sentence at the mission. "Remember Portnoy?"

"I do," Helma said. It was between servings in the dining room, and the room was only half full. Helma knew that in another half hour it would be packed with the homeless and the hungry, and those who'd run out of money.

"Well, thank God there aren't any kids here today," Ruth said. "That's a good sign."

Helma nodded toward a table near the back of the room. "There he is."

The man who called himself the Homeless Citizen sat by himself, a wall of salt and pepper shakers and glasses around his space, just as he'd formed a wall with book ends at the library.

He watched Helma and Ruth approach, his face twisted into a suspicious frown. "I gave it back," he said. "I fixed it."

"Did you give it back to the proper person?" Helma asked.

With his arms, the man pulled in his salt and pepper

shakers, tightening his defenses. "I gave it back," he said, sticking out his lower lip. His face was unshaven, caught between stubble and beard.

"Will you please tell me what in hell you two are talking about?" Ruth demanded. "Who gave back what to who?"

"Whom," the Homeless Citizen corrected Ruth with easy authority.

Ruth looked up at the ceiling. "And whom cares?"

"When you left the library to smoke a cigarette," Helma reminded him. "You picked up an item from the circulation desk."

"What's that: a circulation desk?"

"The library desk where you check out books. No one was at the desk when you walked past, and you reached across it and … " Helma had dropped her voice, keeping her tone encouraging.

Ruth snapped her fingers and said in a loud voice that caused several diners to turn and the homeless man to rock his chair. "The cell phone. You took Dutch's cell phone. *You* detonated the—"

"Ruth," Helma said sharply, and Ruth held up her hands.

"Sorry."

"I gave it back," he insisted stubbornly.

"To Dutch?" Ruth asked. She leaned down, closer to the Homeless Citizen, and he vigorously jerked his hands up and down, extending his wall upward until Ruth backed away.

"I gave it away to a man who needed it," he said, his voice growing louder with each word. "What I did was expiation, karma replacement. I fixed it. It's all fixed now. Go away."

"What was the man wearing?" Helma asked. "The man you gave the cell phone to?"

"Was it—" Ruth began, and at Helma's glance, said, "Okay, okay. I quit."

His Adam's apple bobbed up and down as he peered around the dining hall and finally pointed toward a huge man at a nearby table tipping a bowl of soup into his mouth.

The fabric of the man's shirt was faded plaid.

Helma had never spent time in a spa; the closest she'd come was a gift certificate from her mother after she and Aunt Em had splurged on massages and pedicures for each other for Valentine's Day. "It will be good for you, dear," Lillian had said. "Be sure to ask for Wendy." Helma had traded the certificate in for two haircuts and a new earthenware canister set.

In a curious way, the Cocoon Day Spa reminded Helma of the casino: that sense of timelessness and, well, "cocooning" from the outside world. The spa was on a lower floor of the Lagoon Hotel—"See, there's no lagoon, anymore," Ruth said—and had no windows.

"We're meeting Frances Harrington," Ruth said airily to the young black-clothed receptionist seated at a table that held only a computer.

"She's softening," the receptionist told her, her eyes darting back to her computer screen.

"Don't get up," Ruth said. "I know the way," and to Helma she said through gritted teeth, "Come *on*."

"But—" The receptionist began, half rising from her swivel chair.

"Thank you," Ruth sang out over her shoulder.

They found Frances in a cushiony small room that smelled of lavender and spices and echoed with gentle flute music. At first Helma thought they were in the wrong room. Without makeup, Frances lost the definition Helma was used to. She looked more anonymous—and younger. Frances lounged in a huge white fabric chair in a white terrycloth robe, an expression of contentment on her face. Until she saw them.

"What do you want?" she demanded.

Helma took the lead. "You *did* talk to Randall the morning your father died," she said, leaving room for Frances to fill in the blanks.

"So?" Frances said. She sipped from a cup of tea on the table beside her, then looked up at Ruth. "And now she's blabbed to you about my personal life."

Ruth laughed. "You didn't think people knew? Not about that cozy window table at that little restaurant, or that private place on the bay? And what about—"

Ruth was embellishing, sailing into the dangerous waters of fabrication, so Helma cut her off. "You were worried about your father. You didn't know where he was. And the weather was dangerous."

All defiance left Frances's face. She set down her teacup, and tea sloshed onto the saucer. "I *didn't* know where Daddy was," she agreed. "He had these habits he was so stubborn about: every day the library, the construction site. And in all that snow ... " She rubbed at her eyes. "I was so worried."

"So when you couldn't reach him, you asked Randall to look for him?"

Frances nodded. "Randy was in his office. Snow didn't stop him from working. He said he'd run over to the library for me and check if Daddy was there."

"But your father wasn't at the library and Randy called you to tell you that," Helma guessed. "Did he call you from the library?"

Frances shook her head. "It was from outside, I could tell. He said he'd borrowed a cell phone."

"Randall didn't own a cell phone?"

"No," Frances told her. "Randy didn't like how they intruded on life. He said Daddy had left the library and was out in the snowstorm and he'd go look for him. He told me not to worry, he was sure he'd find Daddy for me." She rubbed her hands together, one over the other, wringing them. "And that was the last I spoke to him."

"The softer side of Randall Rice," Ruth said, and Frances looked at Ruth but the comment didn't appear to register.

"I see," Helma told her, waiting while Frances composed herself. "What time was that?"

Frances shrugged. "Around eleven."

Around eleven. The explosion had taken place at 11:08.

"Would Randall have phoned your father?" Helma asked. "On your father's cell phone?"

"Daddy didn't have a cell." Frances said, calmer now. "He would have gone back to candles and crank phones if he could have."

"Maybe he bought one without you knowing," Ruth suggested.

Frances shook her head. "I had to teach him how to use a microwave oven."

"Thank you, Frances. Let's leave now, Ruth."

Frances hugged herself. "Who killed them? Do you know? Will you tell me? I can't live, not knowing."

"I don't know," Helma told her, "but I believe the police will have the answer soon."

"Not Uncle Del, or Uncle Rosy," Frances said as Ruth and Helma turned toward the door. "Not them."

"Drive to the excavation site, please, Ruth," Helma said. Ruth's Beetle was so low to the ground, Helma heard the remnants of the gravel the city had spread on the icy roads, clattering against the undercarriage.

"What for?"

"To look at something," Helma told her.

"The place has been scoured by the police already, what's the point?" But Ruth turned up the street that led to the site. "Or do you want to take one last look before it becomes Harrington condos?"

"I need to sort out my thoughts before we get there, Ruth," Helma said.

"Okay, okay, my lips are zipped."

The yellow police tapes were gone, the snowy tracks melted. The bulldozer had been removed from the pit, too, and the site was vacant.

"I'd like to look at the spot where Randall was found," Helma told Ruth, heading to the north side of the excavation. They passed the shallower pit made by the explosion and entered the small stand of trees.

"This is creepy, Helma," Ruth said, looking around at the disturbed earth, the scattered dirt, the broken tree limbs. "Nobody in their right mind would build condos here, now."

"That's what Ms. Moon said," Helma told her as she peered down at the grass.

"That cheers me way up, to know I'm in agreement with your Moonbeam. But she still wants the library here?"

"She claims she does," Helma told her.

"Do you?"

Helma paused to glance around the sad scarred site. Slowly she shook her head. "No," she said. "No, I don't."

"Good. That's clear. What are we looking for, anyway?"

"I'm not sure," Helma said. "Randall was looking for Franklin in the snowstorm. He didn't own a cell phone but he told Frances he borrowed one to call her."

"Says Frances," Ruth countered. She stood straight, arms and feet together as if she were afraid to disturb hallowed ground.

"The Homeless Citizen's story supports hers," Helma reminded her. She touched the bright and jagged end of a snapped fir branch.

"You believe him? All that 'expiation' and 'fixing' stuff he was talking about?"

"Yes, I do," Helma said, ignoring Ruth's snort, surprised to realize that she truly did believe the Homeless Citizen. "If the police suspect that Dutch is involved, they could have simply checked his phone records and arrested him."

"Unless they need more evidence, maybe the phone itself for fingerprints or something. Let's say Randall ended up with Dutch's cell phone. He calls Frances to say he's out rescuing Papa, who he hated, by the way. But no way did he have time to sit down in the snow, rig up a bomb, and blow up himself and Franklin."

"Randall could have set it ahead of time and detonated it when Franklin arrived," Helma suggested, parting the glossy leaves of an Oregon grape plant and finding nothing. "Except it was Franklin who wanted Randall to meet *him*."

Ruth turned in a circle. "Who knows. Geez, I wonder if you married the guy if he could simply *tell* you the details over a pillow instead of making us do all this guessing."

"We'll walk around the site and look for anything unusual," Helma told her, leading the way toward the excavation.

"Listen, Helm. Take a look around you. This whole place is 'unusual.' Franklin was found in the pit, Randall in the snow under the trees. Dirt was scattered everywhere. Let's say Randall *did* use Dutch's phone to detonate a bomb that just happened to kill Franklin and himself, the phone could have been blown sky high."

"Ruth, that's excellent reasoning."

"*What* is? What'd I say"

"Sky high. Look *up*." Helma rose from the ground and began looking up into the winter-bare trees around them. "The phone could have been blown upward out of Randall's hand and landed in a tree, not on the ground."

They peered up into the trees until Helma's neck ached, slowly circling each one, squinting at thick limbs and tree crotches without spotting anything unusual. The deciduous trees were gray and cold, the evergreens still winter green.

"If it *was* here, it was blown to bits," Ruth said.

Helma was not an expert, but she *was* observant. She returned to the explosion site and studied the way the dirt had been blown to the south and west. Then she walked in a straight line toward a lone vine maple that stood thirty feet away. The vine maple was old and ragged, multitrunked with broken crowns fifteen feet above the ground, the way the weak trees often grew and died.

She stood before the tree, walked around it, then caught sight of the end of a small black object caught in a broken limb. "There it is," she said, "where it logically should be."

"I bet I can get it," Ruth told her, taking a step toward the tree, already stretching out an arm.

"Don't touch it," Helma warned, feeling justifiably flushed by the discovery. "*Now* we'll call the police. Do you have a cell phone?"

"Hah. Not a chance," Ruth told her. "But there's a pay phone across the street."

Wayne Gallant, with Carter Houston at his side, arrived at the excavation site five minutes after Helma's call.

"You've been busy, Miss Zukas," Wayne said.

"I've only been trying to fulfill my responsibilities to the library," Helma told him. "And if anything I've learned tangentially will aid the police, I'm happy to share it."

Ruth rolled her eyes. "You're stretching 'devoted public servant' to glop, Helma. Cut it out. Just show the nice men the phone."

Carter Houston's head raised; his nose actually quivered. "Phone?" he asked. "Cell phone?"

After Helma pointed out the object on the broken vine maple, Carter returned to the police car to "call in the crew."

Over the next forty-five minutes, Ruth and Helma told the policemen about Randall's possible appearance at the library, about the homeless man, even Bonita Wu, and while not exactly saying that Randall and Frances were having an affair, Helma suggested they talk to Frances, that she may have sent Randall searching for her father.

As they spoke, Wayne asked questions and Carter wrote in his notebook. Once, Ruth leaned over Carter's shoulder to peer at his notebook and said, "Did you get an A in fifth grade English, Carter? You know, when you learn to make outlines for essays, with all those Roman numerals and stuff, I bet you made it all the way down to the lowercase letters with half parentheses."

"Fifth grade was a long time ago, Miss Winthrop," Carter said, his pencil poised. "For all of us."

"Ouch," Ruth told him, her smile widening. "Touché, Carter. Good job."

Wayne walked with Helma to the Volkswagen, while Ruth lagged behind for a few final jabs at Carter. "This is good information, Helma," he said, dropping his police mask. "We'll follow up on it."

"What do you hope to learn from the cell phone?" she asked.

He touched her elbow, warning her of a strip of metal near her feet. "First, we'll check it for fingerprints, and go from there," he said.

"Naturally, you'll expect Dutch's fingerprints to be on his own cell phone," she told him as she stepped around the metal strip.

He only smiled at her.

As Helma and Ruth pulled away from the site, Helma realized that, without actually having made a decision to do it, she had kept Cornelia Settle's association with Franklin Harrington totally out of the conversation.

Chapter 30

A Pack of Lies

On Monday morning there was no sign of the winter storm that had brought Bellehaven to a dead stop only five days earlier. In fact, a haze of yellow-green clung to lawns and fields as if the snow had shocked an early spring into life. Tips of tree branches swelled red, crocuses and daffodils resumed their upward thrusts.

There was nothing new about the murders in the *Bellehaven Daily News*, nor on the morning news. In fact, only one brief sentence indicated that "the police are still investigating." An unnamed city official had berated a child who'd ridden his bicycle into the side of his car and the parents were threatening to sue. The sink hole on Fifth and Barrywood was finally filled and resurfacing would be completed by noon. The TV station was sponsoring a contest for photos depicting the recent blizzard.

Helma told herself that Franklin and Randall's deaths might never be solved. The principals were both dead, and the secrets of the "bad blood" between them irrevocably lost when they died. If only Wayne Gallant was more generous with the facts of their investigation. For a wild moment she wondered if Ruth was correct, that a married policeman could safely share his investigations with his wife.

But no; certainly a married librarian wouldn't share the secrets of library patrons with his or her spouse, so she supposed a married policeman wouldn't, either.

Before she left her apartment, Helma bundled up the three-ring binder of Franklin's Harrington history and tucked it into her blue bag beside her pumps. It was a jaundiced recounting, Harrington myopic, but still, it deserved consideration for the library collection.

"Did you settle anything regarding the library site since we last spoke?" Ms. Moon asked, her eyes alight with eagerness as Helma removed her coat and buttoned it onto a hanger.

"That was only last night, Ms. Moon," Helma reminded her. Ms. Moon had called at 9:00 P.M., and Helma almost didn't answer. The director had wanted to send bottles of wine to Del and Rosy to "lift their spirits, so to speak," and Helma had suggested she wait.

"Without a signed legal document saying otherwise, you must be prepared for Delano and Roosevelt Harrington being the rightful owners of the property," Helma warned her.

Ms. Moon's lip trembled dangerously. "You couldn't change their minds."

"The last option would be a protracted legal battle, I fear," Helma said. "And that wouldn't garner favorable publicity for the library. You and the Harrington brothers *could* come to an agreement that would benefit both the library *and* the Harringtons."

"Me? Del hates me."

"Perhaps," Helma agreed, "but he does have enormous regard for people who refuse to give up." She paused and buttoned one more coat button. "And you *can* be very persistent."

"Why, Helma," Ms. Moon said, smiling and swaying a little. "Thank you."

Helma was still in her cubicle, making last minute changes to her order for new U.S. government materials, conscious that in fifteen minutes she was scheduled to begin her two-hour shift on the reference desk. She had expected a phone call from Wayne Gallant regarding the cell phone found at the library site but hadn't heard from him. She was reaching for her phone when Dutch appeared in the entrance to her cubicle.

"We have a curious situation," he said. He was the same Dutch as always. No hint in his eyes of their late night encounters and conversations. No hint of any confrontations with the police. There may have been a slightly warmer tone in his voice when he spoke to her, but that could have been her imagination. He glanced toward the director's office and said in a lowered voice, "Could you take a look at it before I show Ms. Moon?"

"Of course," Helma told him, and he led the way to the work area behind the circulation desk where he'd been sorting the contents of the lost and found box into piles of jackets, umbrellas, scarves, cups, notebooks, stray gloves, and nonlibrary books. Items were gathered up daily and sorted by the staff under Dutch's purview every Monday morning.

A red backpack lay on Dutch's desk. He picked it up and reached a hand inside. "I was looking for identification and found these items." He pulled out a white box clearly marked with the Bellehaven Public Library's ownership stamp.

"It's microfilm," Helma said. She read the label aloud. *"The Crier.* September, 1872," one of the earliest, sporadically published Bellehaven newspapers. "Someone was attempting to steal it?"

"And these." He slowly reached into the bag again and carefully pulled out a long object wrapped in newspaper and a small white paper bag with contents that rattled softly when he lifted it out. He handled the packages with curious reverence.

"What are they?" Helma asked.

Dutch pursed his lips, then spoke quietly. "Unless I'm mistaken, ma'am," he said as he unwrapped the long package first, "this is an ulna bone. And these," he opened the small sack so she could see the ivory objects inside, "are distal and middle phalanges. Finger bones."

"Human?" Helma asked. She stared at the bones, so shockingly delicate. They glowed as if they'd been polished.

"I believe so." He hesitated. "I've seen human bones before."

"How long has this backpack been in the lost and found box?" she asked, her eyes still on the bones.

"Only a few days. Since the snow."

She knew the red backpack, but she couldn't bring herself to say it yet.

But Dutch wasn't finished. "One more thing," he said softly. "When I opened the pack, I caught an odor I recognized." He looked away.

"What was it?"

"C4. Sometimes called Composition Four because of its four ingredients, the main one being cyclotrimethylene trinitmarine. It's an explosive."

"You're sure?" Helma asked.

"Yes," he said simply, and when he looked into her face, she recognized a man who, without a doubt, had intimate knowledge of C4 in all its forms.

Helma gripped the microfilm box so hard the edges bent inward. She loosened her grip and took two fortifying breaths. "I'm going to look at this microfilm first, and then we'll call the police," she told him.

Dutch nodded and gently replaced the bones in the red pack as Helma carried the box of film to a microfilm reader with an automatic threader. Whatever fingerprints had been on the box had been obliterated by their handling it, but the film itself was a perfect receptor. The police should be able to lift prints from it.

Helma paused. This *was* evidence, but her curiosity could not be denied. She slipped on plastic gloves the staff wore to change toner in the photocopier, and touching the film as little as possible, set it in the threader. The machine whirred and in a few seconds an image appeared on the oversized screen: the September 1872 editions of *The Crier*. The original of this newspaper had deteriorated profoundly, and physically existed only in the local museum in a protected climate-controlled room.

Helma began methodically going through the filmed newspaper, day by day, reading headlines. The newspaper had been brief back then, each issue only a few pages, sometimes only a single blurred sheet.

The woes of a new city: budgets, crime, politics, lingering Indian wars in the West, births and deaths, new store openings and closings. And fires, such a common occurrence they rarely rated as lead stories.

Then, on September 17, she saw a headline that read, HARRINGTON MINE PLAYED OUT, CLOSING IMMEDIATELY. The article quoted Albert Harrington as saying it was a choice between bankruptcy and ceasing production. He'd shut down coal mining operations the day before and was about to seal the mine entrance. The site outside of Bellehaven would then become the new Harrington headquarters as the Harringtons cut their losses and expanded into shipping and logging concerns.

Helma searched through the article for the address of the mine entrance. There wasn't one. But the article said the mine site would become the Harrington headquarters. The only headquarters Franklin Harrington had mentioned in his history had been the site where the new library was planned. Wouldn't he have known it was the original mine entrance? It was right there in the newspaper; it wouldn't have been a secret.

Yet at the same time, she remembered reading of the early chaotic history of the region, the lost and destroyed records, lawlessness—even in Bellehaven.

She continued skimming and reading. Nothing more about the Harringtons until the September 23 issue. Inside, at the bottom of page 3, there was a small article headlined: CHINESE LABORERS VANISH IN MIDDLE OF NIGHT.

A group of Chinese laborers had apparently fled, leaving behind food, clothing, and effects in their tent camp outside of Bellehaven, as well as leaving behind unpaid bills with local businesses. At the bottom of the article, the last line reported the city had ordered the Harringtons to clean up the camp since the Chinese had been miners at the now closed Harrington coal mine.

Helma sat back, the seemingly insignificant article blaring at her from the screen. Chinese miners who'd left Bellehaven in the middle of the night? Who'd worked in the Harrington mines? She pressed the Print button. A chill swept through her, hearing in her mind Boyd Bishop say, "People came and went and hardly left a mark. Brutal times."

Or had these been Chinese laborers who'd *never* left Bellehaven?

Mines had been haphazard in the early years of Bellehaven, disappearing just as gold seekers and businessmen had. And laborers, too. It had been rough country, the last land before the sea, a jumping off point.

But she remembered Franklin Harrington and his history, his Harrington legacy. "Isn't that a coincidence," he'd said to her when he saw the Chinese women in the library. "The past belongs in the past," he'd told Bonita.

And Franklin had asked Cornelia to tell Randall to meet him, that he could prove that he—Franklin—and not Randall, was right.

She rewound the microfilm, returned it to its box, and took it to Dutch at the circulation desk. "Can you keep this? I have to leave the library for a half hour, then we'll deal with … " She saw Glory coming their way. " … all of it," she hurriedly finished.

"Oh, Helma, Ms. Moon would like books on negotiation strategies," Glory said.

"I'm sure you can find several for her, Gloria. Check the catalog under the terms, *Negotiation*, or *Conflict Management*. If you'll excuse me."

"Please, call me Glory," Glory called after her.

As she pulled her coat from its hanger in her cubicle, Helma's eyes fell on Franklin's history. She hadn't read *every* page of the three-ring binder. Had he treated the subject of Chinese miners the Harringtons had employed? There was an index, she recalled.

In her hurry to flip to the index at the back of the binder, the covers jammed and the loose pages she'd inserted in the front flap when Rosy had given her the book slipped out and floated to the carpeting, spreading across her cubicle floor.

"Oh, Faulkner," she whispered as she stooped to pick them up.

Notes of Franklin's, mostly. His Palmer method handwriting led straight across the unlined pages: indented paragraphs, numbered sentences, arrowed points. She thought she'd gathered every paper until she spotted the fluttery edge of one last page beneath her desk. She knelt and reached underneath. Fortunately, she was not a woman to store files, books, or boxes beneath her desk, and within seconds her hand touched the page and she pulled it into the light.

Instead of Franklin's identifiable writing, the upper half of the page contained a drawing. Helma studied it: lines led from a small shape to a crudely drawn blob. She squinted at the shape and held it up to see more easily by her desk lamp. On the blob was written: "C4."

And beneath the drawing were lines of crossed-out writing. Helma was not as accomplished in forgery detection as her cousin Ruby, but surely this writing was also in Franklin's hand. The same perfectly formed ovals of the capital letters, the careful spacing learned under rigorous training as a child and undeniable even as an adult.

She held the paper so it was backlit by her lamp. The two top lines of writing had been totally blotted out with a black marker. She could only make out the letters S and M.

But the third and fourth lines were nearly readable: "S blank, blank, f, blank 1. SW corner." In light of the microfilm she'd just read, she wondered if the first word was "Shaft," meaning coal mining shaft. Shaft number 1. In the southwest corner. Of the old Harrington offices site? The original Harrington mine? The library site?

How better to hide a crime scene than to build on top of it?

She steadied the piece of paper and examined the fourth line, concentrating, blocking out every thought and distraction. A slash between numbers, like a date: 2/15, and a time?

Could 2/15 be February 15, the previous Wednesday, the day of the explosion that killed Franklin and Randall Rice and forever destroyed the dreams of a new Bellehaven Public Library on historic Harrington land?

In a fluid series of movements, Helma entered a side door of the Silver Gables, hurried up the stairs to 402 and rapped on the door.

This time, Cornelia Settle herself answered it. She didn't smile in greeting when she saw her. "Somehow I thought you'd be back," she said. "Come in."

She motioned for Helma to take a seat at the dining room table. "Would you like a cup of tea? A glass of water?"

"No thank you. May I ask you a few questions?"

"I imagine that if I said no, you would ask me anyway," Cornelia said.

"I would," Helma said, "but the convention of politeness removes some of life's harsher realities."

"And your questions will be harsh?"

"Only the answers, I'm afraid."

Cornelia nodded. "About Franklin and Randall."

"You *did* reach Randall with Franklin's message on

the day of the explosion, didn't you?"

Cornelia held her hands together so hard they turned white, in an emotional display for the composed woman. Finally, she nodded. "Randall answered his phone himself; most of the staff had stayed home because of the weather. I gave him Franklin's message, and he said he already knew the old fool was out in the snow."

Helma nodded. By then Frances had called Randall and asked for his help, worried because she couldn't reach her father.

"What was it Franklin wanted to show Randall at the library site?"

"I don't know." Nothing changed in her voice or her expression, but Helma did not believe her.

"There was *another* phone, wasn't there, Cornelia?" Helma asked. "Franklin had a cell phone."

Cornelia didn't answer. Her telephone rang and she ignored it.

"Franklin had a prepaid cell phone that couldn't be traced, didn't he?" Helma asked. "And he'd also devised a plot—on paper. He carelessly left his notes inside the manuscript of his Harrington history."

She pulled a folded sheet of paper from her purse and held it so Cornelia could see it. "I found them."

She wasn't saying that *this* was a copy of Franklin's plans; it was merely for illustration. The actual paper was safely stored behind January's reference question statistics in the bottom right drawer of her desk.

Cornelia's eyes widened. She looked at the paper in Helma's hand with apprehension and—yes—fierce longing.

"We both did," she said quietly, looking down at her hands. "So we could stay in contact privately, so there wouldn't be messages that our children would hear. He never wanted anything to be traceable that might taint his reputation. He didn't even use his name to purchase the phones."

"And you gave Franklin's cell phone number to Randall?" Helma asked.

Cornelia was silent, but Helma folded her own hands in silence, and finally Cornelia said, "Franklin told me not to use the phone for a couple of days because he was going to spend time with his daughter, but Randall was afraid Franklin was in danger, so I gave the number to him."

"Why didn't *you* call Franklin yourself instead of giving *that* cell phone number to Randall?" And more softly, "Didn't you realize what calling that phone number would *do*?"

"I ... I just wasn't thinking straight."

Helma studied the strong tilt of Cornelia's shoulders, the proud head and cool eyes, and wondered.

"Did you know about the Chinese laborers killed in the Harrington mine in the 1800s?"

"That's an old tale," Cornelia said. "A myth."

"Until Franklin found bones," Helma guessed. "That's why he was at the site so much, not because he was interested in the building process, but looking for proof of a horrible crime that was committed over a hundred years ago—by a Harrington. So he could destroy the evidence. And Randall had discovered the truth, too, maybe first. They were rivals in local history.

You were a party to luring Randall to the site where Franklin intended to set off an explosion. Was his plan to kill Randall as well as collapse the excavation?"

Cornelia closed her mouth tightly, and Helma continued, "But Randall went looking for Franklin because he was *worried* about him. In his haste to find Franklin, he accepted the cell phone when it was offered to him by a homeless man. He didn't see Franklin in the snow so he called Franklin's cell phone number, not knowing how close he was to him."

Cornelia looked at Helma coldly. "You're a woman of your word, I could tell that when I first met you. Catherine can't know of our association with the Harringtons, the publicity would destroy her. You promised not to inform the police, and I expect you to keep your word."

"No," Helma corrected her, rising from her chair. "What I said was I wouldn't tell as long as your association didn't have bearing on the deaths of Franklin and Randall. And as you can see, it was instrumental."

Chapter 31

Just a Phone Call Away

"To construct his explosive," Wayne Gallant told Helma, "Franklin studied books and a few vague articles on Middle East terrorists. We found them in his den and their illustrations were a close match to the drawing you found. I'm surprised he didn't blow himself up while he was building it."

They sat side by side on Helma's sofa, two glasses of wine on the coffee table, one red and one white. Boy Cat Zukas lay in his basket with his back to them, his tail occasionally twitching.

"The ABCs of explosive building is hardly part of the Bellehaven Public Library's collection," Helma said. "He could have found better information on the Internet, though. I found several sites with more complete directions—and clearer illustrations—myself."

"Why, Miss Zukas, I'm shocked."

"Purely an academic exercise," she told him. "I never saw Franklin using one of our computers, and he still used a typewriter to write his histories. He wasn't electronically savvy."

"I don't know about that. The cell phone detonator worked."

"Do you think Franklin really intended to kill Randall Rice?" Helma asked. Wayne shifted his legs and his thigh brushed against hers. He worked out, sometimes in a gym sparring with TNT, and he ran, too. She felt the hardness of his thigh muscles through the fabric of both their clothing.

"We'll never know for sure, but it looks that way. Why else ask somebody to meet you when you're carrying an explosive? And in the middle of a snowstorm, which would have given him perfect cover, by the way. He appears to have decided on the time as soon as he discovered the bones and realized that old tale was true."

"If the construction crew had discovered the bones, they'd have had to stop work," Helma said. "Archaeologists and the authorities would be called. He didn't dare wait."

Wayne nodded "The storm played right into his plans. He could have left the explosive on the ground near the old mine shaft and set it off when Randall stepped near it."

"If he'd intended to dial his cell phone number from the pay phone across the street, and even *if* you'd been able to trace the call from the explosive device to the pay phone, there would have been no way to trace it to

Franklin. " Helma took another swallow of her white wine. Wayne had arrived at her door with both bottles, one to suit each of their tastes. "Randall must have already been convinced the mine deaths were actual."

"Frances thinks so. She wasn't interested in local history so she didn't pay close attention to what he said. My guess is he challenged Franklin about the Harringtons murdering the miners. We don't know if this was news to Franklin or not, but he considered his family's history as a sacred trust."

"How many miners died?" she asked. Handel's Water Music played on the new CD player her brother had sent her for her birthday last fall. She'd set it on replay so she wouldn't have to rise from the sofa to change CDs.

"We won't know for months," Wayne told her. "It's a crime scene now and archaeologists will have to go slow. There are no records to help us out on this one. We'll probably never know who any of them were."

They sat silently for a few minutes, both of them considering not just the crime a few days earlier but what had happened nearly 150 years ago. The darkness underground, the blocked escape. Helma closed her eyes a moment, then swallowed.

"Franklin's gift to the library was just a ruse," she said, feeling bitter disappointment, not for the loss of the site, but because she'd *believed* Franklin, had respected and, yes, trusted him. "He used it as a cover until he did his digging and discovered if the story of the Chinese miners was true. That's why he was underfoot when the contractors were excavating, so he'd be first to spot any evidence. And that's why he was there every night when they finished: looking for signs. Either way it turned out, his motive was to protect the Harringtons' place in history. Did Cornelia give you any more information?"

"She's a hard nut to crack. And in fact, she's backed off on why she gave Franklin's cell phone number to Randall." Wayne tapped his wineglass, then swirled the red liquid so it swished up the sides. "But with Franklin's notes that you found, and what we're learning from Frances, Cornelia is looking more implicated every day. She's fiercely protective of her daughter—and herself, actually."

"I suspect she's been that way since she left Bellehaven as a young woman," Helma said, recalling the picture of beautiful young Cornelia and Franklin's child. "Cornelia led a secret life for decades, denying the truth to her daughter, Bellehaven, and herself. It would cause resentments in most women."

Wayne nodded in agreement. "Seething resentments. We'll be spending a lot of time with her in the next several days."

"Delano and Rosy must have been close to Cornelia," Helma said. "They participated in Franklin's subterfuge to keep Frances from discovering Cornelia or Catherine."

"We're satisfied that was the extent of their involvement. Neither brother knew about the dead miners. They'd heard the stories, sure, everybody has, but you expect tales like that when a city is built over old mines."

He smiled as if recalling talks with Del and Rosy; and Helma remembered what Ruth called Rosy's "Oscar Wilde complex."

"Nope, " Wayne went on. "Both men are more interested in the future than the past. I got the idea they'll be shifting their attention to Frances. Can you imagine life with those two as your guardian angels?"

In his basket, Boy Cat Zukas suddenly raised his head and swiveled to stare at them. He froze, ears forward, eyes turned to black and gold discs. "What's that about?" Wayne asked, frowning at the cat.

"He does that sometimes," Helma told him. "Animals are unfathomable."

He gazed at Boy Cat Zukas for a while longer, during which the cat never blinked once. "How is Ms. Moon feeling about the library site?"

"She came away from her meeting with the Harringtons believing it's most fitting that the property become a memorial park."

What Ms. Moon had actually said was that the beneficial forces of life had been violently sucked out of the site and no one could ever read for pleasure under its influence, that it was only suited to be a grave. Helma dearly wished she could have attended the meeting.

"So it's back to the drawing board for the new library, then?"

"Ms. Moon thinks public sympathy for the library's situation will carry a new bond issue."

Wayne Gallant chuckled and placed one arm along the back of Helma's sofa. He lifted his glass of red wine to her and smiled. "Here's to your curiosity. Well done."

She lowered her head demurely. "Thank you."

The Penny Whistle Gallery was packed. Art appreciators and the curious spilled out the front door, chatting and laughing and drinking wine from plastic glasses. As Helma threaded her way inside, snatches of conversation swirled around her.

"Did you see the one she called *Dead Man Gawking*?"

"What about *The Bad Lover Pays the Piper*?" which was followed by uncomfortable laughter.

"I think *Shiny Waters* is a hit," someone else said. "What great stuff." Helma hoped Ruth hadn't overheard any comments like *that*.

Someone handed her a glass of wine, which she held without sipping. Glasses that held any type of liquid gave one an errand for the hands. She glanced at her watch. Wayne would be meeting her in twenty-five minutes, but she'd felt it best to see Ruth's show on her own first.

As usual, Ruth's head was visible above the crowd. She stood in the center of the gallery, trying to tame her smile, which Helma thought seriously triumphant. This night, Ruth was dressed entirely in white, "in honor," she'd told her, "of our recent interesting weather." She spotted Helma and beckoned with her glass of wine.

Helma worked her way between people toward Ruth. She glanced left and right and in Ruth's immediate vicinity. There was no sign of Paul. She hadn't seen him standing outside the Penny Whistle, either.

But what she *did* see was a man at Ruth's elbow: a beautiful blond man with high cheekbones and broad shoulders. He was tall, taller than Ruth in her high heels, which Helma couldn't see but knew she wore. The blond man was at least six-foot-six, and his eyes, bright blue even in the dim light, shone on Ruth.

"Helm," Ruth said, beaming. "Meet Shiny Waters. Shiny, this is my friend, Helma Zukas"

"*You're* Shiny Waters?" Helma said before she thought.

He laughed warmly, shook her hand, and said in a Scottish accent, "Aye. It's my given name. Blame my parents, who were fans of your American blues."

"Except they wanted to skew his name to the sunnier side of the street," Ruth said in a voice like a purr. She bumped shoulders with Shiny Waters and he gently bumped back. "Shiny's a fabulous artist," Ruth continued. "I'm so proud to be sharing a show with him."

"I can see that," Helma said judiciously.

"Take a gander," Ruth told her, waving toward both sides of the gallery: her work on the left, Shiny's on the right. "Shiny does oils, too, even bigger than mine."

More well-wishers approached Ruth and Shiny, and Helma made her way toward the windows, edging slowly closer to the art. For a moment she was hemmed between a man and a woman and closed her eyes until they'd passed and the constriction of her throat eased.

"Hi, Helma. Isn't this so fun?"

It was Gloria "call me Glory" Shandy. She beamed

at Helma, her hair fastened back with girlish barrettes, her short pink dress tight across her midriff. She held two glasses of wine, one in each hand. Glory glanced behind Helma. "Are you alone?" she asked.

"Glory," Helma said, suddenly weary. "He's not coming until later."

"Oh," she said in a small voice.

"But you're with someone," Helma said, nodding toward the two glasses.

Glory shook her head. The perky smile flattened. "No. No, I'm not. I'm here alone. I just carry two glasses so it looks like I'm waiting for my date to come back." She swirled both glasses and white wine rose dangerously close to the rims. "I'm alone," she repeated. "People don't like me like they do you. I'm alone a lot."

Helma stared at her. Glory gave a little regretful shrug and grimace. "I don't know why; that's just the way it is."

The crowd eddied and surged around them, voices blended to inarticulate tones. "Why don't you look at the art with me?" Helma asked her. "Ruth said Shiny's work is ... fabulous."

"Oh goody," Glory said, recovering her indefatigable buoyancy. "That'll be so fun. And when Wayne gets here, we three can go out for a drink together."

"No, Glory," Helma said in a firm voice. "We will not."

Ruth's skills ran the gamut from purely representational to totally incomprehensible. Helma was never sure what to expect when she attended a display of her art. Ruth *had* warned her that she'd recognize the piece she'd finished the night before. "Call it prescient," she'd said, "but watch out, it's still wet."

Finally the crowd parted and Helma, with Glory at her side, stood with a clear view of Ruth's painting, her "prescient" painting.

It was called *Out of Circulation*, and in it, a stylized but recognizable Cornelia Settle sat erect on a straight-back chair, hands folded in her lap, her face a study in emotionlessness. The shadow of a man stood behind her, his features invisible. There were no doors in Cornelia's painted room but there *was* an abundance of windows, and each one cast a shadow across Cornelia's figure, forming a pattern of bars.

Check out librarian of excellence, Miss Helma Zukas. She's left her tangled Lithuanian family in Michigan to forge a life of order and certainty in Bellehaven, Washington.

But far is never far enough. One by one, they find her, beginning with her outrageous artist friend, Ruth. Murder finds Miss Zukas, too. But what might throw anyone else for a loop doesn't faze Helma Zukas. She is a professional.

Armed with prodigious library skills, she's a match for the craftiest of criminals. And if life sometimes tosses her an oddball question, she may not know the answer, but she definitely knows how to find it.

Miss Zukas and the Library Murders

Introducing Wilhelmina (Helma) Cecelia Zukas—that's Miss Zukas to you. Sure, Helma Zukas lines up her pencils and never shouts in public. But Miss Zukas understands the power of knowledge, whether she's facing a library patron or a murderer. She caresses the library wealth at her fingertips. She has a book and she knows how to use it. Go ahead: make her day.

Who better to research a body discovered in the Belle-haven Public Library than the premier librarian of the Pacific Northwest herself? When the murder weapon turns out to be a piece of library history, and the clue a bit of her own Lithuanian heritage, Miss Helma Zukas's skills will not be denied. Chief of Police Wayne Gallant enters the scene, and the attraction between them can neither be denied *nor* accepted. With the aid of Helma's not-so-proper best friend, Ruth, a six-foot-tall bohemian artist, the two are soon in hot pursuit of the truth.

Chapter 1

Murder. Murder in the library.

Helma allowed herself a dismayed shiver and then she firmly put the horror of it out of her mind. It was done. It was too late to alter what already existed. Only the facts could be dealt with now.

A yellow plastic tape stretched across the ends of the fiction stacks, separating the crime scene from the rest of the library. It read: POLICE LINE DO NOT CROSS

Helma lifted the tape with one hand and smoothly ducked beneath it.

Four uniformed policemen and two men in suits stood talking beside the green-sheeted bulk on the floor. A red-headed policeman cleared his throat and caught the others' attention, nodding toward Miss Zukas, who had invaded their cordoned area.

"May I look?" she asked, stepping closer to the body.

It lay on the gray carpet under the green sheet, one dirty-knuckled hand peeping past a hem.

There was a man, a murdered man beneath the green sheet. Helma paused, swallowing when there was nothing to swallow. No, it was no longer a man. It was a body, just a body. Inanimate.

"The janitor will have a difficult time removing that stain," Helma observed, motioning to the deep red stain that curved beyond the sheet like a setting sun.

An ambulance attendant browsing through *Lolita* looked up and said, "Probably have to replace the carpet."

"Ma'am," the red-haired policeman said, reaching for Helma's arm. "This is a police . . ."

"Excuse me," she told him and pulled back the green sheet.

The dead man lay on his stomach with his head turned to the side, toward Helma. "I've seen this man before," she said to the policeman reaching for her arm, dropping the sheet so it billowed and settled back over the body.

They all turned their cool, detached policemen's eyes toward her. She felt the stillness of their attention, their unblinking scrutiny.

"Yesterday afternoon he asked for one of the reference materials we keep behind the desk."

"Which reference material?" the chief asked.

Helma tried to remember. It had been a very busy day.

Rainy days frequently drew the public into the library. "I'm sorry," she told him. "I can't recall right now but I may later. I frequently do."

"Can you remember anything he said?"

"He requested a quarter to make a phone call."

"Did you give it to him?

"I never give money to strangers," Helma assured the chief.

Miss Zukas and the Island Murders

An anonymous note in the morning mail reminds librarian Helma Zukas of her long forgotten promise to plan her twenty-year high-school reunion. She meant what she said and she said what she meant, so now Helma transports her class from Michigan to an island off the Washington Coast for a celebration "to die for." When fog descends, classmates die, and old animosities resurface, it's up to Helma, along with an assist from her raffish friend Ruth, to save the stranded group.

Chapter 14

Droplets adhered to Helma's hair like a fine spray. Dense fog fingers swirled lazily into the light, forming eerie shadows that took shape and then, just when she thought she recognized them, dissipated.

Beside her the door opened and Ruth slipped through. "Helm?" she whispered.

"I'm right beside you," Helma said.

"Geez!"

"Shh," Helma cautioned her.

"I hope you have x-ray vision," Ruth said. "This could be our last ride together. End up in the drink."

"All we have to do is follow the road," Helma assured her. "No turns, just stay on the road."

Gravel crunched beneath the tires and the car began to roll, first slowly, then alarmingly fast. Helma left the headlights off and steered by the feel of the tires in the worn ruts.

"Are you trying to kill us? Slow down."

The sound beneath their tires changed and Helma hit the brakes. Ruth braced herself against the dashboard. "Now what?"

"We're at the road. You have to drive."

"I'm not driving."

"You have to."

"I can't. Why do I *have* to?"

"Because I left my driver's license in our room."

"Oh, for pity's sake, Helma. That's the last thing in the world we have to worry about. There are no police here, remember? And if there were, we'd be *grateful* to see their little flashing light behind us, believe me."

"I'd feel better if you drove."

"I don't drive without my glasses."

"I thought those were just sunglasses."

"Well, they're not 'just sunglasses,' okay?"

Helma turned on the engine. "It wouldn't matter. You can't see anyway."

Miss Zukas and the Stroke of Death

When she reluctantly agrees to resurrect her canoeing skills for Bellehaven's annual Snow to Surf race, Miss Helma Zukas finds herself paddling through a murder that points to her flamboyant friend, Ruth. The "Snow to Surf" is based on the Ski to Sea race in Bellingham, Washington, a torturous 85-mile relay race from the slopes of Mount Baker to Bellingham Bay during a seven-to-eleven-hour period every Memorial Day weekend.

Chapter 16

Helma dashed toward her canoe and employed a maneuver the cousins had used as children to launch themselves onto their sleds. She grabbed her canoe by the gunwales and pushed it and herself into the river, landing stomach-first on the center thwart, slapping the water with a smack, splashing, barely brushing the rocks.

Her canoe tipped but held, the bow end catching the current and turning before Helma had righted herself. She loosened her paddle from beneath the seat and dug awkwardly into the water, splashing backward but swinging the canoe straight. She began paddling downriver in long, efficient strokes, her knees out and braced, getting her bearings.

The little canoe sped along the river's surface. Ahead of Helma, a brown canoe as thin as an arrow rounded the bend, bent paddles flashing in unison.

Then Helma firmly put the other canoes—those ahead and

behind—out of her mind and concentrated on the river, its currents and eddies and obstacles. She focused on her paddling and the breeze and the position of her body and shoulders, envisioning it all as a single whole, a unit, movements orchestrated to perfection.

And in her concentration she failed to notice the spectators lining the bridges and parked beside roads as the canoeists passed beneath, didn't notice how the crowds went silent as this solo upright woman, her hardwood paddle cadently flashing, her strokes a piece of poetry and her canoe a work of art, passed by as swiftly and timelessly as a vision from a James Fenimore Cooper novel.

Final Notice

Aunt Em is the only sensible member of Miss Helma Zukas's boisterous extended Lithuanian family, an aged, calm and orderly woman. When Aunt Em suffers a mysterious "brain incident," just before a visit to Helma, the aunt Helma picks up at the airport is more akin to her bawdy friend Ruth than the aunt Helma has known all her life. Mysterious deaths, robbery, and chaos now accompany Aunt Em, along with a past Helma never could have imagined.

Chapter 4

"Who's Lukas?" Helma asked.

Aunt Em set her glass down so hard, whiskey sloshed onto the counter. Helma wiped it up with her napkin.

"I don't know any Lukas," Aunt Em told her.

"You said that was his suitcase, with the flamingo."

"I did?"

Helma nodded.

"Long ago," she said slowly, as if she were forcing up memories, "he was a good friend, the best of friends." She clasped her hands together and tightened them once to illustrate. "Like you and Ruth, only he was a man, but we didn't . . . you know." She made incomprehensible motions with her fingers.

"In Michigan?" Helma asked. "A friend of yours and Uncle Juozas's?"

"No," she said, picking up her glass. "Before that. Before Michigan."

Aunt Em had lived her entire life in Michigan; how could there possibly be a "before Michigan"?

Bookmarked to Die

On the morning of Miss Helma Zukas's forty-second birthday, she awakens to discover her world precariously out of kilter, an unaccustomed state of affairs, for certain! One disaster piles on top of another. Ms. Moon, the library director, blackmails Helma into attending self-help groups, Wayne Gallant appears to be having a crisis of his own, murder stalks Helma's well-laid plans for a local authors' collection, and worst of all, Boy Cat Zukas disappears. Mix in the return of her troubling friend Ruth, running from love gone wrong, and things can only get worse.

Chapter 5

"An author killed her?" Ms. Moon's voice rose. She clasped her hands to her bosom, her eyes staring into the shocking middle distance. "Authors killing authors in *our* library?"

"Nah," George said. "Authors killing authors on our *streets*."

Glory Shandy suddenly appeared beside George, touching his arm and rendering him momentarily befuddled.

"We all knew Molly as a regular patron," Glory told Ms. Moon who appeared ready to swoon. "Helma's right, it was an unfortunate accident that had nothing to do with the library."

"I hope not," Ms. Moon said darkly, recovering herself. "It would be an untenable situation if a murder were connected in *any* way to the Local Authors project. *That* would naturally mean the end of the program."

"A death knell, so to speak," George agreed, nodding gravely.

"Wasn't it exciting?" Glory said, "All those writers in one room? I could hardly breathe being so close to them all." She shoved her hands into the pockets of a girlish pink jumper. "The whole project is fantastic: you and everything you know about the community and the library. Your institutional memory is such a help to all the younger people hired after you."

Helma nodded, deciding it was best not to examine Glory's fulsome admiration too closely.

"The death *was* accidental, wasn't it?" Glory asked, her forehead wrinkling. "A *real* writer would never kill another writer, would they?"

"Why ever would they?" Helma asked, rhetorically of course.